Also by Rick DeStefanis

The Vietnam War Series
Melody Hill
The Gomorrah Principle
Valley of the Purple Hearts
Raeford's MVP
The Birdhouse Man

Southern Fiction Series
Tallahatchie

The Rawlins Trilogy
Rawlins, No Longer Young
Rawlins, Into Montana
Rawlins, Last Ride to Montana

Find all of Rick's books on Amazon at
https://www.amazon.com/-/e/B00H2YO2SS

Miss Molly's Final Mission

RICK DESTEFANIS

MISS MOLLY'S FINAL MISSION
Copyright © 2021 Rick DeStefanis

Excerpt from *Raeford's MVP*
Copyright © 2015 Rick DeStefanis

ISBN 13: 978-1-7367120-1-6

Acknowledgments

Several people contributed their time and expertise during the development and writing of this story. Their contributions ranged from technical to creative, and I believe their input took this story to a level beyond that of the average genre novel. I consider all these folks my friends and wish to express my sincerest appreciation and thanks for their help. Listed in somewhat of an alphabetical order, their names are below.

Amy Atwell is an author and a guiding light in my writing endeavors. Her expertise lies in such a variety of areas it would take much too long to describe them all. Suffice to say, when we first met, she reminded me of the first time I parachuted from an aircraft and looked up to see a beautiful nylon canopy blossoming above. The adrenaline rush defies better description. Amy and her husband live with a complement of cats on a barrier island on Florida's First Coast.

Carol Carlson, a friend since childhood, was the "girl next door." She is also a writer who provides me an invaluable amount of feedback in many areas, including the "woman's perspective," event time-line accuracy, and innumerable other aspects of the novel-writing process. Carol currently lives in Cordova, Tennessee.

My friend, Cord Foster, worked as an agricultural pilot (also known as a crop duster pilot) all over the Americas, including a stint with the United States Department of State spraying illegal drug crops in South and Central America. A Texas A&M alum, Cord was born and raised in the Mississippi Delta Region near Clarksdale, Mississippi. He flew his big yellow air tractor at the bottom edge of the sky, spring, summer, and fall. Cord's wife, Roxanne, called me early one summer morning just before this book was published. She told me that Cord had died in the crash of his airplane. Words cannot describe the depth of my grief.

Edward G "Buddy" Klein is an old high school classmate and fellow Explorer Scout who went into the military a year ahead of me in 1969. As a chief warrant officer with the United States Army Special Forces (AKA the Green Berets), Buddy's first assignment was with MACV SOG in the Republic of Vietnam. He has also served in Saudi Arabia, Kuwait, Iraq, Afghanistan, the Caribbean, and Central and South America. He retired in 2003 as the Command Chief Warrant Officer (CW5) of the 20th Special Forces Group. His help and suggestions, based on his time served in Central America during the time in which this story occurs, were invaluable. Buddy is now retired and resides near Jackson, Mississippi.

Elisabeth Hallett is a writer and editor who puts the manuscript through a final rigorous vetting. Commas, semicolons, and other punctuation all have an ongoing feud with me, which she manages well. Elisabeth lives out in the Bitterroot Valley south of Missoula, Montana.

Ellen Morris Prewitt is an author I first met in a writers' group many years ago in Memphis, Tennessee. We have remained friends and continued to trade manuscripts over the years. Ellen's 3-4 pages of detailed feedback were integral to the development of this story and the development of its characters, especially the female protagonist. Ellen and her husband Tom reside in the "Big Easy" (otherwise known as New Orleans, Louisiana).

Maria Razura is a dear friend whose first language is Spanish. Maria was very helpful with her guidance for the dialog in that language. She has lived in Memphis, Tennessee, for twenty-three years.

Robert "Enz" Enzenauer is a retired United States Army Medical Officer, Special Forces Senior Flight Surgeon, West Pointer, pediatric ophthalmic surgeon, and heaven only knows what else this man does in his spare time. As with most of our Special Forces, Enz has served in many areas of the world, including Afghanistan, Iraq, the Philippines, and Central America. I am honored to have him as a friend, and proud to have been dressed down by a retired brigadier general for inadvertently writing "505th Parachute Infantry Brigade" instead of "505th Parachute Infantry Regiment." Yes, I knew better. I blame it on a senior moment. Seriously speaking, Enz made many critically important suggestions and edits to various parts of this story. He and his wife Jill live in Denver, Colorado.

Todd Hebertson is my cover designer—the man who has designed every single one of my book covers. The thing I like best about his work is that it is not only creative but totally unique. His contact information is mypersonalartist@hotmail.com and his website is bookcoverart.webs.com/. Todd and his wife Beam live in Salt Lake City, Utah.

A Note to the Reader

Although, this is not a sequel nor directly related to my other novels, you will find some of the same characters from them appearing in this one. Buddy Rider, the male protagonist, first appeared in *Valley of The Purple Hearts*. Buck Marino from the same story also makes a cameo appearance of sorts. Others include Son Freeman from *Tallahatchie* (only a mention), Billy Coker from *Raeford's MVP* gets a mention, and Curtis Teague from that same story plays a major role in this one. I believe these connections lend a certain degree of interest, satisfaction, and continuity to readers. Enjoy.

—Rick DeStefanis

Dedication

This book is dedicated to my friend Cord.

Fly high, buddy.

Robert Cord Foster
1966 – 2021

CHAPTER ONE

Flying at the Edge of the Sky

January 1981

Buddy Rider lay on his back beneath the love of his life. Yes, he loved her, but like most of her type, she could be a bit high maintenance at times. A lot of girls were that way, and Miss Molly was no exception. He had spent most of his life savings and much of the profit from his crop dusting business on her, and despite all his loving attention, she occasionally gave him trouble. There was little to do in the Mississippi Delta other than farming, fishing, and duck hunting, and he was certain Molly had no use for those…. Something liquid struck his eye.

"Shit," he murmured. "What now?"

Wiping a sleeve across his face, he gazed up into her magnificent twelve-hundred-horsepower radial engine. The wheeled scaffold he lay on was cold beneath his back, but the heaters were warming the air inside the old hangar. He spotted the culprit running down the side of a fuel line. Swiping at it with a finger, he rubbed it with his thumb and held it out in the light. It didn't feel oily and there was no tell-tale rainbow. He touched it to his tongue and tasted it—condensation.

"Thank God," he muttered.

It was only a few years after Buddy returned from Vietnam that he found the old girl in an aircraft junkyard in Arizona, scheduled to be cut up for scrap. Turns out the old C-47 was a relic of World War II and had flown paratroops into Normandy the night before D-day—*D-minus* they called it. They went in before the actual D-day assault on the beaches. The crew had named her Miss Molly, and she had carried men of the 82nd Airborne's 2nd Battalion of the 505th Parachute Infantry Regiment into battle, but unlike many of her sister aircraft, she had returned safely to England. And years later she was unceremoniously abandoned in an Arizona scrap yard.

He had purchased her, along with parts from several less fortunate C-47s, with cash, multiple credit cards, and promises. It was an impulsive buy driven by two things, or perhaps many, but one was nostalgia. The others were women, the living, in the flesh type. Buddy's many failed relationships since the war had driven him to this mechanical bitch under which he now lay.

Molly could be almost as demanding as some of the humans, but as long as you treated her right, she was easy to live with. After four and a half years restoring her, and several test runs, they had made their first officially announced flight a few days ago. The newspaper and even a TV station had shown up to record the event. For Buddy, it was love at first flight, and though it was only January 1981, it was already becoming a pretty good year.

"Sir. Hello?"

It was a woman's voice, and she was standing back near the entrance to the hangar. Since all the hubbub had passed after the flight, it had been quiet, but this was probably another newspaper reporter wanting to do yet another human-interest story. It wasn't like he had something else to do today, but he would rather be left alone for a while. Buddy grasped the motor and pulled himself along with the scaffold from beneath the wing. Sitting up, he wiped his hands with a shop rag, while the woman walked closer.

"Are you Mr. Rider?"

He pushed himself from the scaffold and landed in a crouch on the floor.

"Yes, ma'am, that's me. What can I do for you?"

He eyed the young woman—mid-twenties at best, but she wasn't wearing a hint of makeup and her dress, plain gray, extended well below her knees. She wore little black shoes, and her hair was pinned atop her head. Despite all this, one thing stood out. She was strikingly beautiful. With auburn hair and the kind of light brown eyes that probably drove men crazy, she also struck him as one of a kind. His first thought was Mennonite, but there were none he knew of around Clarksdale. Regardless of her affiliations, this one seemed struck mute. He raised his eyebrows and she seemed to awaken.

"Uh, yes. I mean, hello, Mr. Rider. I'm Sister Elizabeth Anderson, and I came to talk with you about your airplane."

"Sister?" he said.

"Uh, yes. I'm a lay missionary, and I currently work with the Maryknoll Sisters out of New York. I'll get right to the point. I—uh—*we* need an airplane."

"For what?"

"It needs to be large enough to transport twenty-five or thirty people home from El Salvador in Central America. Is this it?"

She stepped toward the plane and gazed up at it while clasping her hands behind her back.

"A friend told me he saw a television news piece about your plane. It should suit our purposes well."

"Miss—uh, I mean Sister, uh, Elizabeth, this C-47 is better than forty-five years old, and I've just spent the last four of those years restoring her. She's a fine lady, and I am sure you are too, so I don't want to seem rude, but I'm not interested in the job."

"So, how do you make your living?"

"Most days I make it flying at the bottom edge of the sky."

The nun wrinkled her brow and cocked her head to one side.

"I'm a crop duster pilot, Sister, and this plane is just a hobby. She's not for hire."

"Mister Rider, please, hear me out. I'm not asking for charity. I have sufficient funds to pay for all your expenses, including fuel and whatever payment you may require."

"I'm sorry, Sister. It's not about the money. I just don't want to risk flying her all the way to Central America and back."

"Please, Mr. Rider. Let me at least explain before you make up your mind."

Buddy exhaled. He didn't want to be a jerk, and what the hell would it hurt? He threw his hand up. "Go for it."

There was no way she was going to change his mind, but at least this nun could tell her friends she tried.

"Mister Rider, just a little over a month ago, four women— three nuns and a lay missionary—were murdered by government troops in El Salvador. I personally knew one of those women. She was a mentor of sorts to me. They were good people, missionaries working hard to help others. They were only trying to help the poor, but they were murdered—tortured, raped, and killed. Do you hear me? They were innocent women only trying to help those poor people."

Her eyes reddened. Buddy had been a Green Beret and later flown a spotter plane, an L-19 bird dog, back in Nam. He had already seen the innocent dead—the cold ugly result of war in the villages. And this poor woman apparently thought there was a way to bring them back. A frustration like hers was one that had burned in his heart long after returning to the States. Yet there was no reprieve. He lived with it almost every night.

His war was one without end. He saw them night after night—the innocent dead and the young warriors who fought for them. This same war was fought again and again in the minds of men like himself—the ones who made it home and were unjustly blamed for things they hadn't done. Yes, just like those missionaries in El Salvador, Vietnam had been raped and tortured, and a damned good many innocent Vietnamese had been killed, but the vast majority of American soldiers had done their duty—nothing more.

"And the Archbishop was murdered only ten months before them."

"Sister, what the hell? I mean, I'm sorry. That's not what I meant to say. Look, I can't bring them back. What is it that you want?"

And it came back to him—twenty-something people needed a ride back to the States. There was no way he was going to fly into a revolution. He had seen enough killing for one lifetime.

"There are five more missionaries who have an orphanage in a mountain village near the Guatemalan border. Four are Maryknoll Sisters and one is a lay missionary like me. They are in danger, and so are the children in their care."

"Sister, do you have any idea what it takes to fly into a foreign country and fly out again? I mean, there are visas and clearances required, and fuel, and God forbid we have mechanical problems—and, oh by the way, there's also a war going on down there. Jesus!"

He again caught himself. "I'm sorry. I didn't mean to use his name—whatever. Look, have you tried contacting the State Department?"

The nun pulled a small white kerchief from her skirt pocket and wiped her eyes.

"Why don't you come over here and let me pour you a cup of coffee?" Buddy said.

This was a hell of a way to begin his day. He didn't want to be mean, but this woman had no grasp on the reality of what she was asking. Taking the young nun by her elbow, he led her to a corner of the hangar where the coffee pot sat with a couple of open boxes of leftover pizza. He wiped the residue from two cups that were stained and cracked with age.

"It's probably a little stout," he said as he poured the coffee. "I made it early this morning."

"Do you have any cream or sugar?"

"Sorry, Sister. This isn't Waffle House."

She cradled the cup in her hands and gazed down into the thick black brew.

"Look, Sister, I know of a guy down in New Orleans who owns some aircraft and from what I've heard, he has a lot of experience flying into Central America. Maybe you can give him a call and—"

"Yes, I know the man you're talking about. His name is Barry Seal. He turned me down, and he was rude about it as well. Said he didn't have any planes available."

This wasn't surprising. Seal was a shady character with more rumors floating in his orbit than the average spook. Buddy had heard a lot about him—ex-Special Forces pilot, CIA connections, lots of wealth, and rumored to have gone to the dark side. He had too many loose ends, all of which seemed to wrap around and point in one direction—the drug trade in Central America.

Seal had tried to recruit him to join his private air force not long after Buddy returned from Vietnam, but he smelled the stench of a rat and declined. He would pick up the remnants of his father's crop dusting business and do well enough without getting mired in a morass of drug running and God only knew what else. Life was too short for that crap.

"I figured if you were so intent on making this flight to Central America, he was probably the man with the most experience, but he probably did you a favor, turning you down. Rumor is he's running drugs. Have you tried contacting the State Department?"

The nun sipped the coffee and wrinkled her face, staring at the cup as if it were a snake.

"Yes. I've even talked with the American ambassador, Mister White."

"And?"

"He said we have to go through proper channels."

Buddy looked across the top of his cup. "Proper channels?"

"Yeah, I know—sounds like bullshit—oh, sorry, I shouldn't—"

It was an accurate description, but a colorful one for a nun to use—or at least it seemed so from his experience. The only nun Buddy had ever seen was Sally Field as the Flying Nun on TV, and he was pretty sure she never uttered a single expletive.

"It's okay, Sister. The government can bring out the worst in all of us. And I'm assuming you've been through those proper channels. What did they say?"

"They said they were working on it, but none of them could tell me what they were actually doing, and none of them seemed to know anything about the situation when I pressed them for details. They're just a bunch of bumbling bureaucrats."

"So why would the El Salvadoran government want to kill a bunch of nuns at an orphanage?"

The nun cast a paranoid glance at the hangar doorway. Buddy looked past her.

"You expecting someone?" he asked.

"No," she said, an obvious lie.

Buddy had not survived the war in Vietnam by being a dumbass.

"So why are you looking over your shoulder?"

The nun's eyes darted nervously about. It was clear she was groping for a response.

"Uh, I'm not—I mean—Oh, Mister Rider! Can't you see I need your help. Yes, someone has been following me. I don't know why, and I don't know who they are, but I haven't done anything wrong—yet."

"Okay. Tell me a little bit about yourself. Where are you staying? I mean where is your convent or whatever? Is it located somewhere around here?"

The woman went flat-lipped and rolled her eyes. "Mister Rider, we are missionaries and as a rule we do not stay in convents. I am currently staying at a hotel in Memphis, while I try to find an aircraft."

Buddy had no intention of getting drawn into this shitshow, but he had been the beneficiary of helping hands himself—twice in Vietnam.

"Sorry, Sister. Look, this is in no way a commitment to fly to El Salvador, so don't go getting your hopes up. Frankly speaking, it would be damned near—excuse me—I mean it would be near impossible without a lot of financial and logistical support. I'm going to make some phone calls and try to reach an old friend. Last I heard, he was somewhere in Central America. Maybe he can come up with some more realistic options for you to consider."

"I can't thank you enough, Mister Rider."

She stepped forward, grasped his hand, and gazed up at him. Slowly and deliberately, he pulled free of her grasp. Nun or whatever, she had the beguiling beauty and manner of a Venus Flytrap.

"Then don't. I haven't said I would do anything other than ask around."

A wisp of her auburn hair had worked its way loose and now dangled across her face. He drew a deep breath as she self-consciously brushed it aside.

"I'll be back tomorrow afternoon. What time is good for you?"

"No. Don't come back here. Meet me at the Blue and White Café in Tunica around ten. The breakfast crowd will be gone, and the lunch crowd won't be there yet. And don't stop if you think you're being followed."

"Who do you think they are—the ones following me?"

"Given you spoke with Barry Seal, it could be some paranoid drug trafficker who works for him, or a CIA spook, or maybe just a DEA investigator."

"DEA?"

"The Drug Enforcement Agency."

The nun's face paled and her lips parted as her eyes fell into a vacant stare.

"Believe me, the DEA wouldn't be near as dangerous as a paranoid drug trafficker, but do you see now why I'm not flying to Central America? And since you've already visited Mister Seal, that makes me even more certain. He's probably trying to make sure you're not somehow connected to the government.

"The good news is I'm a sucker for damsels in distress, and I have friends. I'll call around and see what I can learn about what's happening down there and why no one is willing to help. I'll offer my advice free of charge, but that's all you'll get. Outside of that—you're on your own."

Too Much Paranoia

E lisabeth Anderson found herself looking into the rearview mirror as she drove her rental car back to Memphis that day. She wasn't sure what to think of Rider, but his paranoia was contagious. She had to make this work, but his mention of drug traffickers, the CIA, and the DEA made him seem a bit of a conspiracy nut. There really was someone who seemed to be following her, but she had broken no laws, and there was nothing they could do to her—she hoped.

It wasn't that the things he said couldn't be true, but his fears were probably overstated. The government might be doing some background checks, but that was hardly a reason for her to give up on doing the right thing. And how complicated could it be, flying to an airstrip adjacent to a village, taking the nuns and children on board, and flying them home? She had to remain positive and hope this crop duster pilot and his old airplane were the solution, because she had searched far and wide to find him.

A commercial charter was out of the question. Besides the required visas, which were unlikely to be granted, no commercial pilot would land on a grass strip in a war-torn country. Her sponsor had researched the possibilities and pointed her toward the outliers such as Rider. A crop duster pilot who lived out in the sticks of Mississippi, he would have been one of her last choices, but Rider was at least somewhat clean-cut and despite his redneck accent, spoke decent grammar. It seemed this quest had become a continual string of tradeoffs.

For now, he had at least agreed to help, and if he had some brains to match his rugged good looks, she could handle everything else. Earlier that morning, when he leapt from the scaffolding beneath his plane and landed on the hangar floor, she had been taken aback by his blazing blue eyes, deeply tanned face, and lady-killer smile. She had expected an older man, pudgy perhaps, with some gray hair, but he was lean and looked to be in his late twenties or early thirties. If it weren't for his oil-stained gray coveralls and the grease smudges on his face, he might have been a handsome man.

Her only doubts about him now came from the things she had learned about southerners from her college professors, her parents, and other men like him she had dated over the years— men too cocky and too self-assured—mostly high school and college jocks with big egos and only one thing on their minds. The temptations had been many, but two things saved her—her scholarship to the small Catholic girls' college and the promise she made her mother.

With her college years now behind her, and the promise fulfilled, she decided to try lay missionary work as a way of giving back, but she had to admit, it was also a way to test the waters of life—to re-engage perhaps. She would do this while learning to cope with her new freedom—no school and out in the world on her own. That at least had been her plan until this problem in El Salvador arose. People now depended on her, and she carried the full weight of that responsibility.

She could not fail them, especially since she had convinced

one of them—her best friend and college roommate—to become a missionary like her. After listening to her describe the possible adventures of visiting exotic countries and doing something unselfish, Melissa Hanahan volunteered and was called first. Traveling to El Salvador, she went to work in a small village with the nuns already there. Elizabeth now felt duty-bound to rescue her.

Her life had taken some radical turns in recent months—her mother's death, her college graduation, her new commitment to missionary work, and now this. It was overwhelming at times, but she was determined to figure things out. Hopefully, Rider's friend could help him work out the details. They could all go together and rescue the nuns, Melissa, and their orphans. When they were out of danger, she could again be at peace with herself.

It was noon when Elizabeth pulled into the motel lot and parked in front of her room. A strong wind had come up, sending trash, paper cups, and other litter tumbling across the lot. The door opened down at the motel office and the clerk was looking her way. This was strange—or was it simply more of that contagious paranoia? She let herself into her room and found the phone ringing.

"Hello?"

It was the desk clerk. His accent was Middle Eastern, and he was polite as he apologized for his call.

"You had a visitor earlier today. He asked for your room key—said he was your friend. I sent him away. I don't mean to pry, but were you expecting someone?"

"Uh, no. No, I wasn't."

"In that case, I would suggest you take precautions, madam."

"Yes. I mean, sure I will, but what did he look like?"

"He looked like a policeman, but when I asked him for identification, he said that it wasn't necessary."

"Can I move to another room?"

"Most certainly, and might I suggest you don't park your vehicle in front of your room? Come by the office and get the new key."

"Thank you. I appreciate it."

She hung up. This was crazy. And she thought of Rider's warnings. Perhaps he wasn't paranoid after all. And perhaps he was more than the redneck crop duster pilot she assumed him to be. He was smart enough to become a pilot, and he seemed to know things about Barry Seal and the DEA that were suspicious. Perhaps Rider was involved in the drug business. What other explanation was there?

She needed him and his airplane, but at what cost? Employing a criminal, no matter how well-intentioned the cause, was a dangerous exception to her morals. Giving up on Rider was perhaps the better decision, but she decided to wait until after their next visit. She wanted to hear what he learned from his mysterious friend—the one who he seemed to think would know a lot about El Salvador.

The door to her room rattled and she spun about as a burst of adrenaline sent her heart into overdrive. Only then did she realize it was the wind. Still, it was a reminder that this room was no longer safe. Grabbing her bag, she tossed it on the bed and began gathering her things. For now, the car could remain parked where it was, but it was time to get moving. Making no pretense of organization, she threw toiletries and clothes into the bag and zipped it closed.

She was beginning to feel like a character in a redneck spy novel.

CHAPTER THREE

Jungle Jim Parker

Later that day, after the nun left, Buddy replaced the cowling on the motor, padlocked the hangar, and drove home to Sunflower County. His plan was to call around and try to find an old friend who was his commanding officer and backseater on more missions than he cared to remember. He was a man Buddy respected. Whatever Jim Parker could tell him about El Salvador that wasn't classified, he would pass on to Sister Elizabeth Anderson.

He reflected back on his old commander. When Captain James "Jungle Jim" Parker put his Special Forces teams on the ground in Laos and Cambodia, he didn't always remain back at the Tactical Operations Center. The TOC was relatively safe, but Jungle Jim led from the front, and riding backseat with his spotter aircraft was one way of doing it. He was a true leader who had saved his men from more than a few tight spots.

Buddy first served under Parker on an A-team—crossing the fence into Laos and Cambodia where they ghosted along the Ho Chi Minh Trail. Later, when Parker discovered his flight experience, he insisted Buddy could better support him by moving to an aviation unit and qualifying to fly observation aircraft. Within a short time, his CO pulled enough strings to get

Buddy trained and officially designated as an army aviator with the 220th Aviation Company. From that point forward he became Jungle Jim's pilot.

That was a decade ago and, finding him now could be problematic. This long after the war, he might be anywhere in the world. Buddy had heard Jim was still on active duty and was rumored to be in Central America, but the way the Army Special Forces operated, only God knew for sure if that was true. There was one way to find out.

He picked up the phone and dialed 411 for information. There was but one place to begin—Special Forces Headquarters at Fort Bragg. It was the home of the Green Berets and he had been to Smoke Bomb Hill more than a few times, but he was prepared for the worst. Getting information from his old buddies would be difficult at best. Surprisingly enough, he got a number and got through to someone immediately.

"23884," a voice answered.

"Hello, I'm trying to reach a friend, Captain James Parker—goes by Jungle Jim Parker."

"He's not here."

"Can you tell me how to reach him?"

"Stand by," the voice said. "I'm transferring you."

Buddy got nowhere as he answered the same questions for the next person.

"Yes, he was my commanding officer in Vietnam. No, I resigned my commission after the war. We were friends, and I just want to look him up. I believe the last time was around September of 1968."

The officer was terse and, not surprisingly, tight-lipped.

"I'll check around," he said. "Give me a phone number."

After the call, Buddy's yellow Labrador retriever, JD, must have sensed his frustration. The dog stood, stretched, and ambled over, pressing his head against his leg. Buddy rubbed his ears.

"I wish I had your good sense, boy. I'd stay curled up in front of the fire and mind my own business."

Sitting at the kitchen table, Buddy stared out across the vacant mud fields toward the far horizon. It wasn't always obvious, but the Mississippi Delta had a unique beauty. You only had to know where to look. He gazed up at long V-formations of snow geese, strung for miles across a deep blue winter sky, brilliant white dots shimmering in the late afternoon sunlight. It would be dark in a few hours.

He dropped a couple of ice cubes into a glass and poured a shot of bourbon over them as he thought about his meeting with the nun that morning. She was unlike any nun he had ever imagined. She was also desperate and needing help, but he had worked hard since the war, building his crop dusting business and making peace with the past. He wanted to help her, but he had no interest in another war. Once in a lifetime was enough for him. Yet, there was this niggling thought—one he could not deny. He owed his fate to the heroic efforts of others.

He took a sip from the glass. The bourbon was usually reserved until after supper but not today. This business with the nun had brought back memories, and they were haunting him. There had been those saving angels in his life who had risked everything for him when he thought there was no chance of survival. Jungle Jim Parker was one, and he was the one person who could likely provide the information the nun needed. There had to be another way of contacting him. As he sipped his drink, Buddy thought back to that fateful day.

Someone needing help—that was the issue, and it was the same that day when he and Parker were shot down over Laos. A team of Parker's Green Berets and their Montagnard guerrillas were trying desperately to break contact with half the North Vietnamese Army that morning while Buddy and Captain Parker skimmed the treetops in the Cessna dropping grenades and smoke until the F-4s arrived. The metallic impacts of bullets striking on each pass had Buddy studying his wings for telltale fuel leaks and the gauges for other signs of damage.

"Bravo Delta One Niner, Angels Delta Five on station in one mike. Over."

It was the inbound Phantoms. Buddy glanced over his shoulder at Captain Parker who shot him a thumbs-up and keyed the mic. It was time to climb and take advantage of some of that empty air overhead. Jungle Jim was an old hand at this, and Buddy had only to fly the aircraft while Parker directed the airstrike. With his low-level passes no longer needed, Buddy knew the hairy part was done, but he continued to jink the aircraft left and right to avoid ground fire as they climbed.

Far up the valley, he spotted the first F-4 dropping into its bombing run, its wings loaded with enough ordnance to stop the NVA pursuers in their tracks. Low, fast, and lean, it was a beautiful sight as the vapor streamed off its wingtips. Buddy was about to turn and give Parker a thumbs-up when he spotted orange blobs the size of grapefruits floating upward from the jungle below. He slapped the stick to one side, but it was too late.

Two, then three streaked past the cockpit—misses, but the plane jolted and shuddered as it apparently took two hits. The little aircraft began a slow turn on its own and he glanced back. Pieces of the plane were fluttering earthward below. Part of one elevator and a piece of the rudder had been shot away.

Parker pointed to his mic and yelled, "Radio's dead."

Buddy turned to find the windshield spattered with oil. The wind streaked it upward as he gazed down at the oil pressure gauge. It was dropping fast. Only then did he notice several holes in the cockpit dash and the telltale wisp of smoke. The odor of hot oil filled his nostrils.

He turned back to Parker. "We've got to find a place to put down quick," he yelled.

A glance at the surrounding terrain and an instant decision were his only options. Buddy fought the stick, slowly correcting the sluggish little bird, and aiming it toward a ridge on his right. Reaching the next valley was a long shot at best but becoming a prisoner of war was something he had decided long ago to avoid, no matter what the risk. Even if he cleared the ridge, there was no guarantee he would find a clearing in a thick canopied jungle that stretched for miles. The aircraft skimmed the treetops across the ridge and shot out over the next valley.

The engine sputtered, vibrated, and went silent. There was only the eerie whispering of the wind outside the plane. He searched the valley for someplace to put down. The terrain below was furrowed with deep ravines, but it flattened further out in the valley where the jungle gave way to a boggy, bamboo-filled lacework of creeks and water-filled potholes. It was his only hope. Pushing the nose over, he fought to maintain airspeed, but the altimeter spun down. The last thing he remembered was flaring hard as the plane sailed into a large bamboo thicket.

It was the first time a soldier had carried him out of the jungle. When he awakened, the painted faces of Parker's men were looking down at him from a hovering chopper while pulling him on board. The downdraft was thunderous, and the rotors clacked loudly as the helicopter pulled vertical and rose out of the bog. He escaped death that day and was medevaced to a hospital in Phu Bai. That was the last time he had seen Jungle Jim Parker. A month later he was back in the cockpit and flying as a spotter for the 101st Airborne Long Range Reconnaissance Patrols. But it happened again.

This time it came after crashing his smoking Cessna L-19 Bird Dog into the mountainous jungle and awakening to find himself hanging upside down, still strapped in his seat twenty feet above the jungle floor. Groggy and not thinking, he unbuckled his seatbelt and plummeted to the ground, snapping his ankle. His chances for survival were bleak at that point, but another one of those angels of the infantry came for him. This time it was Buck Marino—an Army Ranger who carried him on his back out of that place they called the Valley of The Purple Hearts—the A Shau Valley of Vietnam.

Buck now lived with his wife Janie and three kids up in Montana. Buddy talked with him on the phone at least once a month, and they had traded visits several times over the years. Buck would also be a good one to call and discuss this issue. He had connections and might have some helpful ideas as well, but Jungle Jim was the best choice. If he heard from him at all, it would likely take a day or two. He decided to wait and see before contacting Buck.

———————————

Two hours passed as he sat there at the kitchen table lost in thought, and when the phone began ringing, Buddy glanced out the window. Clouds had moved in, and the January sun had dropped into the distant trees, setting them aflame with an orange glow. The phone was relentless as it continued ringing. Too soon for Jim Parker to be calling back, it was probably some farmer wanting to get his order in ahead of the competition. Buddy would not begin spraying pre-merge until sometime in February, but they would all want it at the same time.

The phone kept ringing.

"Oh hell," he muttered. He picked up the receiver. "Hello."

"This is Colonel Parker. I'm trying to reach some derelict flyboy named Rider."

Buddy sat upright. The voice on the other end was distorted as if coming from an echo chamber—likely a satellite phone.

"You got him, Jungle Jim. Hell, I didn't expect to hear back from you this quick."

"You should damned well know I would return your call even in the middle of the night."

"I appreciate that, Jim. Sounds like you're coming up in the world. When did you make colonel?"

"Oh, a while back."

"Hell, you must be doing *something* right."

"Well, likewise. I mean, since you're still around, I'm figuring you found a better way to land airplanes since I saw you last."

"You walked away from it, didn't you?"

"How the hell are you, Buddy?"

"Doing well right now, but I need some information."

"What'cha got?"

"I had someone show up at the hangar today wanting me to use an old C-47 I restored to fly some nuns out of an orphanage in El Salvador. They're in a small village near the Guatemalan border west of San Salvador."

The silence on the other end lasted several seconds before Parker cleared his throat and spoke. "Ummm. El Salvador. That's not good. Who is this person? Do you believe him?"

"It's a 'she,' and I don't know. She seems legit."

Again, there came another extended silence.

"There's more I *can't* say than I can, but you need to be careful."

"What's going on down there?" Buddy asked. "From what I hear, there's a lot of foreign influence—Russian, Cuban, and the whole region is a mess."

"Sounds like you've got it wrapped up in a nutshell. Some of the governments have gone the way of Cuba while some are fighting rebels of the same ilk. Problem is it's a lot like Nam. There's no simple black or white. The damned drug cartels are involved, and there's a lot of money passing hands with some real sleazeballs involved. Our people tiptoe around and try to sort the good guys from the bad guys."

"Are you involved?"

"Can't say."

"Sorry, didn't mean to—"

"Don't worry about it. I'll be at Eglin to pick up some assets in a few days. I've got your number. Get some more information from this woman. We need to make sure she is who she says she is. We'll talk then."

Buddy set the phone carefully back in its cradle and again stared out the window. The wind had come up, and from somewhere outside the house came the calls of geese still flying in the night sky. They were looking for the telltale shine of a field or lake, someplace to land for the night. Tomorrow he would meet with Sister Elizabeth and hopefully learn more about her mercy mission. He couldn't believe he had allowed himself to get involved in this crap.

CHAPTER FOUR

The Spooks

Leaving the house that morning, Buddy headed north up 49-West to Highway 61. On the radio, George Jones was singing his recent hit, "He Stopped Loving Her Today," and Buddy found himself aggravated—too many bad memories associated with that one. He punched a button to the next station—disco music. "Crap," he muttered.

Twisting the knob in frustration, he turned off the radio. Silence broken only by the hum of his mud tires on the pavement was a better option. The drive to Tunica took him past the Clarksdale airport, and he glanced at his watch. He was running early. For no particular reason he turned off the highway and drove down the road toward the hangar. There was probably no one around, but it wouldn't hurt to drive through.

As he approached, he spotted an unfamiliar car—a late model tan Ford. It was parked beside one of the faded yellow buildings on the ramp. He let the pickup roll to a stop. A man was peering through the window of his hangar. With his hands cupped on either side of his face and his forehead pressed against the glass, he hadn't yet noticed Buddy's approach. Probably just another reporter, but no sense in being unprepared.

Reaching beneath the seat he retrieved his .45 automatic, slipped it in his coat pocket, and stepped from the pickup. A building provided a convenient screen as he trotted up the road. Still unaware of his approach, the man was now testing the door to the hangar. Buddy walked to within a few feet of him before the man, clearly startled, straightened and spun about. He was wearing a suit and a tan trench coat—law enforcement perhaps.

"Are you the security guard for this place?" the man asked.

"How can I help you?" Buddy asked.

"Do you know the person who owns the aircraft in this hangar?"

"Who are you?"

The man's face reddened slightly—not a good sign. Buddy wrapped his hand around the .45 in his coat pocket. His thumb rested on the safety.

"I just need some information."

"That's not what I asked you."

"I'm a private investigator."

"Do you have some identification?"

"Look, mister, if you're not going to help me, you need to stand aside. I'm here on official business."

"Well, unless you have a warrant of some sort, you're trespassing, and since you refuse to show me any identification, how about I get the local law over here so you can show it to *them*?"

The man reached up and thumbed open a button on his trench coat. Buddy thumbed the safety on his .45 and cocked the hammer as he drew it from the coat pocket.

"If you come out of that coat with anything other than some identification, I'm going to shoot you. So, why don't you try being a little more cooperative, and maybe I can help you?"

The man held his hands up, palm outward.

"Okay. That's enough. My name is Benson. I work for the State Department, and I'm looking for a man named Rider who owns the plane inside this hangar."

"Good enough, Mister Benson. Now we're getting somewhere. I'm Rider. What can I do for you?"

"Have you been approached by a woman named Elizabeth Anderson or anyone else about the possibility of renting or leasing your aircraft?"

"Why do you ask?"

"Because she and others may be planning an unauthorized flight into Central America that may well interfere with both DEA and State Department business in the region. Trust me. It's not something you want to get involved with."

It was time to feign ignorance. "Who is this Anderson woman? Is she a drug runner?"

"Mister Rider, I'm going to reach inside my coat now and get a card for you with my contact information. So, just relax."

Benson pulled a wallet from a side pocket and handed him a card with an official-looking State Department logo.

"We know the Anderson woman flew into the Memphis airport a couple days ago, and we know she's made a number of inquiries about aircraft. If she approaches you, I'd like for you to get as much information from her as you can and contact me. She's not only a danger to herself, but to anyone she recruits, and to our people down in Central America."

"Isn't there a civil war or something going on down there? I thought I saw something like that on TV a while back."

"Mister Rider, it's a hell of a lot more than a civil war. The entire region is in turmoil. Every major city between Mexico and Colombia has antiaircraft weapons atop their buildings. Only a fool would fly down there without proper authorization or knowing exactly where in hell he was going. Like I said, if they contact you, don't be a fool. Call me."

The man turned to walk back toward his car but stopped and turned. "Do you know anyone else around here who owns a relatively large aircraft?"

"There's a fella up at Covington, Tennessee, a crop duster. He owns a Twin Beech they use for skydiving."

"Covington, Tennessee, huh?"

"Yeah, his place is out east of town a few miles."

"Thanks. I'll check him out."

There were others closer but driving sixty or seventy miles north to Covington would likely keep Mister Benson tied up for a day or two. Buddy's planned meeting with Colonel Parker had now taken on a greater sense of urgency.

Following at a safe distance that morning, Buddy watched as Benson blew through Tunica on his way back to Memphis. The tan Ford disappeared up Highway 61, and Buddy pulled into the parking lot at the Blue and White. The nun was there, sitting in her car. He got out and walked past as if she weren't there. Going inside, he found an empty booth in the back where he waited. A few moments later she came through the door but stopped and glanced back. Clandestine ops were definitely not her forte.

"Have a seat," Buddy said.

"Thanks."

"Coffee, please," Buddy said to the waitress.

"I'd like coffee as well, with cream and sugar," the nun said.

"Y'all gonna eat with us today?" the waitress asked.

"Maybe, later," Buddy said.

"Just give me a shout when you're ready."

When she was gone, Buddy gazed across the table at the nun. "Tell me a little bit about yourself, Sister. How long have you been a nun?"

She smiled and blinked. "I'm not a nun. I'm a lay missionary."

"Then why do you call yourself sister?"

"I'm not sure. That's what the Maryknolls call me."

"The Maryknolls?"

"Yes, they *are* nuns."

"You seem mighty young to be a missionary. I mean, how long have you been at it?"

"I just finished college last spring and I've been training. I haven't actually been on a mission trip yet."

"So, it's a calling, I suppose?"

"You could say that. I planned to be a counselor and a teacher, but now, I just want to give back to others what I have been fortunate enough to inherit."

"Sounds noble. Where are you from?"

"Chicago. That's where I went to school."

"What does your family think about this trip you're wanting to take?"

She paused, her lips parted, and she seemed momentarily confused.

"They don't know anything about it. Almost no one does, except for a donor who is sponsoring this trip as long as he can maintain anonymity."

"And you're the point man, so to speak, right?"

"Yes. I suppose."

"Well, Sist...Since you're not a nun, do you want me to call you Sister or Elizabeth or what?"

"You can call me Elizabeth."

"Okay, Elizabeth, I'm going to shoot straight with you. I don't think you've told me everything. I want you to tell me all you possibly can about this mercy mission you're planning."

"A Panamanian physician visited the mission in late November. That was the last time anyone heard from the sisters. He said they were not well. Two nuns and several of the children had fevers and he treated them, but they are in danger. The doctor said there are many government troops in the area. He also said rebels are around there as well. He thinks the government is involved in drug running because there is some type of facility nearby that is used either for consolidation or manufacture of cocaine and heroin. They have forced many of the villagers to work at the facility, and some who refused have simply disappeared.

"The orphan mission is all that's left of the village. It's located in a remote mountain area near the Guatemalan border northwest of the capital, San Salvador. The missionaries live in very primitive conditions, as do the children. They have little food, almost no medical supplies, and the government troops harass them continually when they come to search for rebel guerrillas.

"The doctor said there's an airstrip on the mountain near the village and government trucks come and go there once or twice a week. He observed them from a distance, but he's almost certain some of the people coming and going on the aircraft are Americans—I mean from the US—which makes sense, because our government is working with the current regime to fight the rebels.

"A Catholic charity recently sent the mission a truckload of supplies. It was just before Christmas, but the government troops turned them back before they could depart San Salvador. According to the doctor, the airstrip is guarded only when an aircraft arrives, and the soldiers leave to return to the compound as soon as it takes off. There isn't much we can do except hope to fly into the airstrip to take out the nuns and children before the government troops know we are there."

"Do you realize just how dangerous this harebrained scheme of yours is?"

"Of course I do, and I don't think it's harebrained. We can't just leave those nuns to die there in the jungle without trying to help them."

"I don't think you do. One of your State Department friends paid me a visit this morning down at the hangar, and you're right. The spooks are following you."

The young woman's face paled.

"Spooks?"

"Not sure—DEA or CIA, I figure."

"What did he say?"

"He said he knows you're trying to lease an aircraft to fly down there and that it would be ill-advised for me to become involved. Do you realize that even if you are able to pull this off, you and anyone else involved could go to prison?"

A pall fell over her face as her eyes again sank into thought.

"Oh, hell," Buddy said. "Relax. The pricks are just fishing. I'm going to meet with my friend in a couple days. He knows a lot about what's happening down there. Go back to your hotel, and if you call anyone, don't use your room phone. I don't think that guy is who he says he is. I think he works for the company, and they have a nasty habit of bugging phones."

"The company?"

"The CIA. If you call anyone, use a pay phone. I'd also change hotels and register under another name as soon as you can. Call me every night at seven beginning tomorrow evening. We'll talk after I meet with my friend."

"Why would the CIA be—"

"Elizabeth, go to a pay phone as soon as you can and tell the people you're working for not to call you at the hotel. I can't answer any of your questions right now. Just lay low and call me like I said. After I meet with my friend, we'll meet again."

Rider stood to leave. Elizabeth wanted to tell him about the man trying to get the key to her room, and there was the truth about her sponsor and the real motivation behind this entire mission, but she was afraid Rider would quit altogether. He seemed so paranoid and distrusting, and perhaps it was her own bias, but he also seemed especially distrusting of her as a woman. Yet, it was a nun at the college who once told her a lie chains you while the truth leaves you free. Elizabeth considered herself a person of morals. She had to tell him everything.

"Mr. Rider…" She hesitated.

"It's okay," he said. "Just be smart and keep your eyes open."

She looked down into her empty coffee cup. Despite his paranoia, he seemed so self-assured.

"Are you okay?" he asked.

"Yeah."

She would tell him later. For now, it was good that Rider was taking control. He dropped a ten on the table and winked at her.

"At some point you're going to have to trust me and start telling me everything."

She could hardly breathe. It was clear he knew she was holding back. Her face felt hot and flushed, and again she started to tell him, but he smiled and walked out.

A Mexican Standoff

B uddy had just finished supper that evening when the phone rang.

"Hello."

"Hey," was all the caller said. It was Jungle Jim Parker. "I got here sooner than expected, and we're flying out again in thirty-six hours. Can you meet me tomorrow around noon at a place called Sam's Oyster House in Fort Walton?"

Having to travel all the way to Florida was not what Buddy expected, but he had told the woman he would get her some information, and Parker obviously didn't want to talk on the phone. Determined to keep his word, Buddy realized there was but one viable option. He had to go to Florida. He would get her the information she needed and let her decide what she wanted to do. Then he would bow out. Besides, Jungle Jim's terse communication was evidence that he knew a lot about what was happening in Central America.

"I'll be there."

The phone clicked and the dial tone returned. With such short notice, flying down, even in one of his crop dusting planes, would require too many arrangements. Buddy's only practical means of transportation was his pickup. It was over four hundred miles and nearly seven and a half hours by highway to Fort Walton. Best to leave now.

He put a pot of coffee on to brew and threw a change of clothes and shaving kit into his bag. After pouring the thermos full he glanced at the clock. With fuel and rest stops, he could make it by four a.m. Once there, he would get some sleep.

It was a straight shot down Highway 49 to the Gulf Coast, but passing through Jackson, Hattiesburg, and Mobile would cost him time, plus he had to top-off the tank in places like Hattiesburg or Mobile because nothing would be open in the middle of the night. The time slipped by as he drove, and Buddy found himself wondering just what the hell he was doing. He was just like the young woman—an altruistic fool, bent on doing some magnanimous act of kindness with no real idea what all it might involve.

Parker was being super-cautious. That alone did not bode well, and the further Buddy drove the more his doubts increased. He should have simply told Elizabeth Anderson it was too risky and dropped it. Yet here he was on a midnight ride to Florida and for what? With the federal government on this woman's trail, it wouldn't be long before they would be on his, and he sure as hell didn't want to go to prison. This was insanity.

Six hours later he passed beneath the giant live oaks on the quiet streets of Mobile, Alabama, and crossed Mobile Bay. The strong, clean scent of coastal pines and salt water filled his nostrils, and it was still a couple of hours before dawn. If nothing else, it would be good to see Jim Parker again. Jim would shoot straight with him and hopefully give him the skinny on the situation in Central America. He would also know if the odds were worth the risks, but even that idea was ludicrous, because Buddy had made up his mind—come hell or high water, he was not flying to Central America.

———————

After a long nap in his pickup, Buddy found Sam's Oyster House later that morning, but it wasn't exactly what he expected. There was no restaurant. It was a shanty with a menu printed on colorful boards hanging over the service windows. The only things keeping him from judging it too quickly were a parking lot full of vehicles and the intoxicating aroma of fried fish—one that had him practically drooling.

He glanced at his wristwatch. It was only eleven. There was one parking place and he pulled in. With another hour remaining before Jim was to arrive, it was terribly tempting to order something, but that would be classless. He closed his eyes and drifted into dreams of tables piled high with seasoned fried shrimp and fried Amberjack sandwiches.

It reminded him of a hot Thanksgiving dinner he'd had in Saigon in '67. There was no turkey and no cranberries that day, but it was the best Thanksgiving dinner he'd ever had. Shrimp fried with rice and spiced with nuoc mam, lo mein noodles in a soup of bamboo sprouts and soy. And of course, it didn't hurt that he'd just survived another mission where his little Cessna barely made it back while smoking and looking like a piece of olive drab Swiss cheese.

Buddy's memories faded and he slipped into a restless sleep, drifting in and out of his dreams as the aroma of fried food filled his head. He was in fried seafood heaven.

"You gotta be dreamin' about a woman, dude."

The voice didn't fit his dream.

"Hey! Wake up."

Buddy's knee banged against the underside of the dash as he sat bolt upright. Only then was he fully awake, and he turned to look up at the person standing beside his pickup.

"Jesus, Jim! You scared the shit out of me."

He pushed the door open and got out of the truck, standing face to face for the first time in eleven years with Jungle Jim Parker. The colonel still had that deep patina from years in the tropical sun, and he may have had a few more creases around his eyes, but he looked almost exactly as Buddy remembered him.

"You never age, do you?" he asked.

Parker grinned. "Apparently not as much as you chickenshit flyboys."

The two men clutched one another with mutual back slaps.

"Let's not get too intimate, Kemosabe. I've been down there in the jungle too long and haven't seen my wife in months."

"Damned if you lifers aren't a bunch of sex-starved perverts."

Jim laughed out loud. "Don't worry. She's flying in from Bragg tonight. Let's go order something, and we'll drive someplace where we can sit and look out at the Gulf."

When they received their food, Colonel Parker rode with Buddy in the pickup down to Okaloosa Island. It may have been January, but the Florida Gulf Coast was warm. Buddy quickly shed his flannel shirt and hiking boots. Walking barefoot in the snow-white sand, the men hiked over to a private military beach where they found a wooden picnic table amongst the sand dunes. The sun glittered on the Gulf waters, and emerald-green waves gently pounded ashore. Far out on the Gulf, the hazy gray silhouette of a ship passed slowly on the horizon. The men opened their sacks and spread the food on the table.

"You can pay more money, you can have fancier surroundings, but you will never get better food than they have at Sam's Oyster House."

"How'd you find that place?"

"I went through Ranger training down here in '65. That's when I met old man Taylor. He owns the place. Treated us soldiers like V.I.P.s."

"Sounds like good people."

"He is."

Buddy took a huge bite of his fish sandwich.

"Anything I say to you today could get me in deep shit," Parker said.

"Anything you say to me today will never be repeated."

Parker eyed him across the table. His eyes had the natural squint of a hunter, a man-predator who had been in the jungle for so many years until he now resembled the big cats that roamed there. Parker was a patriot and a man who believed in his oath to protect and defend the Constitution. Yet his was not a blind allegiance. Even the Asian followers of Jainism occasionally stepped on a bug, and governments did so often, no matter how well intentioned. Jim did his best to keep that from happening.

"As you well know, Special Forces have a code of silence that is unlike that of other branches of the military. Ours is absolute. We talk to no one. The only reason I am telling you any of this is because you were Special Forces, and we've faced the beast together, up close and personal. I know you, and I trust you. I expect you will die or go to prison before you reveal any of what I am about to tell you."

The warning was not needed, but it was Jim's way of telling him he was about to receive some highly classified information.

"Well, Jim, I'd say that's a fair and accurate description of how we operate. What I need, now, is your assessment of the situation in El Salvador and an assessment of what I am about to share with you."

"You first," the colonel said. "Tell me the *what* and *why*, and we'll go from there."

"Fair enough," Buddy said.

Sea gulls flashed in the sun overhead, their squawks echoing over the white sand dunes. A warm Gulf breeze swayed the sea oats, and the men ate their sandwiches with relish.

"It's like I told you on the phone. This missionary woman showed up at my hangar in Clarksdale wanting me to fly her to El Salvador to bring back a bunch of nuns and orphans."

"First thing I want to know is how you knew to contact me," Parker said.

"I heard rumor that you were in Central America, and I know S.F. is always trying to save the world. I figured you might know what's happening down there. Hell, I wasn't even sure you were still active military, but you were the only one I knew well enough to try to contact."

"So, you're saying contacting me was strictly a shot in the dark?"

"Yeah, why?"

"All I can say is you hit the jackpot as far as getting information on the area, but first let me ask you this. Do you trust this woman?"

"I believe she's telling me the truth about wanting to rescue these people from the Salvadoran government."

"How the hell are you going to rescue people with a crop dusting plane?"

"I have an old C-47 I restored."

"Oh, yeah. I forgot you mentioned that."

Parker gazed out at the Gulf. Along the water's edge, sandpipers scurried away from the waves as the foamy surf slid up onto the beach.

"Buddy, I'll tell you what I can, but don't expect me to tell you it's all bubble-up and rainbow pie. It's a tough scenario down there. Our government is supporting the current Salvadoran junta—the ones who came into power during the October '79 military coup. The leftist rebels have valid gripes, but they are being led by the Communists. The Cubans, with Russian support, are in there selling them a bill of goods, much as Castro and Guevara did with their people. You know how that turned out. The problem is it's the same as it was in Cuba. The ones in power are a bunch of sleazeballs, but they're the ones we have to support."

"Sounds like a real shitshow."

"It's the big picture we're looking at. If we take care of the assholes in power, we're gambling that will protect the hemisphere from the Russians and other Communist influences. Meanwhile, the poor get shit on. These missionaries are in the middle of it, and the paranoid assholes in the current Salvadoran government fear them. They don't want them to leave the country because they already know too much. That's why they're in danger. Do you know what liberation theology is about?"

Buddy shook his head. "Not really."

"Well, it's what has put your lady-friend's fellow missionaries' necks in the noose. Don't get me wrong. Their intent is noble and well-grounded in religious belief, but it's the same old story of the path to hell being paved with good intentions. It's problematic and a classic Catch-22 strategy because liberation theology naturally gravitates into the political realm, and the Marxists and Communists have latched onto the movement like bloodsucking leeches. They feed the peasants weapons and money along with a line of bullshit three feet wide and ten yards long. The poor buy into it and end up swapping one form of dictatorship for another."

"Is this liberation theology some sort of official church policy?"

"Not really. The popes, bishops, and other church leaders have been at odds over it for a long time. You know yourself that our Special Forces motto is 'De Oppresso Liber – to Free the Oppressed,' and this mess puts us at odds with our own belief structures as well. Meanwhile, people die while we try to influence the politics of their oppressors to cut them some slack. I'll tell you more later, but what do you need to know now?"

"Can you tell me anything about that orphanage west of San Salvador on the Guatemalan border?"

The sun glinted in Parker's eyes as he squinted at the Gulf horizon.

"Like I said, you hit the jackpot. I am directly involved, and I have men on the ground in that area, as well as all over Central America. Our mission is classified, and we're operating totally in the dark. Officially, we are supporting the Salvadoran government and training their troops, but lately they've been slaughtering people wholesale. So, our higher-ups have ordered us to stand-down for now, but my men are still ghosting and reconning in the area. No one, not the rebels nor the Salvadoran government, knows where we are or what we are doing, but we have eyes on them.

"My orders are to do only that—at least for now—and here's the skinny on the local AO. There's a large compound there, and there's an airstrip nearby, and the Salvadoran Government is either complicit with those using the compound or else directly involved and using it themselves. That's where their troops are housed, and they aren't allowing us anywhere near it, but I've had my men check it out.

"It's a drug facility. There are drugs being flown in by the cartels from Nicaragua and Colombia. We think they're consolidating shipments and perhaps processing drugs there as well. Best we can tell, if the Salvadoran government isn't running it, they're guarding it and likely collecting some hefty kickbacks. The sad part is we saw some Americans there, and some of the drugs are being sold right here in the United States. I don't know it for a fact, but my guess is they're former CIA guys who are running drugs now. Yeah, it's a sad fact. We're supporting these sleazeballs selling dope, in hopes of keeping the Communists at bay.

"The village, or what's left of it, is only a couple klicks down the road from the compound, between it and the airstrip. As far as we can tell, there are only a few old people left there along with the nuns and orphans. Now listen carefully. What I'm about to tell you could be detrimental to U.S. interests and get us all in deeper shit if it gets out.

"Our people are at odds with one another. By that I mean the DEA, the military, and the State Department are locked in a classic Mexican standoff. The DEA wants to bust the drug runners. The military wants to bust the chops of the Salvadoran National Guard, because of their wholesale slaughter of the peasants, and the State Department wants to play politics. Fact is there's no exit strategy where anyone comes out squeaky clean, but the simple fact is the State Department has the trump card, and they're giving everyone a 'hands-off' for now. They feel the Salvadoran government will eventually allow the nuns to leave the country, but State doesn't want to force their hand and possibly cause them to do something rash."

"You mean like kill them?"

"There are a lot of innocent people getting hurt, and I would like to say that won't happen, but we're between a rock and a hard place. We have eyes on that village twenty-four/seven, but if the government goons come in there and take those nuns, my men have standing orders not to interfere. I would like to do more, but like the oath you took when you served, I have my oath as well. Interference of any sort could create difficulties with the current regime that the State Department wants to avoid."

"Is it possible for some idiot to fly into the airstrip and bring out the nuns and orphans?"

"It's about timing. And it would require some solid ground support."

"I understand, but do you think it can be done?"

"It's possible, but there are a lot of variables. Let's assume you're lucky and everything goes well with the flight and landing. What if the government troops in the area are alerted, or what if the rebels show up? What if the weather goes to shit or you have mechanical problems after you arrive? It's not quite a crap shoot, but it would take a lot of communication, coordination, and a hell of a lot of luck to succeed. You're not really considering doing this, are you?"

"Oh, *hell* no! I mean, I'm just trying to get some facts for that woman."

Parker turned his gaze back to the horizon, and it was clear he was masking a grin.

"Rider, you are one lying sonofabitch."

"What do you mean? I'd be crazy to try something like that."

"How long before you try it?"

"Look, Jim, I'm not.... Shit! Okay. Maybe. I've been telling myself there is no way I'll do something like this, but I really don't know. My plan was to get some information for the woman and maybe talk her out of it. I thought she was like all the other women I've known since returning from Nam—you know, not a clue about war, death, and the sacrifices our buddies made over there. I still think she doesn't understand what could happen if we fail, but the more I think about it, I believe it's something I have to do."

"Why?"

"I've asked myself that same thing since that woman first came to me. I reckon it's because of people like you and Buck Marino."

"What do you mean?"

"I was carried out of the jungle in Vietnam twice—once by you and once by Buck. I think it's *my* turn to carry someone out of the jungle."

Parker stuffed the empty food containers into the sack.

"I'll contact you at your house telephone on a secure communication link three days from now. It will be around nineteen hundred hours your time. Make sure your line is clear and uncompromised. Check it carefully for me. I don't need to get my ass in a bind by sharing classified information. If an operator gets involved, she will say the call is coming from somewhere in the states, Fort Bragg, Benning, hell, I don't know. Anyway, I'll update you then.

"I'm going to have our people do a background check on the woman—make sure she's not media or something. If her story checks out, and my men there in El Salvador think this is something we can do, I'll contact you with our next move. Keep your cards close to your vest and watch your back."

Buddy walked back over the dunes with Jim to the pickup. This entire affair had taken on a life of its own, racing ahead faster than he could comprehend. It was a sucker hole that had lured him into the comfort of a blue sky, while his own steadfast refusals had provided the false sense of security that convinced him he would never do something so stupid. He had said it repeatedly, but the clouds were now closing in around him.

The warm breeze was cooling as the sun sank into the Gulf.

Flying to El Salvador was something he did not want to do. Yet, if there were no other options, he knew now that he would try. He would try to save these nuns and their orphans, because he owed it to the ones who had twice saved him from a similar fate.

After a night in a motel, Buddy made the long drive back home to Mississippi, and he thought about the situation the entire way. The good Lord had given him the grace to survive two near misses with death in Vietnam, and now he was considering something that was likely just as dangerous. He had to be out of his mind. First, he would try to make Elizabeth Anderson understand the dangers, but if she insisted, he would work with her.

CHAPTER SIX

How to Fly Under the Radar

B uddy checked the phone as soon as he arrived home. Elizabeth Anderson had left a recorded message, saying she would call again the next day. Another meeting with her could bring the feds down on them both, but he was committed. Buddy examined the telephone and checked all the wires around the house and out to the service pole. There was no evidence of tampering, but he was taking no chances. A face-to-face meeting was the wiser option. At precisely seven p.m. the telephone rang. He picked up the receiver.

"Yeah."

"Uh, is this Mister—?"

"Yes. Meet me at Overton Park Zoo tomorrow at ten a.m. I'll be leaning against the pillar with the statue of a lion on the left side of the main zoo entrance. I'll be wearing a dark green hooded jacket. Drive by twice, but don't look my way. When I see you coming the second time, if you're being followed, I will walk away.

"If I don't walk away, park and come inside the zoo. I will find you. If I walk away, don't follow me, but park anyway and go inside the zoo. Wait ten minutes and come back out. Walk briskly to your car and leave quickly. Drive to the south park entrance and turn right on Poplar Avenue. Drive into downtown

Memphis, park, and walk to Court Square Park. I'll be there near the fountain. You got it?"

"Yes."

"See you then."

He hung up.

The first time Elizabeth Anderson passed the zoo entrance that morning, Buddy saw a car nearly two blocks away following slowly behind her. It was the same tan Ford that Benson had been driving when he was snooping around the Clarksdale Airport. Turning away, Buddy pulled the bill of his cap down low and the hood of his jacket close around his face. Thankfully, despite being January, the southern sunshine had brought out a decent crowd. Cutting his eyes as the vehicle passed, he recognized the driver. It was Benson.

A couple minutes later Elizabeth's car approached again with Benson still following. Turning, Buddy mingled with the crowd and walked casually away. Making his way into the trees near the parking lot, he waited and watched as Elizabeth parked and walked toward the zoo entrance. Benson pulled in, parked several rows over. He paid admission and followed her inside. There came the roar of a lion and the children near the gate screamed and giggled.

After scanning the lot to make sure he hadn't overlooked anything—like a second spook—Buddy walked quickly to Benson's vehicle. Lifting the hood, he went to work. After loosening the coil wire, he did the same with several more wires on the distributor cap. This would get Benson off her tail for now. When he was done, Buddy hurried to his truck and drove into downtown Memphis.

After feeding every squirrel and pigeon in the park, Buddy had developed a following of sorts as he walked around the big fountain. It was 11:30. She should have already been here. Tossing the empty peanut bag into a trash bin, he shooed away the pigeons and scanned the park. If Benson had approached Elizabeth while still in the zoo parking lot…. Buddy spotted her walking his way. She shot a quick glance over her shoulder.

He studied the crowded sidewalk behind her. The people hurried along while pulling their coats tighter as a cloud layer moved in, and the temperature dropped rapidly. It was always cooler downtown near the river, but it seemed a cold front was approaching. No one seemed to be following her as Elizabeth entered the park. She was wearing only a light jacket. Her cheeks had reddened, and her breath vaporized in the chill breeze that blew between the buildings.

"I saw him," she said. "It was the guy in that tan-colored car that was following me, right?"

"Did he realize you saw him?"

"I don't think so. I mean, I tried not to be obvious about it. Why?"

"As long as he thinks you don't know he's following you, he'll stay predictable."

Elizabeth shivered. "It's getting really cold."

"Okay. Let's go. We'll find someplace warm and get some coffee."

They walked out to Main Street and turned south. The downtown odors of sizzling burgers, the peanut store, and diesel fumes were complemented with honking horns and an Elvis song coming from a nearby record store.

"Did you talk to your friend?" she asked.

"Yes. And I learned a lot."

"Did you learn enough that you want to help me?"

Buddy had already determined this woman was a stubborn one, and decided finesse was the better part of good judgement. Instead of telling her she was batshit crazy, he tried to modulate his response.

"Elizabeth, I want to help you, but you're taking on a mission that requires a lot more expertise than either of us possesses. My friend said there are lots of Salvadoran troops in the area around the village, and there may be drug runners involved as well. We would have to be mighty lucky for this to work out in our favor. The question is, do we want to dive into the fire in an attempt to rescue your friends—even if we are likely to be consumed by the same fire?"

"No, but God tells us He expects us to be our brother's keeper, and sometimes a person has to act on conviction even when the odds are not very good. You sound like you're giving up before we've even begun. Are you?"

"I am trying to reason with you, and like I said before, I'm not committing to anything without knowing *all* the facts. My friend is gathering more information about the situation in El Salvador. You need to tell me everything you know about these missionaries, the people helping you, and anyone else who may be involved. Let's take it one step at a time and determine if we can accomplish this without ending up dead or in prison."

Telling Rider everything so soon could be risky if he backed out. She looked over at him and shrugged. "There are only five or six close acquaintances involved, but I really don't know what else to tell you or where to begin. What do you suggest?"

They stopped in front of a small grill. "Let's go inside and see what's for lunch."

He pushed the door open for her, and she again glanced back before going inside.

"To answer your question: the first thing I suggest is that you begin learning how to fly under the radar."

They sat at a small table near the window. A city bus rumbled past, trailing a cloud of diesel fumes. Buddy noticed the Christmas wreaths still hanging from the lampposts up and down Main Street. It reminded him of his Mississippi neighbor who left his Christmas lights up year-round, but then this *was* Memphis, the metropolis of the Mississippi Delta.

"What do you mean by *fly under the radar*?"

"I mean you've got to start thinking more like a fox and less like a lamb. Take for example how you keep looking over your shoulder. That's a dead giveaway that you know someone is following you."

"What am I supposed to do?"

"If you think you're being followed, stop and look into a store window or pretend you're looking for something in your purse, and carefully watch your back-trail from the corner of your eye. That's only one small thing, but how about we begin there? You have these people tailing you, and the way I figure, they're probably CIA, trying to make sure you don't interfere with whatever it is they're doing with the Salvadorans. Right now, it looks like there's only one of them following you, so how do we get rid of him?"

She looked up from the menu, startled and wide-eyed.

"What do you mean—get rid of him?"

It was clear she misunderstood and assumed the worst. Buddy did his best to remain poker-faced.

"Well, I'll have to off him—know what I mean?"

"Off him?" she whispered. "You mean *kill* him?"

She took it hook, line, and sinker.

"Yeah."

"No!" she said too loudly.

People at the adjacent tables glanced around at them.

"No," she hissed—this time quieter. "I can't believe you wou—"

"Calm down. I was kidding."

Her lips flattened hard as she glared at him.

"I don't think you're funny."

"Okay, seriously, we have to find a way to get him off your tail. We can't accomplish anything as long as this guy is following you around."

"So, how do you propose I do that?"

Buddy thought about it while the waitress took their orders.

"I'll have this cheeseburger with mayonnaise and lettuce please," Elizabeth said.

"Fries?" the waitress asked.

"No, thank you. Just the sandwich, please."

"You, sir?"

"A hamburger, with mustard and onion, and fries."

"Drinks?"

"I'll have water," Elizabeth said. "No ice."

"Sweet Tea," Buddy added.

When the waitress was gone, he again studied the woman sitting across from him. At least seven years younger than himself, she seemed intelligent, but this idea that she could simply rent a plane with a pilot, swoop into a war-torn Third World country, and rescue her friends, was largely premised on her ignorance. Yet, the more he thought about it, the more he realized he was encouraging her by participating in her surreal world of make-believe. It was one much like his old friend Buck Marino had described as his view of the war in Vietnam—the one Alice found down the rabbit hole.

The girl gazed across the table at him but said nothing. She was waiting for him to start the conversation, but his plan was only partially formulated. The first thing he had to do was throw the feds off her trail, then take her somewhere to lay low until Jim Parker called back. He was no super-spy, but he had to think this through and come up with a plan.

"Okay. We need to send this guy following you in another direction. If we're successful doing that, then we can take the next step, which is to go somewhere and lay low until we hear back from my friend."

"Are you saying you're going to help me do this?"

"I'm saying we'll take this one step at a time. I still want to know about everyone involved, but we'll discuss that later. Right now, I'm going to call the airlines and find out when the next flight departs for Miami. That will likely be tomorrow morning. When we know, I want you to go back to your hotel and pack your bags. In the morning, about an hour before the flight is scheduled to depart, call the airlines from your room phone, and ask when the next flight to Miami departs. I'm banking on the spooks having the hotel phones bugged.

"Once you've done that, go to the front desk and check out, and while you're there tell the clerk you couldn't find what you wanted here in Memphis, so you're going to Miami. Try to emphasize it so he remembers what you say when the one following you comes around and questions him."

"Then what?"

"Go to the airport. Turn in your rental car and go into the terminal and purchase a ticket for Miami, Florida. Don't check your bags and make sure you're not being followed. Walk like you're going to the departure gate but go to baggage claims instead, on the bottom deck. I'll be waiting out front to pick you up. I'll be in a late model Chevrolet, probably a Malibu with a dealer tag, but I'm not sure about the color yet."

"You got it?"

She nodded rapidly. Elizabeth Anderson was young, naïve, and hopelessly altruistic, but she seemed quick on the uptake.

"Good. We'll discuss the rest after we get this bozo off your tail."

That afternoon he borrowed a loaner car from a friend who owned a car dealership in Tunica—something the spooks would not recognize as his—a Chevy Malibu.

The next morning, Buddy was parked in the drive lane outside baggage claims at the Memphis Airport when Elizabeth hurried through the door. He grabbed her bags, pushing them into the back seat.

"Come on. Get in," he said, "and buckle up."

Ten minutes later they were headed south from Memphis on I-55 into Mississippi. It was a cold and dreary day, but it fit his mood. He still could not believe he was going through all these motions when every ounce of his common sense said it was a Quixotic mission. This one though possessed windmills with real dangers, and the consequences for knights in shining armor were potentially fatal.

"Where are we going?" she asked, glancing over her shoulder at the highway.

"If you're going to look back, use the rear-view mirror or a mirror from your purse, but you need not worry. There's no one following us. I'm going to exit the interstate down here and head west over to Highway 61. I'm stopping at the hangar in Clarksdale to check on the plane."

"Did your friend call you back?"

"Not yet."

Buddy couldn't help but notice she was now wearing a somewhat more stylish white blouse and had unpinned her hair, letting it fall below her shoulders. A little lipstick and this woman could pass for a fashion model. A smattering of wet snowflakes began hitting the windshield.

"I didn't think it snowed this far south," she said.

"It doesn't much. We'll get a few inches, two or three times during the average winter."

"I hope it doesn't snow much today," she said. "They said it would be warm down here, so I didn't pack any warm clothes."

"Who are *they*?"

"My friends from the college. I don't think any of them are from this part of the country."

Buddy bit his tongue. The people from the college were her apparent mentors, many of whom had apparently been cloistered in academia and traveled little.

"So, is it someone from the college who is sponsoring you?"

"No, I just have lots of relationships there—old teachers and such. I stay in touch with them."

He decided to let it drop for now. The hangar was cold and dark when they arrived. After turning on the lights, he climbed into the C-47. Elizabeth followed as he made his way with a flashlight up to the cockpit. Despite refurbishing most of the mechanical components and some external surfaces, the decades of wear on the cockpit controls and instrument panel were still evident. Flipping several switches, he brought the instruments to life. Elizabeth stepped over into the right seat and smoothed her skirt back over her knees.

"Don't you have some slacks and long-handles?" Buddy asked.

Glaring at him, she snatched the hem of her skirt further over her knees. "I told you I expected it to be warm down here. Besides, I'm not sure that my clothes are any of your business, Mister Rider."

"Look, it's thirty-two degrees out there right now. It's going into the twenties tonight, and tomorrow you're going to find this cockpit mighty damned drafty. It will probably warm up in a few days, but I suggest you put that little outfit you're wearing away and dress for the weather."

"Are we flying somewhere tomorrow?"

"Like I said, we're going somewhere to lay low. We're relocating the aircraft until I hear back from my friend. Do you have any warmer clothes?"

"Other than my jacket, I have some khaki slacks and a sweater."

Buddy used a shop rag to wipe the dust from the instrument panel.

"I didn't realize this airplane was as old as you said."

"She's a good old girl, but she does show her age."

"Why do you call your airplane a girl?"

"I did a lot of research on this plane. She was originally dubbed 'Miss Molly' when she arrived in England in 1944."

"Hmmm—1944. That was a long time ago. According to what I've learned, there are some high mountains in El Salvador. Do you think this old plane can get over them safely?"

"Perhaps you'd rather do like Sister Sarah and climb them with two mules, Sister Elizabeth."

Her eyes widened with anger. "Mister Rider, your joke is stale and frankly, it's really not that funny. Do you have to be such a smarta—"

She caught herself and went silent. Buddy stifled his anger as he killed the switches one by one.

"You know—this old girl has flown across oceans, been in wars, fought through storms, and has always been there for her crew and passengers. That's something you can put your trust in and that's the reason I love her like an old friend. This plane will take you anywhere you need to go. Fact is I trust Miss Molly a lot more than I trust you, and trust is really important in a mission like yours. Think about it."

He stood and squeezed from the cockpit. Buddy wanted to like this woman, but something about her didn't set well with him. He wasn't exactly sure how she felt, but to him it was much like the impersonal and cold January breeze that was blowing that afternoon. He and his airplane were mere assets to her—nothing more—someone and something to be used and discarded, as if this mess she was proposing were a simple business proposition.

CHAPTER SEVEN

A Quick Relocation of Assets

Buddy completed a walk-around and finished prepping the aircraft for the next day's flight while Elizabeth stood by, hugging herself and shivering. By the time he was ready to leave the hangar that day, the afternoon temperature had dropped below freezing. When they stepped outside they were met with a blast of bitter-cold north wind. It took several minutes for the car to warm after departing the airport, and Elizabeth was still shaking.

"Where are we going now?" she asked.

"To my house."

"Where is that?"

"About twenty minutes from here, south of Tutwiler, off 49 West."

"Why are we going there?"

"We're going there to get something to eat, and I'm going to pack some clothes and gear. In the morning, we're coming back here and loading the plane with spare parts and supplies."

"Are you saying I'm spending the night with you?"

Buddy resisted rolling his eyes.

"I have spare bedrooms, but if that doesn't suit you, you're welcome to sleep in the car tonight."

Her face blushed a bright crimson, but she maintained a steadfast gaze on the road ahead.

"So, are we flying to El Salvador?"

"I don't know yet."

"When will you know?"

"Possibly when I talk to my friend again. He is supposed to call me tonight. Unless he tells us to do something different, we're going to fly to a private airstrip south of Baton Rouge."

"Why are we going there?"

"To get away from the people following you and lay low while we wait."

Buddy pulled into the Dollar store in Clarksdale.

"Why are you stopping here?"

"We're stopping so you can do what women like to do most. You're going to go in there and shop. I want you to buy yourself a good windbreaker to go over your jacket and get some long-handle underwear. Do you have wool socks and boots?"

"No, and you don't have to be such a smart—" she hesitated "—alec. Besides, I don't have enough money to buy all that stuff."

"Use a credit card. Isn't that the currency of choice for you gals?"

"I still have to pay for it sooner or later."

Buddy found himself checkmated by a woman who practiced his own sensibilities.

"I thought you had money for fuel and other supplies."

"I do, but I want to save it for the trip."

"Oh, for the love of—!" He snatched his wallet from this pocket. "Here's fifty bucks. Buy some cotton-pickin' underwear and a windbreaker on me, or you'll freeze your ass—sorry, I mean you'll get really cold tomorrow—and get some extra socks and some boots!"

His anger must have cowed her because she put up no further argument.

Late that afternoon, Buddy chopped some venison steak into cubes, dusted it with flour and browned it with garlic while dicing carrots, potatoes, celery, and onion. JD had introduced himself to Elizabeth and she was rubbing his head and giving him hugs. The big lab was sucking it up.

"Do you like venison stew?" Buddy asked.

"I don't know. I've never had any."

The aroma of the garlic and venison browning in the skillet filled the kitchen.

"I can't believe a girl from Illinois has never had venison stew," he said.

"We lived in a suburb, and no one in my family hunted. Besides, I've always heard deer meat is gamey tasting."

"It's only gamey when it's not prepared properly, and preparation begins when you line your sights on the deer. You've got to kill it quickly with one shot. Then you skin it and hang it to cool down. And you sure as hell don't put it in your pickup and drive around to every bar in town, showing it to your buddies. You've got to respect the animal and it pays you back with some damned fine venison."

"Mister Rider, I don't want to seem unappreciative, but I don't condone killing animals of any sort, especially deer."

"I suppose you think that cheeseburger you had for lunch grew on a hamburger tree, or is it that you think the little brown-eyed steer they made it from died of natural causes?"

Her eyes widened and her lips squinched into a circle as a certain sort of rebellious look came over her face.

"Where is the room I'm staying in tonight?"

"Down that hallway off the big room, first door on the left. There's a bathroom attached. I'll bring you some clean sheets after we eat. There are towels in the bathroom closet. Let me know if you need anything else."

She grabbed her bags and marched across the big room toward the hallway.

"I won't need anything else!" she shouted.

"Are you coming back to eat supper?" he yelled.

"No!"

The bedroom door slammed shut, and Buddy sighed. He was no expert on female psychology, but this one seemed a bit more sensitive than average. He had dated many women since his return from Vietnam ten years ago, and Elizabeth wasn't much different from the others—temperamental and never happy—but once upon a time there had been one. She had at first seemed different. It was the girl he was engaged to back in the sixties when he went into the army.

Lori, his first love, always reminded him of sunshine—or so it was until two years after he departed for the military. That was when she sent him the same "Dear John" letter so many of his buddies had gotten while in Nam. His love for Lori never died, and he could never hate her, but the broken trust between them would never heal. She married an Ole Miss football player who gave her three kids before his car dealership and a half-dozen girlfriends came between them. Lori had been a fine woman. Too bad. Last he heard, she was single and working as a nurse in Baton Rouge.

She called him one day out of the blue—*just to see how he was doing,* she said. Thankfully, she had the three kids to keep her company, because despite his best efforts toward civility, when she suggested they meet sometime, he said he would rather be lonely than subject himself to another broken trust. That had been five years ago and the last time he heard from her.

It was also when he first realized he had driven away every woman he had known since. He didn't trust any of them—not one. It didn't matter that most never gave him a reason to feel this way, but it beat the hell out of having it happen again.

After eating a bowl of venison stew, he gathered sheets and blankets and went to the bedroom door and knocked. No answer. He knocked again. He heard a shuffling sound.

"Yes?"

She was just the other side of the door,

"I have your sheets."

The door opened. Elizabeth's eyes were red and moist.

"Why are you crying?"

"I'm not crying."

She snatched the sheets from his arms and pushed the door shut.

"You're welcome!" Buddy shouted through the door.

There was no reply, and he walked back to the kitchen where he poured himself a glass of bourbon. He had done what he could to make the woman comfortable. Now he would wait for Jim Parker's call. It came twenty minutes later.

He picked up the phone. "Yeah."

"You need to be in Brownsville, Texas, in three days. I'll have a man meet you there. He will fly copilot with you. He will purchase your fuel and have nav charts and radio frequencies, as well as complete information for your initial destination and secondary airstrips if you need to divert. I strongly recommend you bring along some survival gear and personal protection such as a sidearm. Outside of that, my people will supply everything else. If anyone asks, you're on your way to Cancun for a little R & R. with some friends. Questions?"

"Did you run a background check on the girl?"

"Her story checks out. Anything else?"

"No."

"Good luck."

The phone clicked and the dial tone returned. Buddy stared out the window at nothing in particular. This was it. He was really going through with this thing, and there were other people taking tremendous risks. Regardless of all his reservations, this was going to happen, and he had to stop playing games with himself and zero in on the facts at hand.

The plan for now was to fly with no flight plan to a friend's private airstrip near Houma, Louisiana. Two days later, he would hop to Brownsville and top off the tanks. After that, it would be up to Jungle Jim and his man to take the lead. For now, he had to do his part to get the girl and Miss Molly quickly and safely out of the area.

The diversionary tactics with the spooks would work for only so long, and Buddy set his alarm for four a.m. The sooner he moved the plane out of Clarksdale, the better his chances were of escaping detection. He spent the remainder of the evening preparing, packing gear, and writing detailed letters to leave behind for his closest friend Buck Marino, his accountant, and his lawyer. Hell, he hadn't done this even when he went to Vietnam.

─────────────

One thing Buddy had learned in Nam was how to sleep. No matter how risky the next day's mission, he could fall asleep in minutes. It was a necessity. You slept when you could, and this night was no different. It was a total black-out until the alarm jarred him awake at four a.m. sharp. The house was still and quiet, and he wondered about his guest. He would let her sleep a while longer.

Wasting no time, he took a quick shower, dressed, and started the coffee. With his bags already packed, he loaded the car, and went back inside to start breakfast—sausage, eggs, biscuits, and grits. The sound of a hair dryer came from the bathroom. She had awakened on her own. A few minutes later, Elizabeth walked into the kitchen. She was wearing khakis and a sweater.

"Morning," he said.

"Good morning." She didn't smile, but her voiced lacked the sharp emotion of the night before.

"Are you ready to move ahead with this?" he asked.

She nodded, and he studied her eyes. She masked her feelings well. If nothing else, this woman was stubbornly focused while fighting doubts of her own.

"Bring your bags in here, and I'll put them in the car."

"I can load them." It seemed her voice was softer and perhaps somewhat conciliatory. "Where are we going?"

"We're taking the plane to an airstrip in Louisiana and wait."

"So, we're going?"

"Seems so, but if things get derailed, I want to know we have enough money for fuel to return here. You said your sponsor gave you money for that. How much?"

"I have several thousand dollars."

"Okay. Keep it in a secure place. We may need it to get back home. Go ahead and load your bags."

When she came back inside, her cheeks were red. She exhaled and rubbed her hands together. "I still can't believe it gets this cold down here," she said.

"It should be warmer where we're going."

Buddy pulled the biscuits from the oven and set them on the table.

"Butter those, if you don't mind, and I'll set the table. How do you like your eggs?"

"Over medium, maybe, but I'm not particular."

He wondered why she had been crying last night, but silence was the better part of detente for the moment. He cracked two eggs over the skillet and didn't ask as he put sausage and grits on her plate. The breakfast aromas permeated the kitchen. When the eggs were done, he set the plate on the table in front of her. She looked around the kitchen as if suddenly aware of something that had been forgotten.

"I'm sorry," she said. "I'm just sitting here like a dummy. Can I help you with something?"

His first thought was "go back to Chicago" but he was too far committed to turn back now.

"Keep your seat. I've got it."

After pouring her coffee, he remembered she liked cream.

"Crap!"

"What's wrong?" she asked.

"I forgot you like cream. All I have is milk in the refrigerator."

"That will be fine."

Buddy breathed a sigh of relief.

"You seem a little nervous this morning," she said.

Only then did he realize she was right. He *was* nervous. And it had nothing to do with this wild adventure they were planning. It was her. She was an enigma—a piece of work he couldn't explain, and it was affecting him. He didn't entirely trust her, but he didn't want to hurt her feelings. Why—he had no clue, but it seemed important.

"I'm fine. Eat up. We've got to get moving."

CHAPTER EIGHT

A Sobering Reality

For the first time in two days, Elizabeth was physically comfortable as she rode with Rider back to the Clarksdale Airport. It was the insulated underwear, and the addition of the windbreaker over her jacket. She wasn't an idiot. After all, she lived in Chicago and knew how to dress for cold weather, but as much as she hated to admit it, he was right. The young nuns from the college had simply not realized it got this cold in the South.

Seemingly lost in deep thought, Rider hadn't spoken since leaving the house. They were going to fly in his airplane down to an airstrip somewhere in Louisiana. The whole endeavor was taking on a life of its own and she felt things were spinning out of her control. She gazed out her window. The bayous along the highway were frozen into stillness. Nothing moved. It was as if her world had died, and this was her new and discomforting reality. She was now merely a passenger along for the ride.

The Mississippi Delta was a desolate place—at least what she had seen of it. They passed through Tutwiler—a boggy little town with frozen muddy ditches full of beer bottles and trash, a few ancient brick buildings, shacks, and shanties. In the yards were junk cars, old washing machines, and the refuse of a people lost and abandoned with no hope for anything better. The only sign of life was the smoke wisping from rooftop pipes on this frigid January morning.

The South was as her college professors had always said, a place of poverty and ignorance. It was this ignorance that frightened her most. Rider was typical of the whites down here—perhaps a little better than average—but likely not much different from the others. The only thing that set him apart was his skill as a crop duster pilot. His house was a nice one, and he had somehow learned to fly, but that didn't necessarily make him a member of the cultural elite—whoever and wherever they might be in this place Martin Luther King called a desert state, sweltering with the heat of injustice and oppression.

It was difficult to face this "deal with the devil" she had made, but Rider was now her only hope for saving her fellow missionaries. She hadn't sold her soul entirely to him, but to get his airplane, she was making a deal of sorts. And who knew? Perhaps this opportunity she was giving him to do something redeemable with his life might bring him out of his backward ways. It might make him stand for something better than the redneck legacy of his birthplace. Perhaps he would someday be her first success with the salvation of another soul. Afterall, he wasn't all bad, and with a little enlightenment, he might actually become a decent person.

Elizabeth felt the rising tension as Rider slowed the car north of Clarksdale. They were approaching the airport, and he was scanning every side road, every vehicle, and every patch of woods they passed. He was being ultra-cautious. She was about to glance back but remembered his admonishments and used the sideview mirror instead. There was no one behind them. He turned off the highway and drove down the narrow blacktop road toward the airport.

"I'm pulling around back. As soon as we stop, I'll open the

trunk and go unlock the hangar door. Unload your bags and bring them inside."

Rider returned to the car as she went inside with her bags. The concrete floor of the hangar was hard and cold, and the air inside was frigid. Elizabeth shivered—unsure if it was a result of the cold or the tension. The airplane was a giant dark green shadow squatting silently in the dim light. She was determined to let nothing frighten her, but her heart skipped a beat when Rider returned with a pistol and several magazines of ammo that he laid atop his bags. He hurried toward the big doors at the front of the hangar.

"What are you going to do with these?" she asked.

"I thought we might do a little hunting while we're down there," he called over his shoulder.

"You're not funny."

Rider stopped and turned. His blue eyes glistened in the shadows, and his jaw was set hard. There was a cruel beauty in those eyes not unlike a wolf staring at her alone in the forest. She might have described him as intimidatingly handsome if she were not so totally disgusted with his smartass attitude. He frightened her.

"You don't seem to realize the danger we're facing with this mission. No, it's not funny, and maybe I'm not much of a comedian, but I don't intend to get dead while doing this—at least not without doing something to avoid it. Now, stop your stressing and start loading that stuff on the aircraft while I open the hangar doors."

Elizabeth stifled her anger. Rider was as cruel as he was ignorant—an ignorance no doubt grounded in the same gun-toting mentality of the ones who elected Ronald Reagan president. God forgive her for thinking it, but this man was an asshole. She wanted to tell him as much. She wanted to tell him never mind this mission. She could find someone else—someone with decency and a heart, but she knew better. He was her only chance.

It had taken her a while to find someone who would even try. And he was now too deeply involved for her to simply walk away. He might betray her to the authorities. No, she had to bury her pride and deal with him. She would use him to save Melissa and her sister missionaries. After that, this hick could go back to his selfish, backward ways.

Snatching the bags from the floor, she carried them to the airplane while daylight spilled in through the hangar doors as they slowly opened. After twenty more minutes spent loading the aircraft with parts, tarpaulins, and various other supplies, she climbed aboard, while Rider did something he called sumping the fuel. A few minutes later he closed the cargo door at the back of the aircraft and latched it. Signaling for her to follow, he walked up the narrow interior to the cockpit.

Rider sat in the left seat and motioned her into the right one. From somewhere outside the hangar came a sound like that of a chugging farm tractor. Craning her neck, she looked out to where an old black man in dirty gray coveralls appeared, driving a rust-covered tractor into the hangar. He wore thick, oversized leather gloves and gripped the steering wheel with both hands.

Rider slid his side window open. A few moments later he extended his arm outside and gave the old man a thumbs-up. The tractor engine revved, and the aircraft lurched as it began moving forward. Her heart leapt. This was it. They were moving. Rider was busily scanning the instrument panel, throwing switches, and pulling levers. She again felt her life spinning out of control.

When they stopped outside the hangar, she glanced down at the black man on the rusty green tractor as he pulled away from the aircraft.

"Take care of JD while I'm gone," Rider shouted, "and don't forget to turn the car in at the dealership."

The old man smiled, waved, and shouted back at him. "Yes, suh, Mista Buddy. I got'cher back."

This was strange—a black man so readily helping a white southerner. It made no sense. Her mother and father had told her much about the South, and several of her college instructors had talked about how Jim Crow was still the rule. They said the blacks and whites down here hated one another. But then there were the Uncle Toms who did what they had to do to survive. She felt sorry for the old man. He was probably little more than a modern-day slave.

"Buckle up," Rider said as he donned headphones and pulled a small microphone in front of his mouth.

He gazed out the right-side window and the aircraft vibrated as one of the engines grunted and belched a cloud of white smoke. Its propeller began turning and Elizabeth felt lightheaded. Her world took on the surreal aura of a fantasy, except this was reality and they were really going.

CHAPTER NINE

Strange Relationships

lizabeth felt suddenly alone—almost alienated. Rider had said nothing to her while he prepared for their departure, and this airplane of his was equally as cantankerous. Her hopes were nearly dashed from the very moment when he first started the engines. The motors sputtered, spewed white smoke, and backfired for several seconds— maybe minutes. She wasn't sure. After a while when they seemed to be running normally, he pushed the throttles forward and the airplane began a slow lumbering roll down the runway. Her gut tightened, and all she could imagine was them crashing after take-off into the frigid, black Delta mud.

The engines roared and the muddy farm fields seemed to pass by forever as the aircraft rocked and swayed while slowly gaining speed. She felt the tail lift and up ahead she saw the now rapidly approaching end of the runway. Beyond was a frozen muddy bog full of dead cattails. Rider glanced down at the instrument panel before pulling back on the yoke, and it seemed to take forever before the plane slowly lifted from the runway. How he hoped to fly this thing all the way to Central America was beyond reason. It seemed she had hung her hopes on a foolish pilot and a relic of an airplane.

Rider turned the aircraft into a slow, banking turn, and off to the west she spotted the Mississippi River. Her tension slowly abated as they gained altitude.

"When will you talk to your friend again?"

"I spoke with him last night."

"What did he say?"

"We're meeting one of his men in Brownsville, Texas, in three days."

"One of his men? Who are they?"

"Let's leave it there for now. I'll explain more later."

It was becoming more evident that she had cast her lot with drug runners. It was the only explanation for all his tight-lipped secrecy. Elizabeth gazed out the side window at the Mississippi River far below, winding its way southward. This was so much different from the commercial flights she had flown. She could see so much more from the cockpit, and it seemed they were flying much lower than the big jets she'd taken in and out of Chicago.

Towboats pushing strings of barges left foamy wakes in the river, and wisps of clouds floated by beneath them. A factory far out on the western horizon billowed brilliant white clouds of smoke against a cobalt sky. She suddenly felt alone, ridiculously small, and insignificant.

"So, where is it exactly that we are going?"

"A little airstrip down south of New Orleans and Baton Rouge, near Houma, Louisiana. That's where we're going to lay low at a friend's place for a couple days."

Lay low seemed the words of a man who knew how to dodge the authorities. She was more certain than ever that Rider must be a member of a drug ring. How could he fly this way so freely and know so many people? And this hideout in Louisiana was just another bit of evidence.

"You seem to have friends in lots of places," she said. "How do you know this guy?"

"He's a friend from way back."

"How do you know we can trust him?"

"How do you know you can trust *me*?"

"I don't."

"Hey, why don't we just turn this bird around and go back to Clarksdale, and you can find someone you trust? How about that?"

Making him angry at this point was counterproductive and perhaps a little dangerous.

"No. I'm sorry. I didn't mean—I mean it's just that, uh—"

"Look. You said you live in Chicago. You ever hear of an all-pro linebacker named Curtis Teague?"

"Yes! I have. He played for the Bears."

"That's right. It's his place where we're staying the next couple nights."

"How do you know him?"

"It's a long story I'll tell you some other time."

There it was again. He was hiding something. Rider remained silent and was all business as he scanned the instrument panel and made various adjustments. He had donned a pair of aviator sunglasses. They gave him a certain devil-may-care handsomeness, but Elizabeth would not be distracted. She had no need for a friend in the drug-running business—just this one for as long as it took to save her sister missionaries.

"We're going to skirt Baton Rouge so we can avoid traffic and approach Houma from the west. Right now, I need your help. I want you to scan the sky constantly left and right and watch for traffic. If you see something, sound off."

She knew nothing about flying, but this seemed an odd thing to have to do. Her rush to find a plane and a pilot had led her to this barnstormer, and she was not sure if she should feel fear or disgust. Her doubts continued growing, and she began to think perhaps he was a charlatan intent on cheating her out of her money. Telling him about the cash she was carrying had been a mistake.

That was it. He was taking her to this desolate place in Louisiana to rob her and perhaps kill her. He would bury her in the swamp, and she would never be heard from again. An hour and a half later, Rider put the aircraft into a steep, banking turn and flew back eastward. Her fear grew as she gazed out at endless miles of swamps and waterways stretching away to the horizon.

"If you look down there on your right, you'll see a small airfield. The sock says the wind is out of the southwest. You agree?"

"Sock?"

"Yeah, that orange thing down there on the pole. It tells us which way the wind is blowing."

"I don't see it."

"Never mind. The communication tab said they monitor the radio from oh-nine hundred to seventeen hundred. I'm going to come up on their frequency in a minute. Right now, we're going to fly downwind and set up for an approach."

The cypress treetops grew closer as they descended, and flocks of birds skittered across the water as the aircraft passed over them. The roads were atop narrow levees, and Elizabeth now knew she had made a mistake. Rider's story of knowing Curtis Teague was a lie, and this desolate airstrip could have but one purpose. She had put her trust in a drug runner.

As they taxied back to the metal buildings at the end of the airstrip, Elizabeth spotted a shiny black Chevy Suburban parked there. That figured. These criminals drove only the fanciest vehicles. Beside it stood a black man who made the Suburban appear small. After both engines were shut down and several switches thrown, Rider hung his headphones on the yoke and stood up. He said nothing as he walked to the rear of the aircraft, opened the door, and leapt to the ground.

Elizabeth followed and stood in the door watching as Rider and the man embraced while trading tawdry insults. Only then did the stranger seem to notice her standing there in the doorway. He appeared suddenly embarrassed.

"Oops! I forgot you said you were bringing company." He reached up with both hands. "Here, little lady, let me help you down."

She tried to grab his hands, but he grasped her around the waist, lifting her with ease, and setting her on the ground.

"There you go, ma'am. Mista Curtis Teague at your service."

She blushed. Perhaps he really was Curtis Teague. She unzipped her jacket, already realizing she was overdressed for the balmy Louisiana weather.

"Don't worry none," the man said. "We'll head on over to my place. You can meet my wife and kids and change into something cooler."

Rider jumped back into the aircraft and pushed her bags into the door. Ten minutes later they were in the Suburban and heading south on a rural highway. The two men sat up front while Elizabeth sat in the back. Rider had called him Curtis, and Elizabeth was beginning to believe he really was the famous all-pro linebacker.

"I'm assuming y'all want to go to Mama Cici's place this evening," Teague said.

Rider looked back at her and raised his brows. "It's a local restaurant. I think you'll like it."

She shrugged.

"I'll take that as a yes," he said.

"So Capt'n, what brings you and your girl down this way?" Teague asked. "You weren't too talkative on the phone last night."

She wanted to tell Teague that she wasn't Rider's girl but thought better of it. Best remain silent and let him explain.

"Curtis," Rider said, but he paused for several seconds. "You know I trust you like a brother, and I know you wouldn't say anything if I were to tell you, but for your benefit and mine I'd rather not explain—at least not right now. Let's just say I'm taking this lady down south on a little vacation trip."

Teague turned and looked across at Rider. His eyebrows were folded together, and his lip curled in anger. He was a fearsome sight to behold.

"That sounds like BS to me. You haven't gone to runnin' drugs, have you? You know I've worked way too hard to screw up my life by messin' around with that sort of thing."

Rider laughed.

"Believe me, it's nothing like that, but if you don't know anything it can't come back to haunt you. It's nothing that will get you in trouble. As far as you're concerned, I'm an old friend who came down to visit and wants to show his girl a good time down at Mama Cici's. Fact is I didn't file a flight plan, so we're down here incognito—so to speak."

Teague turned his attention back to the road and said nothing. Despite his denials, Elizabeth was still uncertain about Rider. She glanced out the side window at the sawgrass along the canal paralleling the highway. What she saw made her gasp. Both men turned and looked back at her. Pointing feebly over her shoulder, she felt the heat of another blush cross her face.

"It was an alligator—a really *big* one. It was black. I've never seen a real live one—not even in a zoo."

Curtis laughed. "Where're you from, girl?"

"Chicago."

"No shit?"

"No—I mean yes."

This set off a long conversation, as she and Teague traded notes on the Windy City, and he told her about his years as a linebacker with the Bears. Twenty minutes later he turned the Suburban down a palm-tree-lined drive at the end of which stood a beautiful multi-story stucco home with a red tiled roof.

"Dorie took the kids to make a run to the supermarket, but she left some sandwiches on the bar," Teague said. "We'll unload your bags after lunch, and I'll show you to your room."

"You mean 'rooms,' right?" she asked.

Teague glanced at Rider who gave him a quick nod.

"Yeah, sure—rooms. Whatever. That's what I meant to say."

———————

When she returned from the grocery, Teague's wife showed Elizabeth around the house and took her to her room. Elizabeth inhaled a deep breath of the fresh air in the bedroom. It was spacious with soft pastel colors, high ceilings, lots of pillows, and tall windows full of sunshine. A ceiling fan turned slowly and luxuriously overhead, stirring a wonderful scent from a bouquet of flowers placed on a dresser table. Dorie Teague was a gracious hostess who had thought of everything.

The scent of the flowers was as intoxicating as that of the swamp that began only a hundred yards from her window. It stretched away to the horizon—towering cypress trees laden with Spanish moss, canals disappearing amongst fields of sawgrass, and huge flocks of white birds winging majestically in the distance. A person could lose herself in a paradise like this. This was an exotic land the likes of which Elizabeth had never experienced.

She gazed out the window at the swamp while Dorie Teague turned back the bed covers and fluffed the pillows. It was an intimidating country that reminded her of old pirate tales, men in pirogues, and mysterious Cajun hideaways. Yet it was a strange juxtaposition to stand here in this castle-like home gazing out at such a wild and mysterious landscape.

"It's called the Mandalay," Dorie said.

Elizabeth snapped from her reverie. The name Mandalay had struck home as she remembered her college studies about the Burmese city of Mandalay, its winding rivers, teakwood bridge, white marble pagoda, and red-roofed palaces. She had studied Kipling's poem and its juxtaposition of romance and colonialism. And this place too, deep in the Louisiana swamps, was indeed a land of beauty and deep mystery.

"It's beautiful, isn't it?" Dorie said.

Elizabeth nodded.

"Come on. I'll show you your bathroom."

Mrs. Teague treated her as if she were royalty, laying out piles of fresh folded towels and a basket of exotic soaps as she ran hot water in a marble tub. It was all so strange how these black people, who had obviously escaped the chains of modern white southerners, still maintained such magnanimous and cordial relationships with them. And this apparently well-to-do black woman still acted as if she were a servant. Elizabeth did not expect to be treated in such a manner, but she was not sure how to tell her so without seeming rude.

"Thank you, Mrs. Teague. I appreciate your kindness."

"Girl, please! Call me Dorie. I'm not *that* much older than you."

"Sorry."

Dorie winked at her.

"I'll leave you to your bath. Use the intercom to give me a shout if you need anything."

"Do you know how I should dress for the restaurant we're going to tonight? I don't have much to wear except for some gray dresses and khaki pants. Do you think the khaki pants are okay?"

"Oh, dearie, you don't have to worry about that. Mama Cici's is *definitely* a laid-back kind of place. Do you have some jeans?"

"Uh, no. Sorry."

Dorie placed her hand on Elizabeth's shoulder and looked her up and down.

"Tell you what, we're about the same size. I can hook you up. I'll leave some duds in there on the bed. You just relax and unwind. I'm sure riding in Buddy's airplane wasn't something you were used to. I know. He took me up in his crop duster one time—dang near peed my pants. I'll tell you about it later. Right now, I have to get on the phone and find us a babysitter."

CHAPTER TEN

The Disenfranchised at Mama Cici's

A fog drifted in from the swamp that evening as they rode in the Suburban down a rain-dampened blacktop highway. Elizabeth sat in back with Dorie as the warm gentle notes of a blues song filled the cozy interior, all but negating the low voices of the men up front. This was a new experience for her, and a somewhat frightening change from the austere climate of the religious college she had called home. And it began earlier that evening when she squeezed into the blue jeans Dorie had loaned her. Never had she worn a sequined blouse and jeans, and never anything this tight.

Buddy Rider had done a double take when she came down from her room, and though he immediately went back to his conversation with Curtis, it had been enough. She would have changed immediately had it not been for hurting Dorie's feelings. That was out of the question. This lady had been waiting on her hand and foot all day. Spending this one night looking like man-bait was something she could endure. Besides, it somehow felt both liberating and empowering.

An electric blue and red neon light blazed in the fog up ahead as Curtis slowed the vehicle and turned onto a gravel parking lot. It was full of vehicles, and the sign said they had arrived at Mama Cici's. Elizabeth gazed out her window at rows of pickup trucks and older cars surrounding a gray wooden building built on piers several feet above the ground. Spanish moss hung in shadowy clumps from live oaks and strings of multi-colored lights were strung above the restaurant windows. As they stepped from the car, the muted sounds of music came from inside. The aromas of cayenne, bay, and fried seafood permeated the night air.

Buddy Rider held the door for the others as Elizabeth and Dorie led the way inside. A man behind a cash register shouted at them. "Curtis Teague! *Bon ami. Laissez les bon temps rouler.* Hang on. I gotcha a table almost ready."

And this man was speaking some version of French while people twirled about and clapped their hands to a band playing fiddles and an accordion. It was all too strange, but strangest of all was how the people, both black and white, mingled every-where in the restaurant. It was a mixed crowd the likes of which she seldom saw, even in Chicago, but she never imagined such a thing was possible in the South. There wasn't a frown in the room, and Elizabeth found the atmosphere mesmerizingly pleasant. People greeted Teague, slapping his back and hugging Dorie.

"Mister Broussard, you remember my old friend, Captain Buddy, right?" Teague said.

"Sho do. How you doin', Captain?"

It reminded her of a family reunion she had once attended in rural New York, only this one was even more cordial. It was as if everyone here was family. Platters piled high with food passed in the hands of waitresses as they carried them out to the tables, and Elizabeth suddenly realized she had not had anything to eat since before noon—nearly eight hours ago. Her stomach felt hollow.

"Can I get you folks something to drink while we get your table ready?" a waitress asked. "It's ladies' night—two for one drinks for the gals."

"Hey, yeah," Curtis said. "Bring these ladies a couple of those sweet pineapple and coconut-cream drinks." He turned her way. "Sound good?"

Elizabeth shrugged. Pineapple and coconut sounded harmless enough. "Sure."

Dorie turned to her with a grin. "You will love them. They taste like the tropics."

Elizabeth was surprised when several women, young and old, walked up and introduced themselves as if she were a celebrity of some sort. And they were all so genuine and down to earth. These were real people, more genuine than any she had ever met at the college, and she quickly realized the attention she was getting had nothing to do with celebrity, but a friendliness grounded in the local culture and meant to make strangers feel welcomed.

The waitress returned with two tall plastic cups with straws, but these had no fancy garnishment or little umbrellas like the ones they served at the alumni reception one year. It made sense. These were people without pretense. They were her kind of people—those who no doubt felt as she did about the state of the nation—people who had been disenfranchised by the recent national election yet determined to live happily. She put her lips around the straw and drew from the cup.

"Oh my!" she said, turning to Dorie. "This *is* good."

"What did I say, girl? I'm tellin' you."

Elizabeth drew hard again on the straw, nearly getting brain-freeze. She looked up and smiled at Dorie and Curtis. Only then did she notice Rider gazing at her. He wasn't smiling, but neither was he frowning. He was simply—almost rudely—

staring at her, but she couldn't tell what he was thinking. His noncommittal gaze left her feeling suddenly self-conscious as she checked the buttons on her blouse.

She glanced down at the now nearly empty cup. It was indeed a very tasty drink.

Rider was still staring. He was always so negative toward her—making snide remarks and putting her down. And now he was the only one in the restaurant who wasn't smiling. He probably didn't want her having a good time with people who only wanted to live in peace. She imagined these must be the less fortunate ones the nuns at the college had spoken of—the ones who were wanted only when there was a war to fight somewhere in the world. She had learned in college that this was the way of the rich and their ignorant supporters—people like Rider. The straw burbled at the bottom of the cup as a waitress led them to a table, and despite Rider's judgmental stare, Elizabeth found herself feeling better than she had in months.

CHAPTER ELEVEN

A Concoction of Rum and Politics

Buddy watched Elizabeth suck down her first drink before they were seated. It was clear she had no clue how much rum she was drinking. The others had not yet noticed, but he saw it in her eyes. She was already tipsy. He wanted to intervene and was about to say something when she met his gaze with a rebellious glare. He hesitated. No sense in making a scene. Most people were happy drunks, but there was that small percentage who became fighters. The look in her eyes fit the latter, and Buddy chose silence as the wiser course.

When they were seated, he tugged at Curtis's sleeve and murmured in his ear. "We better order some fried appetizers before our guest gets herself drunk."

Too late, the waitress delivered the second round of drinks, and Elizabeth ordered more. Even Dorie took note.

"Dang it, girl. You better slow down. Mister Broussard don't fool around. He puts that good Trinidadian 151 rum in these. It'll knock your socks off."

Curtis cast a quick glance at Buddy then across the table at Elizabeth. She was grinning like a mule eating blackberry briars. Quickly raising his hand, he flagged the waitress. "Bring us some of those bacon-wrapped jalapeños and some Cajun fries."

He glanced at Buddy and raised his eyebrows as if to ask if that would work. Buddy wagged his head. "The spice will make it worse."

Only Dorie understood what he meant. "Wait!" She stopped the waitress. "If you don't mind, just bring us ladies some crab chowder with crackers. We don't need that real spicy stuff right now. And bring us one of those big fried onions too with some remoulade dip."

Elizabeth, now working on her second drink, seemed oblivious as she gazed about at the people in the restaurant.

"These are *real* people," she blurted.

No one at the table spoke as they traded puzzled glances.

"Oh. I mean these are the real salt of the earth kind of people who believe we're all equal, and they aren't going to hide just because Republicans are in charge now."

"What *are* you talkin' about, girl?" Dorie said.

"I'm talking about how President Carter was voted out of office in November. Some of our college faculty even cried after the election—said the country was set back years. They wanted someone who cares about all people, black and white, regardless of social status, but they got that movie actor Reagan instead. I mean, how dumb is that?"

Dorie's eyes widened and Buddy was thankful the band was playing, preventing Elizabeth from being overheard at the adjacent tables. Curtis, though, turned and bent toward him. "Where in hell did you find this chick, Capt'n?" he muttered.

With her second drink nearly sucked dry, Elizabeth cocked her head sideways and gazed across the table at Curtis. "I have a question," she said, loud enough to be heard over the band. She was now wearing something akin to a perma-grin. "Why do you call Mister Rider captain? Is that an airplane pilot thing or what? I certainly hope he wasn't some sort of *army* captain."

"What's wrong with army people?" Curtis asked.

"Well, you know—I mean it's no secret how they killed all those poor people in Vietnam. My mother and father said…"

She paused and only then did she seem to realize something was amiss as everyone at the table stared at her in silence.

"Oh, uh, well, never mind," she said. "He doesn't seem like the killer type, anyway."

Buddy couldn't believe what he was hearing. The liquor had her mouth writing checks she couldn't possibly cash. He had seen it on television when he first returned from Nam, these same accusations screamed at returning veterans by demonstrators in the airports, but here his guest was spouting them to total strangers. Had she been a man, he would have decked her. Dorie, who seemed dumbfounded, had locked eyes with her husband.

Curtis's jaw flexed, and Buddy didn't know if he should snatch up his guest and gag her or jump between them. Curtis drew a deep breath, slowly exhaled, and took a long pull on his bottle of Miller Highlife. When he finished, he set it aside and folded his hands into a fist in front of his face.

"Don't pay her any mind," Buddy said. "She's had too mu—"

Curtis threw up his hand. "No, Capt'n. I'm okay. Let me talk."

Elizabeth realized the liquor had loosened her tongue in a way she had never experienced. She was a fool. By repeating what she had been taught by her parents and college instructors, she had apparently stuck her foot in her mouth all the way up to her knee. Despite her head swimming about in an alcoholic haze, the painful sting of embarrassment made her again suck madly on the straw. The second drink, now empty, burbled at the bottom of the cup.

"Tell me, Miss Anderson, why do you say that?"

It was the first time Curtis had addressed her as Miss Anderson. She cut her eyes over at Buddy, but his lips were pressed tight and flat. It was clear. The gauntlet was thrown, and she was on her own.

"Well." She hesitated. "I didn't mean to hurt anyone's feelings, but it *is* common knowledge that American troops *did* kill many of the Vietnamese people—raping the women and destroying their villages."

"Really?" Curtis said. "Common knowledge where?"

"You can read about it anywhere. That Lieutenant Calley wiped out an entire village all by himself, and my college professors said he was only a small example of what occurred. My mother and father were both antiwar activists because of the American Air Force killing millions more Vietnamese, by bombing their cities in the north."

"Hmmm," Curtis said. "I suppose your parents and college professors must have been there."

Elizabeth realized she was only making matters worse.

"Uh, no, but—"

Her alcohol-induced outspokenness gave way to an adrenaline-driven flash of sobriety as Curtis stared laser holes through her face. She wanted to crawl under the table.

"I'm sorry, Mister Teague. I didn't mean to make you angry."

She again glanced toward Buddy, but his eyes were on Curtis. Curtis didn't smile. He didn't nod. Instead, his eyes slowly faded into something that resembled sadness, and she became keenly aware that she had somehow hurt him deeply. It occurred to her that both Curtis and Buddy must have been soldiers. That was the only explanation, and everything she had said up to now had been based on her own prejudices and assumptions. Frozen in a drunken stupor, she held the table edge to steady herself.

Buddy watched his friend closely. Curtis seemed to have relaxed, but his eyes were those of a soldier who had been betrayed by his country—a soldier whose legacy was being designed by professors in colleges and political activists who made evil ogres of men like him who had simply done their duty. After a moment, he shook his head in resignation.

"Hell, girl. You didn't make me angry. If I was angry, I'd have put you in my car and drove you down to the cemetery to see the graves of my friends who were killed over there trying to save those Vietnamese people from the Communists. If I was angry, you'd be walking home tonight—and home wouldn't be where *I* live."

He turned and put his hand on Buddy's shoulder. "The reason I call this fellow Captain is because that was his rank when he was a pilot in Vietnam. And before that he was a Green Beret who trained mountain tribesmen called Montagnards to fight the Communists. Maybe he can tell you about all the Vietnamese he raped, killed, and bombed."

She turned to Buddy. Her eyes were like those of a soldier whose foot was tangled in a tripwire and the booby-trap had not yet exploded. "You never said you were an air force captain."

"You never asked."

"And he wasn't in the air force either," Curtis said. "He was an army pilot, and he got shot down twice and was awarded the Distinguished Service Cross, the Silver Star, the Bronze Star, three air medals, and two Purple Hearts. You mean to tell me you didn't know any of that?"

Elizabeth sat bug-eyed and speechless, caught in the glaring spotlight of her own verbose ignorance. Dorie's lips parted as if she were about to speak. Buddy reached across the table and placed his hand atop hers. "Wait," he said. "Let me say something."

He hoped to calm Dorie and give Elizabeth the verbal wake-up slap she needed.

"I'm surprised you didn't notice the medals framed in Curtis's office when Dorie showed you around the house. The one with the gold stars on the blue ribbon was the Congressional Medal of Honor. He earned it after both he and his squad leader were wounded, and he carried the squad leader several hundred yards through heavy enemy fire to safety. And if he were to raise his shirt, you could see the purple shrapnel scars all over his body. You see, one of those other medals was a Purple Heart."

Elizabeth's face paled, and she looked down as she mouthed her words more than said them, "I'm sorry. I didn't know."

The waitress brought the appetizers to the table, along with the next round of drinks. Elizabeth grabbed one and sucked furiously on the straw. Buddy reached across the table and pulled it from her hands. He was too late. It too was nearly empty.

"If you don't slow down, you're going to be sorry tomorrow. Eat some food."

A red-faced Elizabeth tried to cut a portion of the fried onion, but it was clear she was as wasted as she was outspoken. They ordered the rest of the meal, and ate fried shrimp, oysters, Cajun rice, and hush puppies, but Elizabeth was steadily going downhill. She had trouble staying focused, and Buddy was afraid she might pass out. He stood and took her hand.

"Come on. Maybe a little dancing will help."

Still holding her hand, he wrapped his left arm around her waist and guided her to the dance floor. The lights had gone down low, and the band was playing Menard's "Rebecca Ann." Singing the French lyrics in a rich baritone voice, the vocalist made it deeply moving, and Buddy held Elizabeth close, lest she fall to the floor. Her head fell against his shoulder, and he felt the warmth of her breath on his neck. Poor thing was zonkered.

"I'm so—" she hiccupped ever so lightly. "I'm, sorr, sorr— sorry, Bu—uddy. I was wrong about you. You really are a swee…man."

Her full breasts pressed warmly against him, and he noticed men gazing at her sequined jeans. She did them justice—more so than average, but she was a mess, and he realized she would not walk unassisted from the dance floor. The song did not end too soon as he gently pushed his thumb inside the back of her jeans and lifted gently upward. Supporting her this way, he made his way back to the table. Elizabeth's head rested on his shoulder as he stopped and glanced around. Only then did he realize Curtis and Dorie had been on the dance floor with them. They were standing behind him.

"I hate to ruin our evening, folks, but I'm afraid my, uh, guest has had a little too much rum."

Their eyes met and Curtis nodded. He was being the gentleman Buddy had always known.

"Here, take my key," Curtis said. "Go ahead with him, Dorie, in case he needs you. I'll settle up and be out in a minute."

Buddy sat in the back seat holding a now comatose Elizabeth in his arms, while Curtis drove them home. "We'll be lucky if she doesn't puke her guts out," he said.

Dorie glanced over from the front seat. "I don't think she

drank enough to do that, but she's going to have a sure enough badass hangover in the morning. How is it that you know her?"

Buddy froze in embarrassed silence. She deserved an answer, but there was only so much he could tell her.

"Let it go, Baby," Curtis said. "I'll try to explain it later."

When they arrived back at the house, the Louisiana night was quiet, except for the few insects and frogs that braved the cool night air. Dorie opened the door and Buddy cradled the still sleeping Elizabeth in his arms as he carried her into the house and up to her room. Dorie followed.

After laying her on the bed, Buddy removed her shoes and tossed them aside. He gazed over at Dorie. "If she was mine, I'd try to make her more comfortable by taking off her bra and jeans, but she's not."

Dorie gave him a sideways grin. "You have always been such a gentleman, Buddy Rider. Step out in the hall a minute. I'll undress her and find her a gown."

"But what if she wakes up in the night or gets sick?"

"I'll sit up in here with her."

It was too much to ask.

"No, Dorie. She's *my* problem. Get her ready for bed, but I'll stay in here in case she gets sick. If I need you, I'll call you."

After several hours sitting in a chair against the wall and listening to Elizabeth's heavy breathing, Buddy pulled the chair to the side of the bed and bent across the mattress where he rested his head. He fell asleep at her feet, but it seemed only minutes passed before he heard her moan.

Jerking his head upright, he found the room's pastel walls ablaze with the morning sun. Elizabeth had sat up and was hugging a pillow against her chest. She gazed at him through painfully squinted eyes. The sunshine sparkled in her flaming auburn hair, somewhat matching the color of her bloodshot eyes.

"What are you doing in here?" she asked.

The indignation in her voice deserved a fitting answer.

"Babysitting a damned drunk."

Glancing down, she pushed the pillow away from her chest and gasped.

"Oh! How? Where are my clothes?"

"Don't worry. I don't make a habit of undressing drunken strangers. You have Dorie to thank for that. Do you need some aspirin?"

"Good Lord, yes, please. My head is killing me."

Buddy stood and walked into the bathroom. There he found a well-stocked medicine cabinet.

"Are you feeling sick?" he shouted back.

"Yes, a little," she said.

After filling a cup with water, he walked back into the bedroom.

"You're in luck. Here's some aspirin, and I found a bottle of Pepto-Bismol. I suggest you take the aspirin and a couple tablespoons of the Pepto, then try to sleep it off. You should feel better by this afternoon. I'll send Dorie to check on you in a few hours."

He turned toward the door.

"I said some stupid things last night, didn't I?"

Turning, Buddy fixed her with a steady gaze. Her blazing political activist's brown eyes had softened to those of a somewhat more tolerant and less possessed person. And for the first time since they had met, she wore a humbled countenance. He could almost feel a slight sympathy for her were it not for his still simmering anger.

"That might be a bit of an understatement, lady. Calling your host—who by the way is a Medal of Honor recipient—a rapist and murderer is not exactly endearing. And blurting your political opinions to people, many of whom may disagree with you, isn't too cool either."

A single tear spilled from her eye, leaving a glistening track down her face. He walked to the bedside table and snatched several tissues from a box and tossed them in her lap.

"See you later," he said.

"Uh."

He paused.

"You need something else?"

"Was I dreaming, or did we actually slow dance together while someone sang a French love song?"

"You may have been dreaming, but don't worry, if it happened, it was only because I was trying to sober you up."

With that he walked out and pulled the door closed behind him.

———————————

Buddy drank his coffee that morning, and the Teagues were gracious and forgiving as he apologized for the debacle at Mama Cici's. Later, when she awakened, Elizabeth voiced her regrets and offered her apologies as well. The only repercussions were the knowing grins Buddy silently suffered from Curtis. At least he was good-natured about it.

The following morning, Dorie brewed Community Coffee with chicory and made beignets with powdered sugar for breakfast. She packed a lunch of leftovers, as well as homemade sandwiches, and Buddy and Elizabeth departed later that day for Brownsville, Texas.

CHAPTER TWELVE

Jungle Jim's Pilot

Brownsville, Texas Airport

Elizabeth wandered away in search of a lady's room, while Buddy met with Chief Warrant Officer Stein Foster. He was a taciturn man with the close-cropped hair often described as white sidewalls by the military, except his were deeply tanned. After introducing himself, Foster did not waste time with social niceties. He was polite but to the point as he and Buddy reviewed navigation charts, routes, frequencies, and call signs.

Foster said he would fly right-seat as Buddy's co-pilot, and their destination was a remote airfield in Honduras operated by the U.S. Military. The flight, although long, was a relatively simple one with the only weather concern being a small disturbance between Belize and Honduras—one they could skirt if the need arose. The warrant officer addressed Buddy as one would a senior officer, and he was detailed with his briefing.

"Depending on the winds, we're looking at about eight hours. We will depart here at first light in the morning and hug the coast all the way down to the Yucatan where we'll cross into Mexican airspace. Our people in Honduras have us cleared with the Mexican authorities and they'll turn on the ADF beacon when we contact them off the coast of Belize."

To Buddy it seemed simple enough.

"Pray for favorable winds and good weather, because we don't have much down there for runway lights—just some smudge pots. Worst case, if we have enough fuel, we can divert to Tegucigalpa, but we need to avoid that if possible. I'm not going to blow smoke up your ass. My experience is primarily with rotary aircraft, but I logged quite a few hours flying right seat out of Nha Trang in a C-47 Spooky. That was before I switched services and joined Army Special Forces."

"That's okay, Chief, I'm no salt either when it comes to this bird, but we should make it fine. I do have a question or two for you."

Foster raised his chin.

"I've studied the charts. Why follow the coastline? Why don't we take a hundred and twenty degree heading and save ourselves some time and fuel?"

"Because that's what the drug runners do. As soon as we head out into the Gulf, we'll draw the attention for everyone from the DEA to the Coast Guard. My orders are to maintain a low profile. We'll stay twelve to fifteen nautical miles offshore and parallel the coast. That should make everyone happy."

"Makes sense," Buddy said. "What do you know about our mission?"

"Damned little, right now. When we get the word, I'm flying with you in and out of an uncharted airstrip in El Salvador. I know the location, and we already have a team on the ground there. They've been there for a while and know the area well. Outside of that, the particulars are still up in the air. You and the colonel must be pretty tight."

"Why do you say that?"

"The strip we're flying into tomorrow doesn't even exist as

far as anyone else knows, and he's coming up from Panama to personally oversee this thing. He's also keeping it pretty quiet. Other than the team in El Salvador and some ground support at the strip, he and I are the only ones in on this op."

"Jim and I were together in Nam. I was on one of his A-teams when he learned I was a crop duster pilot before going into the military. He talked me into moving to an aviation group where I got qualified in the L-19. After that he flew backseater with me across the fence in Cambodia and Laos."

It was clear that Jungle Jim had shared privileged intelligence with him and was taking a personal risk by becoming directly involved with this mission. This was all the more reason for Buddy to act on his greatest concern— Elizabeth. They had to talk. If they managed to pull this thing off, she and the other missionaries had to remain silent. This was a discussion he would have with her once again.

"Where are you and the lady staying tonight?"

Buddy shrugged. "I'm not sure what she has planned, but I'll be sleeping in the plane."

"Best keep her with you. We need to get an early start and don't need any complications."

"Roger that, Chief."

———————————

Buddy found Elizabeth in a small lounge area behind a hangar. She was sitting in a worn vinyl chair and writing something in a small book. The lounge reeked of stale tobacco, and the ashtrays overflowed with cigarette butts—typical pilot digs. She stopped writing and looked up at him.

"The man your friend sent us seems nice, but he was kind of quiet. Is he a pilot, too?"

"Yes."

Buddy glanced at her book. It was filled with cursive she had written, nearly filling the two pages that were visible.

"What's that?" he asked.

"It's a journal."

"You mean, something like a diary?"

"I suppose you could say that, but it's not as personal."

"What kind of things are you writing in it?"

"Oh, things about our trip, you, and your airplane, Miss Molly, and just whatever comes to mind." She closed the journal. "Is there something wrong?"

"Elizabeth," he paused and took a deep breath. "Do you realize that what you're writing in that journal is all the government would need to put us both in federal prison for a long time?"

"But—"

"You have two options. You can destroy it, or I will cancel this mission and fly us back to Clarksdale. It's your call."

She pressed her lips together as her face reddened.

"Why do you continually threaten to quit at every turn?"

"Why do you continually say and do things that make it necessary? Look, I'm not trying to be mean, but I'm damned serious about this business. Keeping us both safe and out of trouble is my first priority."

She looked down at the leather-bound book and gently brushed her hand across its embossed cover. "Okay. I understand. I'll get rid of it tonight."

"No. Tomorrow after we get out over the Gulf, we'll get rid of it together—page by page."

She bowed her head but said nothing.

"Come on. Let's walk out to the aircraft and eat those sandwiches Dorie packed for us."

He took her by the arm and helped her from the chair.

"Where are we staying tonight?" she asked.

"In the plane."

"Together?"

"I have several air mattresses, and some blankets and pillows we can use, but no, we aren't sleeping together."

"Yeah, but—"

"Look. In case you don't recall, I've already spent one night close enough to hear you snoring off a night on the town."

"I don't snore!"

"How do you know? That rum had you totally K.O'd."

"Don't remind me. My head *still* hurts."

He helped her into the plane and opened the ice chest. After removing cartons of Creole wild rice with shrimp, Andouille po-boys with Creole mustard, and crab salad, he opened a beer.

"Do you want one?"

"No thanks," she said. "Do I really snore?"

"Like a hog rootin' for acorns." He cut his eyes at her.

A shy smile crept across her face. "You liar."

Buddy grinned back at her.

"Actually, I had to check on you a couple times to make sure you were still breathing."

"I'm sorry I put you through that."

"You put yourself through that, little lady. I'm glad I was there to help, but you've got to understand this trip isn't going to get any easier. I want you to listen, now, to what I have to say. If a single word leaks out about this from anyone involved, we could get in some deep trouble. You need to make that clear to your sponsor and the other missionaries."

"I will."

"One more thing: I don't think you fully realize the dangers we're facing. If I began listing the possibilities…well, let's just say I won't because it doesn't help. The thing you need to understand is that this is a *very* dangerous undertaking, and you must do exactly as you are told. If you don't, you could get killed or get someone else killed."

"Do you think we can rescue the sisters and the orphans?"

"Frankly, I have no idea. What I really hope happens is the State Department will negotiate a deal for their release, and we'll fly them out. Otherwise, I believe my friend down there is going to make a call as to whether or not we should try it."

"What if he says we can't go?"

"He knows the situation better than you can imagine. If he says the risks are too high, it means a successful mission is probably impossible. He will not participate, and he will prevent us from trying it alone."

"What about the money from my sponsors for fuel and for the use of your airplane?"

"Keep it in a safe place—preferably on you. With my friend supplying our fuel, we may not need it."

"I have ten thousand dollars in my bag."

"That's a nice chunk of change, but like I said, the man I met with earlier has cash and he's paying for our fuel. What of your money we don't use for meals and if we survive, you can give back to your sponsor. I'm not doing this for the money. Tell your sponsor I'm not a mercenary and he can shove—never mind."

"He's a good person, and only wants to save hi…" She stopped.

Buddy was beginning to put it together. Elizabeth had never made it totally clear who her backer was, only that he was associated with the mission program. He now realized that whoever was sponsoring her had a personal involvement of some sort, perhaps with one of the missionaries. The last few days had been tough on Elizabeth, and he decided not to press her for now.

"Let's just eat. You can tell me more tomorrow when we arrive in the AO and get a sit-rep."

"A what?"

"Situation report. The colonel will have every 'I' dotted, and 'T' crossed, and he'll know exactly where we stand."

"What does AO stand for?"

"Area of Operation."

"Where's that?"

"Honduras. Now please stop asking questions and eat. I'm hungry."

Elizabeth began devouring her sandwich as if she had not eaten in days.

"I take it you like Mama Cici's cooking."

"I've never had food like this," she said, talking with her mouth full. "Even the leftovers are good."

Buddy reached down into the ice and retrieved another can of beer. After pulling the tab top, he held it out for Elizabeth. "Here. Drink this. It will make it even better."

She gazed at the can as if it contained hemlock. "Oh, no. No way."

"You're a bundle of nerves and need to relax. Besides, I'm cutting you off after this one."

Almost reluctantly, she sipped the beer. "Hmmm. It's been a long time."

"Oh, really?"

"We had a slumber party one time when I was in high school, and I stole one of my mother's Old Milwaukee tallboys from the refrigerator."

"Ahh, so prior to becoming a religious missionary you were a juvenile delinquent?"

"No. I was *not*. I mean, I was no saint, but I wasn't a wild-child like some of my friends. Besides, I went to an all-girls Catholic college in Chicago, and the nuns watched over us like hawks."

Buddy contemplated the situation while chewing a bite of his sandwich.

"Tomorrow you will have a lot of time. You should write a letter to your parents, telling them exactly what you're doing."

"Exactly what I'm—? But you said I shouldn't tell—"

"No. I'll give the letter to my friend for safekeeping. You know—just in case."

Elizabeth cast her eyes down at the beer in her hands and slowly wagged her head. "That won't be necessary."

"Why not?"

"About this time last winter there was a fire at our house. My mother died of smoke inhalation."

She took a long drink from the beer, and Buddy wanted to give her a reassuring hug but refrained.

"And your father?"

"I have no idea where he is now."

"I'm sorry to hear that."

"It's okay. I've adjusted. They were just a couple of crazy hippie types who carried me with them all over the country to their anti-war demonstrations and such. Mom went to Vassar and my father went to NYU. They smoked a lot of pot and drank a lot of wine and spent Mom's entire inheritance. Mom's family had a trust fund for my college, but when the rest of the money was gone my father decided he had to *find himself* and went off to France. At least that's where the postcard we received was postmarked.

"It came about a year after he left. That was eight years ago and the last we ever heard from him—said he found a fellow writer named Claudette and they were co-writing the great twentieth century novel. Mom filed for divorce, and we moved to Chicago."

"That explains some things. So, you actually marched in anti-war demonstrations when you were a kid?"

Elizabeth laughed. "Yep—had my own baby-killer sign. Heck, I was even tear-gassed once, and I was only ten years old when we went to the big Woodstock rock festival. They got stoned out of their minds and fell asleep on the ground. I slept under a poncho for two days. It was one of the most miserable times of my life."

As much as Elizabeth had misjudged him, Buddy now realized she was not the only one who had made incorrect assumptions.

"Sounds like you were put through the wringer as a kid."

"It's what led me to this missionary work. So, tell me about Buddy Rider. You seem to have made some loyal friends in the military—like Curtis and your colonel friend."

"How did you know he was a colonel?"

"You let it slip a little bit ago," she said.

Buddy turned up his beer, finished it, and pulled another from the ice. The tab popped with a hiss.

"It's uncanny, but when you told me about your parents, I thought about my closest friend—a guy named Patrick Marino. He goes by Buck. His parents were both killed in an automobile accident just before he graduated from high school. It drove him to join the army and go to Vietnam.

"Buck still owns his old home place just across the county line a few miles from mine. It's near Bois De Arc, Mississippi. Matter of fact he rents the place out when he can find tenants, and I still look after it. He lives up near Bozeman, Montana, now with his wife and three kids. Back then, Buck was a lot like you are now."

"How's that?"

"Well, he went off to the war in Vietnam after his parents died, and now in a way you're doing the same thing, flying into this Central American revolution. Maybe y'all need your wars to help get past losing your parents."

"So, you knew one another before going to Vietnam?"

"No, we didn't. I had the good fortune of meeting Buck when I was shot down and crash-landed in the mountains above the A Shau Valley."

"Good fortune?"

"Well, yeah. I broke my ankle, and he found me. He literally carried me on his shoulders for miles, while we dodged and hid from North Vietnamese troops."

Elizabeth fixed him with those bright brown eyes, staring steadily at him for several seconds. From outside came the sounds of aircraft landing and taking off, and Buddy found himself growing self-conscious.

"What are you thinking?" he asked.

"You know, I don't believe my parents and their friends ever spoke to men like you and your friend Buck."

"That's probably because they never had much life outside of college. They were protestors in the sixties who got a degree or two. Many like them never left school. Some went directly into teaching. I'm not saying they were right or wrong. I'm just saying self-righteousness can be a heady drug, and they never had enough life experiences to understand how totally one-sided their viewpoints were. Radicalism can never see the truth clearly, because the truth usually lies beyond the hyperbole, somewhere in the middle."

Elizabeth wrinkled her brows but remained silent.

"Do you remember Curtis talking about his squad leader, Billy Coker?" Buddy asked.

"Yes."

"Billy was also a highly decorated veteran who was severely wounded, but he actually left his bed at the VA Hospital in Memphis and traveled to Washington, D.C., where he marched with the veterans against the war. He relapsed while he was there, and they say the trip damned near killed him, but that was just how strongly he felt about our involvement in Vietnam."

"Really?"

"Really."

CHAPTER THIRTEEN

The Gulf of Mexico

They had been flying for nearly a half hour that morning when Buddy called back to her. Elizabeth barely heard his voice but saw him peering back from the cockpit and motioning her forward. She stood and braced herself against the inside wall of the fuselage while making her way forward. When she stepped into the cockpit between the pilots, Buddy pointed out the side window on his left.

"Check that out."

The sky was aflame with one of the most magnificent sunrises she had ever witnessed. The morning clouds were billowing towers of orange incandescence sprouting rays of the morning sun, while the Gulf waters below seemed the source of some mysterious fire glowing from their depths. She gazed in awe for several seconds. After a while Elizabeth realized her hand was resting on Buddy's shoulder. Self-consciously she pulled it away and placed it on the back of his seat.

"I hate to ruin this for you, but it's time to bring the journal up here," he said.

His voice, though raised to be heard over the thrum of the engines, was soft and his eyes appeared regretful. She understood. He was right. It was something they had to do.

A few moments later she stood again between the two pilots, ripping the pages one by one from the journal and giving them to Buddy. Stein Foster flew the plane while Buddy shoved the pages through a small opening in the side window, until the entire book was gone, fluttering away to the ocean far below. After sliding the window shut, he reached over, took her hand, and squeezed it.

"Don't worry. This will be a story you can tell your grandchildren someday."

Buddy Rider was an enigma, seeming at times to shed his obnoxious traits for those of a kind and understanding person. She gave him a weak grin and walked to the rear, where she lay on an air mattress. Only now was her realization of who she had been a few days prior becoming clear. Well-intentioned but misguided and in a way sheltered for so many years, she had been too outspoken while possessing a somewhat sophomoric understanding of the world.

Elizabeth wondered if others saw her in this light, and she remembered how, when they first met, Buddy said the path to hell was paved with good intentions. Yet she was changing, and despite these shortcomings, she had doggedly pulled this thing together. They were actually on their way. And the best part it seemed was that Buddy was now standing by her. She could at least be proud of that, except there also came a better understanding of the dangers they now faced.

She could be killed or possibly responsible for the deaths of others. Her altruism had been a strong tonic, but it was now joined by this deeply sobering reality. Facing one's own mortality did seem to lend itself to clearer thought. She wondered if this was how Buddy, Curtis, and their friends felt when they went to the war in Vietnam.

After a while Elizabeth opened her eyes only to realize she had dozed for nearly an hour. Standing, she again wobbled her way toward the cockpit.

The sky was relatively clear, and the aircraft was purring like a big cat. Buddy and Stein Foster had settled in for the long haul, hooking their headsets to a cassette tape player and pouring coffee from a thermos. They listened to Bob Dylan doing his early seventies cowboy movie hit "Knockin' on Heaven's Door." It had become a bit of dark humor for Vietnam vets.

Buddy felt a hand on his shoulder and looked up as Elizabeth stepped into the cockpit. She appeared sleepy-eyed as she gazed out the front window at the endless ocean. Removing his headset, Buddy looked up at her and smiled.

"What's up?" he asked.

Elizabeth studied the tape player hanging from the control panel, while Stein poured more coffee in his cup.

"Are you guys listening to music?"

"Yeah. It's a Dylan song from that old movie, *Pat Garrett and Billy the Kid.* Here, listen."

He gave her his headset, but she hesitated.

"Go ahead. Put it on."

She pulled the headset over her ears. He studied her carefully as her brows dropped, and after a minute she pulled it off and gave it back.

"It's kind of morbid."

"I take it you don't like Dylan."

"I like him. I mean—it's just that song. It's about dying. You guys seem so cynical. How can you listen to something like that while we're on a mercy mission?"

Stein's eyes remained fixed on the horizon—wisely, Buddy figured, electing to stay out of the conversation. Elizabeth probably didn't understand, because she had not seen the darkest side of this crazy world. Despite the hardships she had told him about, the night before, she still had a certain innocence about her that seemed to deny the harshest realities of life.

"Honey, we're all knocking on heaven's door, but some of us have been in situations where we knocked a lot harder than others. It's something difficult to explain to those who haven't looked the beast in the eyes."

"I'm sorry," she said. "I just think you could be happier if you listened to something a little more upbeat—like maybe some disco."

Stein convulsed, blowing his coffee on the windshield as he fought to stifle his laughter. Elizabeth's face paled, and Buddy felt instant sympathy for her as he tried to remain poker-faced. After all, she was at least attempting some sort of conciliatory response.

"It's okay," he said. "Just go on back and lay down awhile. I'll explain it later."

Elizabeth was again feeling like an idiot. She had not meant to anger Buddy, nor did she mean to make herself the butt of some inside joke. It seemed she never said the right things. Lying on the air mattress, she closed her eyes. After a while she was dancing in the arms of a handsome man, holding him close, and feeling the warmth of his body. It was a wonderful dream, until she realized the man was Buddy Rider. Awakening with a start, she shook her head and tried to determine if it was a good dream or a bad one. Regardless, she was vexed and uncomfortable.

The motors were still humming steadily as she rubbed the sleep from her eyes and again wobbled toward the cockpit. Both men turned and looked up at her as she entered.

"Did you get a good nap?" Buddy asked.

"I suppose."

"It sure sounded like it with all the snoring I was hearing back there."

She playfully punched his shoulder and gazed out the cockpit windows. The sky had become a thick milky blue, splotched with clouds above and below. It was beautiful but also disorienting, and in a strange way frightening. There was no visible horizon, and she couldn't tell where the sky ended and the ocean began. It was as if they were submerged in a bowl of blue and white soup with no means of orientation or points of reference.

"This looks strange. How do you know which way is up?"

Buddy pointed to an instrument on the panel above the yoke as he pushed it forward, paused, then slowly pulled back. Horizontal lines separated and closed accordingly. "It tells us when we're flying straight and level."

"Where are we?" she asked.

Buddy glanced out the side window then over at Stein. "I don't know. Chief, do you know where we are?"

The co-pilot glanced out his side window and shrugged as he opened a map. He ran his finger across the chart and stopped over a large blue area. "Let me see. Hell, best I can figure, we're somewhere over the Gulf of Mexico."

She braced her hands, one on Buddy's shoulder and the other on Stein's, as she gazed out through the windshield. "I ask God for pilots, and he sends me comedians."

"Sorry, Babe. We couldn't resist," Buddy said.

His words struck a chord in the form of a huge emotional lump rising in her throat. "What did you say?"

"I said we're sorry, we just couldn't resist teasing you."

"No. I mean what you called me."

"Oh. Sorry, that was a slip-up."

Elizabeth paused and wondered if she had unwittingly let something slip.

"Babe is what my friends called me in elementary and high school. I got it because I could hit a softball so far, everybody on the team started calling me Babe Ruth Anderson."

"No shi—I mean, no kidding?" Buddy said.

"Yeah, I got away from it in college, but they still call me Babe back home."

"Well, we're still about an hour from the Yucatan Peninsula, Babe."

He gave her a smug grin, and she realized she had to set clear parameters on this relationship before things got out of hand. Buddy Rider was not family nor was he a childhood friend.

"Perhaps you should stick with calling me Elizabeth for now."

She returned to her bed and wrapped herself in the blanket.

Another two hours had passed when Elizabeth felt the plane rocking and jolting. This time she had to use both hands to steady herself as she made her way up to the cockpit. Her knees buckled and straightened again as the floor beneath her rose and fell. Outside, billowing thunderheads filled the sky as bright flashes of lightning leapt across the heavens with thunderous booms. The mid-afternoon sun was gone—blotted out by walls of purple clouds that left the sky slate gray, not unlike the last minutes of dusk.

"Are we flying through that?" she asked.

Buddy turned, seemingly surprised by her voice. The dim light from the instrument panel lit his face with a dull glow that revealed a fine sheen of sweat. He pointed down at a panel on the wall behind her knees.

"Unlatch that. It's a jump seat. Sit down and strap in."

She sat on the small metal seat and buckled the safety belt.

"Cinch it up tight," he said.

"We're trying to skirt these storms," Chief said, "but they're moving fast. Worst case, we'll try to fly between them."

"Where are we?"

"Too close to the edge of this damned storm," Chief muttered.

"Off the coast of Belize," Buddy said. There was no humor in his voice.

Elizabeth felt her stomach rising as if she were in an elevator descending a Chicago skyscraper.

"Downdraft!" Buddy said. He quickly pushed some levers. "Okay, I'm increasing power, full low pitch. What's the altitude?" Buddy maintained his focus through the windshield while fighting the yoke.

"Twelve thousand, sir, but we're unwinding quick—a thousand feet per minute."

"Crap," Buddy muttered.

"There's a gap on the left," Chief said. "You see it?"

"Yeah. Looks like a box canyon. Let's maintain our current heading."

Elizabeth could feel the men's tension.

"Check the carb heat."

Foster pulled two knobs. "Looks like another opening up there."

"It may be the best we can do, but we need to climb some more," Buddy said. "If we get caught in another downdraft like that one, we'll be swimming to Honduras."

Elizabeth craned her neck to see over the instrument panel. If she and these two men were twelve thousand feet up in the atmosphere, the storm clouds were towering twice more than that above them. They were flying along a wall of billowing thunderheads that were only a few hundred yards away. The wall stretched downward for over two miles and seemingly forever upward, leaving her feeling like a mere speck in all its vastness.

This sudden realization of her infinitesimal place in God's cosmos ignited something within—fear combined with awe, but it was a fascination unlike anything she had ever experienced. This was real. She was in it, and she saw with clarity that in the next few minutes, she and these two men could perish forever. They could disappear and never be found again. The windshields became blurred gray with scouring rain. She felt a terrible urge.

"I have to go," she shouted.

The aircraft bucked and rolled. Chief looked around at her. "Ma'am, I don't want to be crude, but if you unbuckle and go back there now, you'll probably end up wearing that urinal bucket on your head."

Buddy turned. "Babe, you gotta hold it, but if you can't, just go and don't worry about it. Whatever happens, stay buckled."

Their eyes met. His squinting blue eyes gleamed in the dim light, and she felt a sudden oneness with this person on whom her survival now depended.

"We'll make it," he said. "Just hang on tight."

He turned the yoke and banked the plane into the canyon between the thunderheads. Within a minute a terrible rattle came from outside. It sounded as if the fuselage was being pummeled by buckets of gravel.

"Hail," Chief shouted.

The rattle turned to thunder.

"Check the carb heat, again," Buddy shouted above the noise.

The sky grew even darker as the aircraft bucked, banked, and swayed. They were at the merciless whims of the storm. The sounds grew until they were deafening, but the pilots seemed to communicate without speaking as they worked together, and when Elizabeth thought the flash and thunder would never end, she began hearing the engines for the first time in twenty minutes. Their sound had been totally drowned out by the storm.

Only then did she realize the hail and rain had ceased, and she sent a prayer of thanks heavenward. The rollercoaster ride had now become akin to a jarring ride down a pot-holed road, and both pilots remained fixated on the controls. Violent jolts of turbulence continued, and Elizabeth wondered if the old plane would hold together. As she gripped the sides of her seat, she worried that her prayer of thanks had been premature.

After a few minutes, the turbulence slowly dissipated, and the aircraft was again flying smooth and straight. Buddy had lightened his grip on the controls. Elizabeth looked out over the instrument panel as sunlight broke through the clouds. The sky ahead was aglow with the light of salvation, bright and clear as a new day. Her heart continued thumping in her chest, but she was finally able to exhale. Only then did she realize she had been holding her breath.

"We've got the ADF beacon loud and clear," Chief said.

Buddy gazed at the control panel. "What do we look like on fuel?"

"Not fat, and we're bucking a pretty stout headwind, but I think we'll be okay. It's less than a hundred miles, and we'll practically be there once we cross the coastline."

Only then did Elizabeth realize she still had to go. She didn't ask but unbuckled instead and hurried to the rear of the aircraft.

CHAPTER FOURTEEN

Welcome to Honduras!

"There it is," Chief Foster said, pointing up ahead to a gash in the jungle.

Buddy breathed a sigh of relief. It was the airstrip, and they had fuel to spare.

"I'll do a flyover before I set up for the landing," he said. "See if you can get someone down there to give us the winds. How accurate is the altimeter?"

He felt her hand on his shoulder. Elizabeth had walked forward and stood between them, gazing out the windshield.

"It's not. You're going to have to eyeball it," Stein said.

Buddy throttled back and gazed out the side window as they passed over the airstrip.

"Jesus," he muttered. "It looks like an aircraft graveyard down there."

The wreckage of all manner of planes was scattered in the jungle below.

"That's mostly just old drug runners' crap," the chief said. "We've got twenty-five hundred feet of hardball with matting now. You should be fine."

Buddy banked hard after passing over the airstrip.

"Winds are light and variable from the south," Stein said.

Buddy patted Elizabeth's hand. "Go ahead and sit back in the jump seat and buckle up."

From a couple thousand feet up, the strip appeared as little more than that—just an airstrip for clandestine operations, but he spotted more. Hidden in the surrounding trees were several camouflaged buildings, tents, vehicles, and other aircraft. The landing was a relatively smooth one, and a marshaller appeared to guide the C-47 beneath a camouflaged canopy. When the engines were shut down and the master switch thrown, Buddy exhaled and hung his headset on the yoke. After so many hours in the sky, the sudden silence was amazing, broken only by the ticking of the hot metal in the cooling engines.

"I'm not blowing smoke up your ass, Rider," Foster said. "That was some damned fine flying you did back there in that storm."

"Thanks, Chief. I consider that a helluva compliment."

He turned to look back at Elizabeth. She had that faraway look in her eyes as she unbuckled. It wasn't quite a thousand-yard stare, but definitely the precursor to one.

"You okay?" he asked.

Her eyes were ringed with moisture. She gave him a quick nod. "Yeah. Sure."

"Buck up, deary. We've got a long way to go yet, but just so you know, you have my respect. Most people would not have handled that as well as you did."

"Thanks," she said in a near whisper.

Turning away, she walked unsteadily toward the rear of the aircraft.

―――――――――――

Jim Parker arrived shortly and greeted them with a six-pack of beer as they stepped to the ground.

"Welcome to Honduras," he said. "Does this remind you of someplace you've been before?"

"I'm afraid so," Buddy said.

"Relax, partner. It's not quite as bad as Nam."

Parker popped the tops on two cans of beer and handed one to each man. "I figured you could use a couple of these after your flight." He glanced at Elizabeth. "Don't mean to be rude, ma'am, but I'm assuming you're passing on the beer."

"No, I really could drink one right now, if you don't mind."

Her voice was subdued, and her eyes, although dry now, were bloodshot. Parker popped open another beer and handed it to her with a half-smile of sympathy, but he offered no further niceties. The group walked toward a cluster of buildings hidden back in the trees.

"This is Elizabeth Anderson," Buddy said.

Parker gave her a terse nod. "Pleased to meet you, ma'am."

Buddy glanced about. The base was mostly small prefab buildings and large tents set on wooden platforms. A diesel generator hummed somewhere back in the jungle and several black Huey helicopters with drooping rotors sat in the shadows beneath the camouflaged netting. Located in a relatively flat area near the coast, the air here was warm and thick with humidity.

"I can put you and this lady in a room with electricity, a small fan, and a couple cots with mosquito netting. There's a latrine just down the trail from there, but I have to warn you, it's the same one everyone uses. You may want to escort her when the need arises. And make sure you watch your step. There are a lot of snakes around here. There's a plastic bucket in the room for a chamber pot at night. I recommend you use it."

"We're in the same room?" Buddy asked.

"Best I can do, unless you want a tent."

"I'll take a tent," Elizabeth said.

"No, you won't," Buddy answered.

"Why not?" she snapped.

"Because I'm not sleeping in a tent when we have a building with electricity and a fan, and I can't guarantee your safety if you're sleeping somewhere else. Don't worry. Other than when we're sleeping, you will have your privacy."

"What about when I'm sleeping?"

"Don't snore and I won't mess with you."

Her eyes widened, and her face reddened. She seemed caught somewhere between her anger and a checkmate.

"Buddy Rider, you—oh, never mind."

Colonel Parker showed them to the room. The fan was mounted inside a screened window five feet above a bare wood floor. A single dim lightbulb with a pull-string was suspended from the ceiling. Two canvas cots with mosquito nets were on either side of a small desk with a ladder-back chair in the otherwise spartan room.

"The bulb is only forty watts. Saves on the power," Jim said. "This is actually the executive suite. We hold it for visiting dignitaries. Leave your bags, and let's head over to the TOC and take a look at a map."

"I forgot," she said. "What's a TOC?"

"Tactical Operations Center," Buddy said. "It's where... never mind. I'll explain more later."

"I'm not stupid."

"No one said you were. Just try to be patient, will you?"

They followed a winding dirt path through the trees where geckos scurried and birds flitted.

"Did you guys have a good flight down?" the colonel asked.

"We hit a little weather just off the coast here, but it was pretty routine otherwise."

"You call that a *little* weather?" Elizabeth said.

The colonel glanced back at her, then at Buddy.

Buddy shrugged. "We got caught between a couple thunderheads. It got a little rough."

Elizabeth's eyes bugged. "A little rough? You've got to be kidding."

"He's telling you the truth, ma'am," the colonel said. "When you've been shot down and crash-landed twice in Vietnam like him, a thunderstorm is probably small potatoes."

Buddy could feel her eyes on his back, but she remained silent. The colonel ushered them into one of the larger buildings that had shaded windows and sprouted several antennas. Inside were huge wall maps of the surrounding countries along with numerous more detailed topographical maps under plastic overlays. They were marked with various-colored grease pencils. A half dozen radios were scattered about on the tables. At the moment they were silent.

"Okay, here's what I've been able to learn. There's no certain schedule for the aircraft flying into this place, but all that came in recent weeks have landed and departed before noon. They come in loaded with raw product and leave loaded with finished product. A government convoy with twenty or twenty-five men usually comes down to the strip thirty minutes or so before the aircraft arrives. They transfer the loads and return to their compound when the plane departs.

"Outside of those times, there is normally no one around the airstrip. There are usually only two aircraft a week in and out. Travel from the government compound to the airstrip is on a rough dirt road and takes about twenty-five minutes. The village is about halfway between, and the road runs right through the middle of it.

"The airstrip lies roughly north and south along a ridgetop on the mountain. It's plenty long enough, but it's mostly dirt and grass with only minimal improvements. The Salvadorans have a tractor with a blade they use to smooth ruts and such, but we'll need some dry weather to put your bird in there.

"If we do our homework and maintain good communication with the Alpha Team, you should be able to get in and out inside of twenty minutes. We will notify the team when you depart from here, and you will notify them when you're about twenty minutes out. They will move all the nuns and locals to the airstrip and be ready to load them by the time you taxi and turn. You're going in with a minimal fuel load. This will give you better flexibility landing and taking off, and also help if you have more passengers than expected show up.

"My men will offer what security they can, but we can do only so much. If there are any major glitches anytime during the mission, I may order you to abort and return here. I need to know now if you intend to follow my orders if that becomes necessary."

"I will, sir."

"Good enough. You know I will do my best to help you get those people out of there. First, we need to discuss your approach to the airstrip. You must go straight in with no flyover. There's no other way to do it without being seen. Regardless, we have to assume the government troops at the facility may spot you and react as soon as you land. Therefore, timing is critical."

The colonel walked to a table where an aerial photo lay and pointed at a spot near its center.

"You, me, and Chief Foster will do a high-altitude flyover of this area tomorrow, weather permitting. This is the airstrip." He pointed to a light gray line on the black and white photo and moved his finger across to several lighter colored squares. "These structures up here are the government facility. The road runs down the mountain from the compound, through this village, and turns down this ridge to the airstrip. As I said, the strip lies along the crest of this secondary ridge."

"When are we going in?" Buddy asked.

"After we do our flyover tomorrow, the team will notify us when the next aircraft arrives. As soon as it departs, we go in. Of course, this is contingent on the weather and any other unforeseen occurrences. Remember, there are rebels in the area as well, and they could complicate things severely. Oh, and one more thing. My men are painting over your tail numbers. We'll replace them when you head home."

Buddy never doubted just how difficult this mission could be, and he wondered if Elizabeth now understood as much. He cut a quick glance at her. The TOC was muggy, and her forehead was beaded with sweat as she stood gazing down at the map. The thousand-yard stare he had seen when they first landed was growing. She glanced up at him—seemingly startled.

"You okay?" he asked.

"Yeah, sure," she said.

Her eyes said otherwise. It was clear she had become more aware of the danger they faced, but this was a good thing. It would make her more cautious.

———————

It had been an exhausting day, and Buddy waited outside the room while Elizabeth prepared herself for bed. He rubbed mosquito repellent on his arms and legs. When she called him, he went inside and quickly crawled inside his netting. The canvas cot had one sheet and a blanket, and the little window fan whirred furiously, but it barely stirred the room's dank air. Elizabeth's eyes were closed, but she was still awake.

"Do *not* under any circumstance get out of your cot or leave this room without waking me up. I mean it."

"I won't," she said.

He didn't know if it was trust or fear, but there was a change in her voice that indicated a growing acceptance of his directives. Either way, it was a good thing. He hoped he wouldn't let her down.

"Good night," he said.

She opened her eyes and looked over at him. "Good night."

Buddy rolled away from her and pulled the sheet under his chin. The room was hot and the air thick. He could feel this woman's thoughts as clearly as if she had spoken them aloud. She was in way over her head and only now was she beginning to fully realize just how deep and treacherous the waters could be.

"Don't worry," he said. "We'll do our best to get your friends out of there."

CHAPTER FIFTEEN

Snakes, Steaks, and a Wait

At better than three hundred miles an hour and ten thousand feet up, the flyover was only marginally better than the aerial photo Parker had shown him. Buddy quickly picked out the major landmarks and did his best to imagine how the terrain might appear when they approached at near treetop level in his lumbering C-47. With the volcano and other peaks in the vicinity, a miscalculation could result in what was officially called "a controlled flight into terrain"—otherwise described as a crash and burn.

There were three of them aboard the colonel's small Lear jet that morning, piloted by Chief Warrant Officer Stein Foster. Far below, through a few wisps of clouds, the airstrip was visible. Off to the northeast Buddy spotted the metal buildings of the government drug processing facility. A few klicks west of the compound was the village, and a short distance from there was the airstrip. The rugged folds of the terrain swept away from these mountaintop locations, dropping toward lake Coatepeque on the east side and the Pacific Ocean to the southwest. The highest obstacle was a volcano that, according to the charts, rose nearly fourteen thousand feet above sea level.

Buddy found himself suddenly thinking of the times years ago when he and Jungle Jim had done this same thing for their

A-teams reconning the Ho Chi Minh Trail in Cambodia and Laos. It was a bad déjà vu that brought back memories of some missions that had not ended well. But that was then, and he had to put those memories out of his head and focus. The entire flyover mission lasted less than two hours before they arrived back at the airstrip in Honduras.

The three men were walking to the TOC when Jungle Jim stopped and motioned Buddy to the side. "You haven't said a word for the last hour. What's the problem?"

"What makes you think there's a problem?"

From somewhere out in the jungle came the screech of a macaw. Buddy did not want his old friend to think he had lost his nerve, but neither did he want Jim to think him a bullshitter.

"Extended silence is not your thing. What's on your mind?"

"Nothing in particular—just some memories."

"Are you going to be ready when the time comes?"

"I'm good."

"Don't do this if you think we haven't covered all the bases."

"I'm committed," Buddy said, "but we both know there is no way to cover *all* the bases. We just have to take our chances and give it our best shot."

The colonel pressed his lips tightly together and gave a single nod. "I understand. And let me make this clear one more time. My men cannot engage the Salvadoran troops. They will bring the nuns and orphans to the aircraft and help you load them, but they will standdown if any of the government troops show up and a clash seems imminent. In that case, you may be on your own."

"I understand."

Jim Parker slapped his back. "You're right about not being able to cover all the bases, but we can do our best to game-out some of the possibilities. Let's sit down now and go over the entire scenario again. We'll look at possible contingencies and prepare as much as we can for whatever happens."

Buddy, Colonel Parker, and Chief Foster spent the rest of the afternoon discussing the mission.

———————————

Later that afternoon, Buddy tapped lightly at the door to his room—their room. There was no answer. He pushed it open. Elizabeth wasn't there. He drew a deep breath and exhaled.

"Shit," he muttered.

There was no need for her to be wandering around the base or somewhere out there in the jungle. He stepped outside and looked around. The sky glowed with the orange of the evening sun as it settled into the treetops. The sounds of insects and frogs came from the surrounding jungle, but he also heard voices. They were men's voices—laughing and talking. He walked down a winding path toward the source where he found a group of soldiers gathered at the entrance to the shower tent.

"Surely not," he mumbled, but it was denial of the obvious. She was inside, showering.

As he walked up, several of the men grinned.

"Sorry, sir," one said.

"Sorry for what?" Buddy asked.

"You can't go in there. The lady is taking a shower."

The tent entrance was pulled closed, and the men were all facing his way. Elizabeth was naïve about many things, yet she had a certain degree of self-confidence that demanded respect. These men were by no means angels, but she had apparently gained theirs. Hell, he wouldn't trust one of the horny bastards as far as he could throw him, but once you gained their respect, Army Special Forces soldiers were fiercely loyal.

"You boys keep up the good work," he said. "And if you don't mind, would you escort her back to the room when she's done?"

"Yes, sir."

Jungle Jim had likely read them the riot act—no doubt wanting to protect his guests as well as the reputation of his Green Berets. Jim never talked about operations except to those who had a need to know, and he always expressed a deep obligation for holding his men to the same high standards. It was this personal integrity that drew Buddy toward him. He walked back to the room—confident Elizabeth was in good hands.

Later there came the sounds of voices outside. It was probably the men from down at the shower tent. The door opened, and Elizabeth stepped inside. Only after thanking them and closing the door did she notice him lying on his cot beneath the mosquito net.

"Oh! You surprised me."

"It looks like you've developed a following."

She hung her bath towel on the back of the chair and began brushing her hair.

"They were perfect gentlemen and guarded the tent while I showered."

He watched while she stood before the little room fan, letting it blow through her hair as she brushed and dried it. Even without cosmetics and with her wet hair plastered against her head, she was a nice-looking woman. It wasn't that he hadn't already noticed, but it seemed she had matured in the last few days—something that went far beyond the physical. It made her infinitely more attractive.

"Do you need me to step outside?" he asked.

"No. I'm already dressed for bed."

She wore a football jersey that extended below her knees.

"Where did you get that?"

"Dorie gave it to me. It's one of Curtis's old practice jerseys."

"Okay, but before you go to sleep, there's something we need to discuss."

She continued brushing her hair.

"If something goes wrong and the Salvadoran troops capture me and the aircraft—"

He paused to gather his thoughts.

"Okay, what I mean to say is I think it will be better if you stay here. There's really no reason for you to take the risk."

She stopped brushing her hair, and her eyes turned to stone. "I didn't come here to sit back and let you take all the risks. I'm going."

"Why don't you—"

"No! This is not something up for discussion. I'm going."

She fixed him with a defiant glare. She was stubborn, but this woman was no coward.

"Okay, I admit that we can probably use your help. You already know how the safety straps along the wall work, so you can help Stein buckle the people in as they come aboard."

"Where will you be?" she asked.

"I'll be in the cockpit monitoring the radio and setting up for the take-off as soon as everyone is on board. You better get some rest now. We might go at any time."

Not long after falling asleep, Buddy was awakened by the sound of distant thunder. He dozed again, and sometime in the night a light rain began falling. The stifling heat abated, and the jungle air grew cool. The raindrops pelted the building's metal roof with a narcotic rhythm that drove him into a deeper sleep. It was the best he had experienced in weeks.

Buddy was wrapped comfortably in his bedsheet and lost in a world of blissful dreams when a gut-wrenching scream jarred him awake. He sat upright. It had come from somewhere outside. Tearing away the mosquito net, he leapt to his feet. Elizabeth was not in her cot. He grabbed his flashlight and snatched open the door. A light rain dripped from the jungle vegetation, and Elizabeth's still burning flashlight lay in a puddle on the path twenty yards away. She was nowhere in sight.

Following her muddy footprints, he walked to the flashlight and picked it up, but the tracks stopped there. Shining his light farther down the trail, he saw only undisturbed puddles of water. The rain dripped relentlessly as he pointed his light left and right into the walls of glistening vegetation. It was as if she had simply levitated and disappeared without a trace.

He was missing something, but what? Despite the patter of the rain on the leaves, he thought he heard something— breathing, perhaps—heavy breathing. It was close. And it dawned on him. Tilting his head back, Buddy pointed his flashlight into the trees overhead.

She was there, halfway up a tall slender tree, clinging to its trunk. Probably unaware she was showing more of her legs than she realized, her rain-soaked nightshirt was pulled nearly to her hips. He put the light in her eyes. She blinked like a treed racoon.

"What are you doing?"

"There was some kind of animal." Her voice quivered and her eyes were reddened and watery.

"No. I mean what are you doing out here in the rain at night?"

"I had to go."

It took every ounce of his willpower not to curse her.

"There's a bucket in the room for that."

"I know. I didn't want to go with you in the room."

"For the love of—. Next time just wake me up, and I'll step outside. Now, come down out of that tree."

Her nightshirt slid well above her hips as she shinnied down the tree. He caught her legs and took her into his arms. Despite the cool rain, her body was warm, almost hot, and Buddy had to remind himself that she was some sort of missionary lay nun or whatever.

"Put me down. I can walk," she said.

"Yeah, sure you can, and when one of these vipers latches onto your leg, we'll be medevacing your little butt to a hospital."

After carrying her back up the trail, he pushed open the door to the room and set her on her feet. She quickly snatched her shirt down over her panties.

"Now, go in there and pee, and put on some dry clothes. Hurry up. I'll be waiting out here in the rain. Call me when you're done."

A fresh breeze was blowing, and the sun was well above the trees the next morning when Buddy awoke to the aroma of coffee brewing. Elizabeth was still sleeping as he crept from the room and walked to the TOC. The colonel and several of his men were gathered there.

"Coffee?" Parker said.

"*Hell*, yes."

"Everything okay? Some of my men thought they heard the woman scream last night."

He filled Buddy's cup.

"Some kind of critter scared her. She's okay now."

The colonel gave him a puzzled glance.

"Don't ask," Buddy said. "Just let me drink my coffee in peace."

Parker grinned. "Better you than me, my friend. The meteorologist in Panama reported that the rain passed over the entire region last night. It wasn't a lot, but we'll need at least one good dry day before we can take off or land on the strip in El Salvador. You can rest easy today. I'll let you know if anything changes.

"I special ordered us some charcoal and steaks. We have a chopper bringing it in from Tegucigalpa. They're also bringing rolls, baked potatoes, corn on the cob, and a few cases of beer. I hope you're hungry."

"Care if I bring my date?"

Parker laughed aloud. "Sure, bring her on. You two can be my guests of honor."

The remainder of the day was quiet, and Buddy returned to the room to lie on his cot while Elizabeth walked around the compound. He had nearly dozed off when she returned.

"What are we waiting for?" she asked.

"The airstrip in El Salvador is too soft after the rain. We have to wait at least a day, and then it's up to the people we're watching. They have to make the first move."

"I'm hungry. Can we go get some more of those army rations?"

"How about we go out for a steak dinner?"

"Yeah, I wish," she said with unmasked sarcasm. "I haven't had a steak in years."

"Years?"

"Yeah, Mom always imagined herself a vegan, except when she got stoned. Then she'd take us to McDonald's for Big Macs and fries. And hamburger steaks were the closest thing we got to steak with our college dorm meals."

From somewhere in the distance came the rhythmic thump-thump-thump of an approaching helicopter.

"Do you hear that?" Buddy asked.

"Is it a helicopter?"

"That's right, and it's bringing in steaks and hot food. Let's head over to the mess area."

The colonel met them halfway there. "I came to get our guests of honor. You guys ready to grill some steaks and eat?"

"Sure," Buddy said.

"I just received some intel from our people in Panama. There's a loaded aircraft down south, and if it follows the pattern, it will likely come our way tomorrow. Make sure you prep your aircraft in the morning and be ready. You may be going in as soon as tomorrow afternoon."

"We will be ready."

Charcoal fires were lit, and they stood with the men around the grills cooking steaks and drinking beer. Elizabeth was now a totally different person. She seemed comfortable and at ease as she carried on conversations with them. Charming but not the least flirty, it was as if she were just another one of the guys. Yet, being the only woman within miles of this desolate airstrip, she was the center of attention. This was the kind of woman Buddy could admire, and he found himself wondering if he had judged her too quickly.

CHAPTER SIXTEEN

Flying into a Revolution

U p at first light, Buddy donned his boots and walked to the TOC. Jim Parker was already there sipping his morning coffee and studying the map.

"Coffee?" he said.

"Thanks. Any updates?"

"The aircraft we had under surveillance in Colombia took off at first light. The Alpha Team at the airstrip in El Salvador also reported a fuel truck arriving and a lot of activity up at the government compound. Seems like it's coming our way."

"I'll go pull the props through and sump the fuel. I need your men to tow the aircraft out to the strip when you're certain we're going."

"Will do. There's a case of LRRP rations over there in the corner. Grab what you want and throw them in your bag. Oh, and here's a couple more things—a bottle of purification tablets and a canister of powdered CS."

Buddy took the OD canister of powdered tear gas and examined it.

"Same stuff we had in Nam," Parker said.

Buddy nodded. It was what SF teams used to keep tracker dogs from following their trail.

"I appreciate it. Let's hope we don't need it."

"Chief Foster is going to wear his civvies and knows he will be on his own if things go sideways, so take care of my boy."

"I'll do my best."

"Your call sign is Papa Whisky One. I will be Black Shadow Six for this op. You have the operating frequencies and alternative landing sites. Come back here in a couple hours, and we'll run through the drill one more time."

After prepping the plane, Buddy returned to the room where Elizabeth sat at the desk writing.

"What's that?" he asked.

"Instructions for your friend the colonel in case something happens."

"Oh?"

"There's that ten thousand dollars in my bag. I'm leaving it here. If we don't return, I'm asking him to use it to help other missionaries in the area. Do you think we can trust him?"

"You're trusting him with your life. I think you can trust him with your money. What are you carrying with you?"

She glanced at her bag in the corner and shrugged. "Nothing, really. I don't suppose I'll need much."

Buddy pointed to his backpack. "I want you to put all the socks you have in my pack, along with an extra pair of trousers and a hat of some sort. Toss any personal items you may need in there as well. Oh, there's already a .45 automatic with two extra magazines in there. It's loaded. There is also a very sharp knife in a sheath, so be careful."

"But I thought the plan was to be back here before dark."

He set four LRRP rations on the desk along with the bottle of purification tablets and the canister of powdered CS.

"If you don't mind, shove this stuff in there, too. I'm heading back to the TOC. It looks like a go for today, so be ready."

"Why are we taking all this extra stuff?"

"In case we have to walk back."

After a quick glance his way, her eyes faded into the unfocused world of thought.

───────────

Buddy stood with Jim Parker and Chief Foster monitoring the radio for coded updates. Foster was wearing blue jeans and a faded Lynyrd Skynyrd t-shirt. Apparently, superstition was not one of his weaknesses. He caught Buddy looking and winked. Buddy could only admire this man's confidence as he shook his head in resignation.

The A-team reported a government convoy from the compound had met the aircraft on the airstrip in El Salvador. It was being refueled and would soon be reloaded. From outside the TOC there came the sound of a tractor. They were preparing to tow his plane from beneath the trees.

"Okay, one more time," Parker said. "Green smoke means you're clear to land. Red, you abort and return here. Winds are light out of the south, and you're making a downwind landing. As soon as you land, you'll taxi around and position for takeoff. Chief and Miss Anderson will go back and open the door to help the team load the passengers while you remain in the cockpit and monitor the radio and instruments. As soon as the last person is on board and strapped to the floor, the Alpha Team RTO will give the 'all clear' and they will clear the strip."

"Got it."

"You will climb out and make your turn that will take you

over Lake Coatepeque. Once you're clear, you will radio us with a sit-rep. We'll fire up the ADF beacon and bring you home. Questions?"

"No, sir."

"You better go get the lady and power up the plane," Parker said. "Good luck."

———————————

Twenty minutes later, Buddy sat in the cockpit with Stein Foster, while Elizabeth sat on the jump seat in the alley behind the flight deck. Static popped in their headphones as they waited for the word from the TOC. The motors hummed strong and steady, and the two men went through the final pre-flight check list.

"Gyros set."

"Check," Foster answered.

"Altimeter set."

"Check."

"Oil temp."

"In the green."

"Oil pressure."

"In the green."

"Flaps."

"Ten percent."

Buddy continued down the list and when they were done, he turned to look back at Elizabeth. She rested her hands on her knees and sat rigidly upright while staring straight ahead. Her face reminded him of the young soldiers back in Nam when they boarded the Huey helicopters for their first combat assault. Stifled fear had a somewhat universal appearance.

"We'll be flying into a revolution soon. Are you ready?"

She turned to face him. With her eyes wide, she nodded rapidly. Buddy reached back with his right hand and placed it atop hers. "It's going to be okay. Just stay with me and do what I say."

The static popped again in his headphones, and he heard the colonel's voice. "Papa Whisky One, you are cleared."

"Roger, cleared," Foster replied.

"Tail wheel locked," Buddy said.

"Check."

"Mixture is Auto Rich."

"Check."

Buddy opened the throttles.

"Props full forward, 2700 RPM."

"Check."

"Manifold Pressure is 48 inches."

"Check."

The plane lurched and lumbered forward down the airstrip as Foster read off the speeds. As soon as they became airborne, the aircraft shot out over the wreckage-strewn jungle and climbed skyward. A minute later, Buddy banked southward toward the Salvadoran border. This was it. They were on their way.

A rolling carpet of hills and mountains shrouded in jungle greenery stretched to the horizon. Neither man had spoken for several minutes when Chief Foster looked up from his map and out his side window.

"We're in Salvadoran airspace now. That's the Rio Lempa up ahead," he said. "Once we cross it, we have about twenty-five miles to go. I'm notifying the team."

He keyed the transmitter. "Vacía el gallinero."

There came an instant but staticky response. "¡De acuerdo! Vacía el gallinero."

These boys were good—no wasted words and all in Spanish. It was the same as when he was in Nam. They were professionals who knew their jobs. If things went as planned, the Alpha Team was now escorting the nuns and orphans down the road a quarter mile to the airstrip. Buddy glanced carefully at the instrument panel. Everything was reading normal.

"Just out of curiosity, what did you say?" he asked.

"I told them to empty the henhouse," Foster answered.

Buddy extended the flaps and lowered the landing gear. Lake Coatepeque passed beneath as he throttled back and banked toward the mountain ridge. He peered ahead, trying to spot the airstrip.

"Do you see it?" he asked.

Chief wagged his head. "Not yet. Watch that damned volcano over there."

"I got it," Buddy said. "We're so low over this mountain, we may not see the airstrip till we're—"

"There!" Chief said. "Straight ahead. Twelve o'clock. See it? Green smoke. You're lined up near perfect."

"Got it," Buddy said.

It was coming up fast.

"I know we're going in with the wind, but I'd reduce power some more," Foster said.

Buddy nodded as he pulled the throttles back. The landing was fast but remarkably smooth as they braked hard. Spinning the aircraft at the end of the runway, he set the brake and gave Foster a nod. Things were happening fast.

The chief followed Elizabeth back and opened the cargo door. It seemed an interminable amount of time, although it was no more than a minute before a crowd of people appeared from the jungle and scurried toward the aircraft. Buddy saw almost immediately that there were more than just missionaries and orphans. There were old men and women as well—at least thirty people in all counting the nuns and orphans, but there were no young men. The villagers were escorted by several soldiers in camouflaged uniforms—American Special Forces.

Even with the minimal fuel load, the aircraft was going to be close to maximum takeoff weight. Buddy gazed down the airstrip. He would have to stay out of the grass. After resetting the flaps and locking the rear wheel, he looked back through the cockpit doorway. Elizabeth and Foster were already buckling the first of the passengers along the wall. This was going remarkably well, and he remembered something he had once read in an old flight journal: *When a flight is proceeding incredibly well, something was forgotten.* But he had thought through every contingency—or so he hoped.

CHAPTER SEVENTEEN

Unforeseen Consequences

Elizabeth was buckling a child's safety belt when there came a muted scream and the sound of shouting voices from outside the aircraft. With the noise from the aircraft's motors, they were unintelligible, and her first thought was that the Salvadoran troops had been spotted. Foster, who had been taking the children through the door and passing them to her, was nowhere to be seen. She went back and cast a quick glance out the aircraft door. He was standing with the nuns who were wringing their hands and pointing back toward the village.

"We left an infant behind, and Melissa went back to the village," one of the nuns shouted.

There was no hesitation as Elizabeth leapt to the ground and sprinted toward the road. Behind her she heard the cries of the nuns calling for her to stop, but she hadn't come all this way to leave her friend behind. Breathless, she reached the edge of the village within minutes, but there was no one to be seen. It seemed abandoned.

Running between the thatched roof huts, she began searching. Most had been uninhabited for some time. Calling out for Melissa, she was answered only with silence. But there came a distant sound from farther up the mountain—the sound of vehicles. Her desperation grew as she ran frantically door to door searching every structure, but to no avail. The vehicle sounds grew suddenly louder. They were arriving out on the road near the center of the village.

Buddy leaned over in his seat and looked back from the cockpit. The plan was for Foster and Elizabeth to take the children and nuns aboard as they were handed up by the soldiers, but neither was visible. He couldn't leave his seat, but where were they? Was someone hurt? He felt movement inside the plane and looked back again. Stein Foster was running up the center walkway toward the cockpit. The look on his face said something had gone wrong—terribly wrong.

"We've got problems. One of the missionaries said a kid was left behind and took off back to the village. Elizabeth went after her. Captain Stark sent three men to bring them back."

Buddy removed his headset, stood, and moved to the right side of the cockpit.

"Take the left seat. If I'm not back when you get the signal from the team, get the hell out of here. Don't wait. We can't let them get these people. The tail wheel is locked, and the flaps are set for takeoff. Oh, and do me a favor. If I don't make it back, tell Jungle Jim the plane is his."

Grabbing his backpack, Buddy leapt from the aircraft and sprinted toward the opening in the jungle where the road led to the village. It was a quarter mile run, but he had slowed to a winded trot when he met the three soldiers coming his way. They had a young missionary woman with them. She was carrying an infant, but Elizabeth was nowhere in sight.

"Where's the other woman?" he asked.

"We're sorry, sir. Salvadoran troops came into the village while we were searching. We think they may have taken her prisoner, but our orders are to avoid contact at all costs."

"Crap! Take this woman and the baby back to the aircraft. Tell Chief Foster to get airborne. Tell him I'm staying behind."

"But sir—"

"Do it!"

"Please," the missionary pleaded. "We can't leave her here. She's my best friend."

Buddy stopped and glanced at the young woman. She looked to be the same age as Elizabeth, and "my best friend" explained a lot of what he already suspected.

"Go, now," Buddy said to the soldiers.

"Yes, sir."

"No! Wait."

The men stopped.

"Do you have any frags?"

Two of the men reached into pouches and came out with several fragmentation grenades. The third soldier unslung a canvas pouch from his shoulder and held it out.

"There are four pounds of C-4 in here, sir. You are welcome to it." He handed it to Buddy and reached into a pouch on his web-gear. "Here are some fuses." He held one apart from the others. "Imbed this cap in the plastic and pull this ring. It's a ten-minute fuse."

He gave them to Buddy who shoved them in his pocket. "Thanks. Do you have any trip-wire?"

"Sure." One of them gave him a small coil. "Good luck, sir."

"Thanks. Now, get going."

With no idea what he was going to do, he turned and continued trotting up the road toward the village.

Elizabeth Anderson held her hands high, expecting and wondering what a bullet would feel like when it ripped through her body. The Salvadoran soldiers approached her with their heads bent over their upraised rifles. The sound of the aircraft engines back at the airstrip could have been a million miles away, and already she was gripped by dark thoughts of the nuns who had been raped, tortured, and slain by these same government troops.

Her heart drained of all hope, and although it was too late, she now saw with clarity what she had lacked after four years of college and six months of missionary training. It was the brilliant light of wisdom shining through the cracked door of a newfound realization. She had not realized just how much she did not know—a simple concept once she recognized it.

The soldiers' torturous glares were made worse by the perverted gleams in their eyes, and she knew a horrible death was soon coming. Fervently Elizabeth begged God to let them kill her quickly and forego the rape and torture, but he had given them free wills, and her destiny was written in their eyes. This was to be her end, and her thoughts went to her family.

It was true what they said about life passing before one's eyes. She saw her parents. Her father, a gentle soul with no real backbone or sense of loyalty, had dodged the draft and his family responsibilities by going to France. She hoped he had found whatever it was he wanted when he abandoned them. And there was her mother, the daughter of wealthy parents. She ended her life by falling asleep in bed with a lit marijuana cigarette. They were pitiful people, but she could hate neither of them.

And the memories of the nuns from the college were here now as well. The first time she saw them playing badminton in their robes, there was something strangely unsettling about it. All of them—even some of the older ones—seemed like young girls who had gotten lost in the confusion of life and were still trying to find their way. They seemed more socially ill at ease than many of their students.

Long before she had gone away to school, Elizabeth began realizing the world was, as Buddy said, not a place made entirely of sunshine and rainbows. But she had not understood everything he meant until this very moment. She had learned much from him in recent days, but not soon enough to foresee the worst possible consequences of this rescue mission.

"Ella es una de las monjas," a soldier shouted.

Her years of college Spanish suddenly became relevant. The man had said she was a nun.

"Sí, soy," she said.

"¡Cierra la boca, perra!" the soldier shouted, poking her with his rifle.

He grabbed her shirt and thrust her toward a jeep parked at the center of the village. Another soldier wearing a sidearm stepped from a nearby doorway and grinned. A pudgy man, whose teeth, those that weren't missing, were yellowed and crusty. His dull brown eyes wore a sadistic gleam as he stared at her body. The other soldiers saluted him.

"¿Dónde encontraste a esta puta?" he asked.

One of the others motioned with his chin back up the road. "Dice que es una monja, comandante. Ella estaba en el camino."

The commander continued eyeing her breasts with lecherous eyes.

"So, you tell my men you are a nun, but you dress like a whore. What am I to think?"

"I am not a nun, but I'm not a whore, either. I am a missionary."

"Ahh, I see. Come, let us get out of this sun, my dear missionary."

He turned to the soldiers. "Termina de registrar el pueblo."

The commander stepped back inside of what appeared to be a makeshift medical clinic for the village. Elizabeth looked around at the pitifully understocked shelves.

"Come, let us sit and wait a few moments until the rest of my soldiers to arrive. So, what brings you to our beautiful country?"

"I came here to bring my sisters home."

"I see. And where are the children—the orphans of the Communist guerrillas we have killed?"

"We are taking them as well."

"We? Who is this 'we' you speak of?"

———————————

As he crept closer Buddy spotted an unoccupied jeep at the center of the village, but there was no one in sight. He heard more vehicles coming down the mountain from the government compound. The sooner he found Elizabeth the better his chances were of freeing her. Ducking into the trees, he drew his .45 and moved parallel to the road as he entered the edge of the village.

The engines of the aircraft still hummed back at the airstrip. Foster wasn't moving, and if he waited much longer, the Salvadorans would likely shoot him down during takeoff. Something needed to be done to delay the approaching government troops. He had to create a distraction. The jeep sitting in the middle of the village was his best target of opportunity. Opening the canvas pouch, he stared at the contents and considered his options. Whatever he decided, it had to be done quickly.

Buddy grabbed a frag and sprinted to the jeep. Ducking, he opened the gas cap and pulled the pin from the grenade. He let the spoon fly and dropped it into the opening. A soldier appeared in a doorway several hundred feet away. Buddy turned and ran for cover as rifle rounds snapped past his ears.

Several loud pops came from outside the door, startling Elizabeth. The commander leapt to his feet. Someone was firing a rifle, and men were shouting. Drawing his sidearm, the Salvadoran officer stepped into the doorway, where he was silhouetted by the bright sunlight.

"I believe someone tried to steal my jeep, but do not worry. He will not get far."

Elizabeth leaned to look past him just as an incredible blast sent the commander stumbling backward into the room. What sounded like pieces of metal rained down on the clinic's tin roof as the commander stared at her from the floor with terror-filled eyes. He crawled to his feet and stepped back into the doorway.

"Atrapa a ese bastardo," he shouted.

Her hopes returned. It had to be the American soldiers. They had come for her, but the sounds of the aircraft engines grew louder. The plane was preparing to take off. Buddy was leaving her behind. He wouldn't do that, or so she had hoped, but the reality was undeniable. He would save the others first. From the other side of the village came shouts and the roar of vehicle engines as more trucks with soldiers arrived.

The commander turned toward her. "Now that the rest of my men have arrived, we will stop your friends and we will apprehend this fool, and I will let you watch while I cut off his balls."

She prayed that the soldier who destroyed the commander's jeep would escape. As for Buddy, she now found herself conflicted and hoping he was about to fly the others safely back to Honduras. And it occurred to her that she had developed this fondness for him. After all, he was noble in his own way, and despite all his faults he had tried to help her.

"Who sent you here? You are working for the United States government, no?"

"No, I'm not with the American government. I work for a priv—" She caught herself, but too late. It would have been better to have claimed some type of government liaison. The commandant grinned.

"Ah, so you are *not* with your country's CIA."

"I didn't say that."

"But you *did*. If not, tell me about this government agency for whom you work."

She fought them, but her tears could not be quelled.

"Oh, but your crocodile tears are so sad. You should have thought about all this before you came here to join with your Communist friends."

"I don't care about the Communists. I only wanted to save my sister missionaries."

"Yes! That is it. You *don't* care. You don't care about my country. You don't care about my people. You come here and want to dictate to us from your decadent life in your bourgeois society how we should govern our country."

"You sound like a Communist yourself."

The commandant slapped her with such force she saw stars and stumbled back against the wall. The pain was a thunderbolt that shot through her jaw, radiating into her neck. She touched her face with her fingertips. Her head felt as if it would explode. Stunned, Elizabeth now faced another new realization. She had always been free to speak her mind, but this was not the United States, nor was it a college class debate. Instead, it was an argument with ramifications far beyond a grade on her college transcript. The stars floating in her eyes were proof of that.

"Get up, puta, before I decide to kill you now."

She stood, fell against the wall, but pushed herself upright. "You better hope I die, you bastard." She was ready to fight.

The commandant stepped toward her, but a soldier slammed open the door.

"Comandante, la guerrilla se ha escapado!"

Elizabeth wanted to smile but her face was still shot with pain and unresponsive. The commandant glanced her way, and his eyes were sufficient payback. He was now showing not only frustration but more fear.

"¿Quién era él, un rebelde?" he asked the soldier.

"No lo sé, comandante."

The commander whirled toward Elizabeth.

"You are with these rebels, are you not?"

"I am a missionary," she said.

"You are a bitch!"

He turned back to the soldier. "Reúna las tropas. Iremos a capturar la aeronave."

Elizabeth stood as the commandant walked to her and grabbed the front of her shirt. Producing a knife, he placed the razor-sharp edge against her throat.

"What should I do—cut your throat, perhaps, and be done with you?"

She felt the keen edge stinging her neck. Certain she was about to die, Elizabeth closed her eyes and began praying. She waited, but he flipped the blade and drew it down the front of her shirt, laying it open. With his free hand he ripped her bra to her waist. A trickle of blood flowed from between her breasts where he had nicked her with the knife blade.

"Ahh. You have such big, beautiful tits for a missionary."

"Hate" was a word her college professors said she should never use toward another human being, but at this moment Elizabeth was ready to take full ownership of it. She wanted this man dead. She would do it herself, but she remained physically stunned and unable to respond. He squeezed her naked breast until it hurt, and his yellow-toothed grin made it clear that she too would soon die as the others had before her.

She then did something she had never imagined doing in her entire life. She spit in his face. He drew his fist back, and she raised her chin ready to take the blow.

"That's right. Kill me, you pig. Kill me now."

It was her only way to escape. She was ready, but he hesitated. A knowing grin spread across his face.

"You would like that, bitch, would you not?"

She searched the room with her eyes for some means or weapon to kill him, but there was nothing there.

"Don't worry. You will die soon enough, but not before I fuck you like the whore you are."

CHAPTER EIGHTEEN

The Loneliest Feeling

More government trucks were entering the village when the jeep exploded into a billowing fireball. Buddy glanced back as he fled into the jungle. The trucks stopped, and government soldiers were spilling out and taking cover. The soldier who had been standing in the doorway was now running toward the road. He pointed in Buddy's direction and shouted, but the others were ducking for cover. At the same moment there came the roar of the C-47 engines as Stein Foster advanced the throttles for takeoff.

Threading his way through the dense vegetation, Buddy continued climbing the ridge. He ran, stumbled, and clawed his way up the mountainside, before slowing to a walk. His lungs heaved as he fought to catch his breath. Thirty-one years could hardly be called old age, but he was no longer the soldier he had been in Vietnam. Behind him the shouting of the government troops dissipated as they lost his trail. He circled northward toward the road leading up to the government compound.

The sound of more vehicles came from the road as they sped down the mountain toward the village. Fighting his way through the dense undergrowth, Buddy made his way toward the sounds. His diversion had not only failed, but as the vehicles passed, he realized it had only made matters worse. With so many government troops in the village, rescuing Elizabeth was now impossible. They were likely fanning out and searching for him at this very moment.

Quickly considering his options, Buddy realized there was but one thing he could do—create another bigger diversion and hope the ensuing confusion would enable him to pull off a rescue. He found his way to the road and began trotting up the long uphill grade until the gates to the compound came into view. Easing into the trees, he studied the entrance for several minutes.

The facility was surrounded by a twenty-foot fence, topped with rolls of concertina barbed wire, but the gates were standing wide open. A lone soldier manned a wooden guard tower at the entrance, and there was no movement anywhere in the compound. It was apparent that most, if not all, of the garrison had gone down to the village.

Circling back into the jungle, Buddy paralleled the compound fence, searching for an opening. After walking several hundred feet he spotted a place where the ground beneath the fence was eroded into a deep ravine. He crept closer and glanced both ways. There were no guards in sight. A coil of concertina wire had been dropped into the wash, but it too was undercut by more erosion. There was a hole large enough for him to crawl under.

Dropping to his knees, Buddy leaned forward, but froze as his hands touched the ground. His right middle finger was touching something metallic. Withdrawing the hand, he sat back on his heels and carefully picked away the leaves one by one from a telltale hump of dirt. The sweat dripped down his face and the mosquitos buzzed incessantly. Both were minor distractions compared to the huge land mine he had nearly detonated.

He had been a fool, a lucky one, but a fool nonetheless for not expecting something like this. He redirected his gaze to the concertina and the ground surrounding the ravine. As he expected, there was more. The gleam of a barely visible trip wire caught his eye. It was wound through the concertina and led upward. He followed it to a hand grenade that was hung high on the fence, ready to spray its deadly shrapnel down on anyone who attempted to move or otherwise disturb the coiled barbed wire.

It took several minutes as he inched forward, searching the ground, gently probing, and crawling until he was beneath the wire. After emerging on the other side, he again glanced about. There were several buildings—one an apparent headquarters, another a large barracks, and the largest, perhaps eighty yards away, appeared to be the main processing facility. Beside it was a fuel truck along with stacks of fifty-five-gallon drums marked with flammable placards—no doubt gasoline and the perfect catalyst to destroy the main building and create one hell of a diversion.

He glanced at his watch and marked the time. Whatever time it took to reach the fuel truck would be the time he would need to get back to the fence. Once the fuse was ignited, he had ten minutes to get as far away as possible. Except for the man in the guard tower nearly a hundred yards away, there was no one in sight, but there was a forty-yard stretch of open ground to cross. If he ran it would arouse immediate suspicion. Better to at least seem casual and hope.

He drew a deep breath and sauntered across the open area. The guard in the tower turned immediately and studied him. Buddy cursed under his breath as he smiled and gave him a casual wave without breaking stride. The guard slowly raised one hand and returned a half-hearted wave. After reaching the trees beside the building, Buddy used the shadows to disappear from the man's sight as he worked his way toward the tanker truck.

The building was quiet. Apparently, no one was inside. This was good. He had no interest in killing anyone, leastwise, for the time being. The only sound came from a light breeze rustling the leaves. He crept along the building wall, until a sudden explosion of birds sent his already pounding heart into his throat. It reminded him of reconning amongst thousands of NVA soldiers in Laos. If flying an aircraft in combat required nerves of steel, special operations on the ground required something akin to chromium steel balls.

When he reached the tanker, he crawled beneath it and glanced at his watch. It had taken him over six minutes, still plenty of time to reach the fence and sneak out of the compound before the explosives detonated. He began packing the C-4 between the truck's frame and the bottom of the tank. When he was done, he inserted a blasting cap, held the fuse with one hand and snatched the ring. It ignited with a telltale hiss, and he scooted from under the truck. After a quick look at his watch, he started toward the compound fence, but something stopped him—a sixth sense perhaps.

Whatever it was, it refused to let him move. He glanced back at the tanker and only then did he realize what had happened. The fuse had fallen and separated from the C-4. It was lying on the ground, still smoking, but useless without being attached to the plastic explosive.

Scrambling back under the vehicle, he again pushed the detonator cap into the cottony, white explosive. The odor of the fuel and the burning fuse was something only he would experience if the tanker blew now. It took several attempts before the fuse finally remained in place. Slowly, he pulled his hands away. It rested on a ledge, secured with more of the plastic explosive wedged around it. Crawling from under the truck, he glanced about. All clear.

Coming to his feet, he crept down the side of the building using the trees for cover. This was it. He could feel it. He was about to bring down one hell of a diversion and hopefully more confusion and grief than these tin-horn despots could deal with. And while they were scrambling about in confusion, he hoped to find and free Elizabeth.

Despite her antagonistic attitude, Buddy's respect for her had grown. She had moral courage and unselfish dedication to others—the same traits possessed by men like Jim Parker and Buck Marino—and he was certain if you asked Elizabeth, Jesus too. Halfway across the open area, he cast another glance at the guard tower. The soldier was no longer there.

"Shiiut," he muttered.

The perimeter fence was only twenty yards away when someone shouted at him from behind. Buddy glanced back. It was a Salvadoran soldier pointing a rifle at him. The hole in the fence was close, but it could have been a mile. If he tried to run, the soldier would likely shoot him down, and Elizabeth would probably die at their hands. He had no choice but to stop, raise his hands, and hope to come up with an alternate plan.

"Detente o dispararé," the soldier shouted.

Buddy glanced at his watch. Over eight minutes had elapsed since he pulled the fuse.

"Date la vuelta y levanta tus manos," the man shouted.

Buddy had no idea what he was saying, but he needed to get as far away as possible from the tanker before it blew. With his hands still held high in the air, he turned to face the soldier, but slowly, he began backing toward the fence. They were probably at a survivable distance, but there were no guarantees, especially considering the volume of the flames and shrapnel that would come with the explosion.

The soldier ran forward, brandishing what appeared to be a shiny new American-made AR-15—no doubt supplied to the El Salvadoran government by the United States. It even had one of the new high-capacity thirty-round magazines. The soldier was young, and his face, taut with fear, dripped with perspiration. His youthful indecision would work to Buddy's advantage.

"¡Detente!" the soldier shouted, jabbing the rifle at him.

"What? What are you saying? Do you speak English?"

The soldier cocked his head to one side. "Gringo?" He was apparently surprised by Buddy's English.

"Yes. I am from the United States."

"¿Por qué estás aquí?"

Buddy had no idea what the soldier was saying, but he had to stall him. He continued backing toward the fence. When he stopped, he knelt, and let his feet dangle over the ravine behind him. He still held his hands above his head.

"¡No! Ponte de pie, ahora."

Buddy pointed to his watch and said, "Thirty seconds. Thirty seconds, and this whole place is going to blow."

The soldier again cocked his head to one side. "Thirty second?"

"Yes, one, two, three, four, five, six, seven—"

"Levántate!" the soldier shouted.

Apparently reaching the end of his patience, he motioned with his weapon for Buddy to stand.

Determined to keep the soldier's body between him and the explosion, Buddy again glanced at his watch—ten, nine, eight…. The tanker disappeared in a massive fireball and the blast's concussion blew the soldier against him. It worked. Stunned but conscious, Buddy realized he and the now unconscious soldier had been blown into the ravine below the fence. He glanced up at the grenade still dangling precariously above him. It had not detonated.

Several secondary explosions sent fifty-five-gallon drums skyrocketing hundreds of feet into the air. Most of the main processing building was leveled, and the burning fuel sent a billowing tower of black smoke far into the sky. Buddy slipped under the fence and fled while remnants of the tanker and drums rained down around him. Trees were shattered by the huge chunks of falling truck frame, and a fog of thick smoke rolled down the slope into the jungle.

Still dazed, Buddy ran from his man-made hell, moving down the mountain and circling back toward the road. He had to gather his wits and avoid capture while he searched for Elizabeth. This now seemed impossible, but after surviving two plane crashes in the jungle, he knew fate was not always dictated by reason. As long as there was hope, all was not lost.

CHAPTER NINETEEN

A Hopeless Situation

Chief Warrant Officer Stein Foster had the unenviable task of reporting to his commanding officer that he was returning without Buddy and Elizabeth. When the team returned to the aircraft with the runaway missionary and the infant, they said the Salvadorans had probably captured the girl and Rider refused to leave without her. A little while later when the Salvadoran troops approached the airstrip, Foster did what he had to do. After glancing back at his passengers, he pushed the throttles forward.

Once the aircraft cleared Lake Coatepeque, the chief leveled off and checked the cockpit gauges. All were in normal ranges. The colonel had told him to radio in the clear when airborne, but with Rider and the woman left behind, he was reluctant. He didn't know who was monitoring the frequency and might take advantage of the situation. This was a mess, but his training told him he needed to follow orders.

Stein keyed the transmitter. "Black Shadow Six, this is Papa Whisky One. Over."

"Papa Whisky One, go for Black Shadow Six. Over."

"Black Shadow, we've cleared the henhouse, and are inbound, but we have problems. Over."

"Do you need medical to meet you? Over."

"Negative, but I am solo. My Echo Tango Alpha is thirty mikes. I will give you details then. Out."

The flight ended with a clean landing, and Foster was still in the process of shutting down the engines when the cargo door opened. Colonel Parker walked past the passengers as he hurried up to the cockpit. He glanced at the empty seat and back at the upturned faces of the people sitting along the walls of the aircraft. He expected them to be celebrating, but they were strangely quiet.

"Where are Rider and the girl?"

"One of the missionaries thought a kid was left behind and ran back to the village. Elizabeth went after her. Captain Stark sent three men to get them, and Rider went, too. The team came back with the missionary and the baby but said the government troops had captured Elizabeth. Rider stayed behind."

Foster waited while Parker seemed to consider his options. The CO had already taken a lot of risks with this mission, and no one would blame him if he did nothing more. Yet, there was a brotherhood that went far deeper than government bureaucrats could ever understand. The colonel remained lost in thought, and Foster realized that whatever it was that the State Department didn't want disturbed at that compound no longer mattered to his boss.

"Okay, let's get a team together. You grab a copilot and get a chopper warmed up. I'm going back to the TOC. We'll get a sit-rep from the Alpha Team. If feasible, we'll insert and rendezvous with them somewhere in the AO—probably near the airstrip."

The colonel was well beyond taking a calculated risk. He was putting his career on the line for Rider and the girl. Stein respected him for it, but he had a better idea.

"Sir, why don't you let me put together a team and do this? I can—"

"Chief, I appreciate what you're saying, but this is my baby. Go get the chopper prepped."

———————————

Buddy made his way back to the road near the compound gate in time to see the Salvadoran convoy roaring up the mountain from the village. Armed only with his .45 pistol and three fragmentation grenades, he crawled forward and parted the jungle as he peered into the late afternoon sunshine to watch them pass. The trucks streamed diesel fumes and their cleated tires threw mud high into the air as they sped up the mountain road. It seemed the Salvadorans were fleeing some tremendous threat as the soldiers peered over the siderails with their weapons at the ready.

But then he saw her. She was there. Elizabeth was alive. She was riding in the open bed of a truck with several soldiers. Her hands were tied, and she was blindfolded. When the last vehicle passed, Buddy crept up the road toward the gate. The watchtower had toppled over in the explosion, and the entire compound was in shambles. The main processing building was a pile of smoking rubble, and the surrounding trees were denuded of their leaves and limbs. Only a crater remained where the tanker truck had been parked.

The Salvadoran soldiers climbed slowly from the trucks as their leaders stood gazing in shock at the compound. Buddy caught snatches of their shouts and exclamations. It was all in Spanish, but it was clear they thought rebels had attacked the facility. Nightfall was rapidly approaching, and he needed to move closer to see where they would take Elizabeth for the night. With no guards at the gate, he crept inside and burrowed beneath a pile of rubble.

Well hidden, he watched while the soldiers continued wandering about, seemingly dazed by the devastation of their compound. Elizabeth was shoved from the back of the truck, landing face down on the ground. Buddy felt an involuntary grimace. A soldier jerked her back to her feet. It was difficult to see in the growing shadows of dusk, but her face looked bruised, and her shirt was torn.

"Trae la perra adentro," one shouted.

It was the apparent commander strutting beside her as they pushed Elizabeth into the headquarters building. The door had been blown off its hinges and the windows were shattered. The odor of burnt fuel permeated the air, and the entire compound was shrouded in a haze of smoke. Mosquitoes buzzed incessantly, gnawing at Buddy's bare skin, but he dared not slap them. He took the bites and remained still, lest they spot him. Watching and listening, he waited for total darkness.

After a while, all the soldiers except for the commander departed the headquarters building. Elizabeth was still inside with him. Others began giving orders as men were dispatched to stand guard at the gate and positions around the compound. The Salvadoran soldiers were obviously exhausted as they trudged to their assigned posts. Two walked to within a few feet of his hiding place, and Buddy remained motionless. He held the .45 and his knife at the ready, but they passed, oblivious to their near brush with a former SOG special forces soldier who was now ready to kill.

Elizabeth was likely facing a merciless interrogation, and God only knew what other horrors she might experience. As much as he wanted to prevent her from being tortured or raped, charging inside now was tantamount to suicide. He would bide his time—watch and wait. The soldiers soon dispersed across the compound, and it remained silent inside the headquarters building. He hoped this was a good sign.

After a while, the night sounds increased to a crescendo of cricket, frog, and gecko sounds. A whippoorwill whistled somewhere near the edge of the jungle, and an owl gave a low spooky call. When Buddy was ready to make his move, this cacophony would be to his advantage by masking his movement. For now, with no sound coming from the headquarters building, he decided to wait until later in the night when the garrison had fallen into a deep sleep.

Buddy pulled the knife from its sheath and tested it, pulling the edge at an angle across the top of his arm. The keen edge shaved the hair from his arm. It was straight-razor sharp. If any way possible, he would use the knife instead of his firearm, but if it were needed, he had the .45 under his belt and the extra magazines in his pocket. He was ready.

During his years in Vietnam, he had been in firefights with the North Vietnamese and later dropped a few grenades from his aircraft, but he had thought his fighting days were over. Yet here he was again facing the same possibility for death or injury, and again there were people, or at least one, whose life depended on him. She was a good person, and he would free her or die trying.

From somewhere to the south came the barely audible sounds of a helicopter. Perhaps it was the cavalry coming, but he knew better. It was false hope. He was on his own. Jungle Jim had made it clear that a clash with the Salvadoran troops was out of the question. Buddy's only hope now was to somehow rescue Elizabeth and hook up with the Alpha Team. His thoughts faded and sometime in the night he awakened when something splattered on his face. It was a fat raindrop.

Instantly awake, he studied the surrounding compound. A few heavy raindrops had begun falling—the perfect cover for his movements. It was time. Again, if there were eyes open anywhere, he had to blend as one who belonged. Crawling from his hiding place, he stood erect and walked casually toward the headquarters building. Stepping into the shadows near the door, he stopped, pressed his back to the wall, and listened. There was loud snoring coming from inside. The odors of ash and burned fuel still permeated the night air, but the silence around the compound was broken only by the sounds of the jungle.

The damaged door had been leaned against the opening, and Buddy carefully shifted it to one side. The explosion had apparently knocked out all power, and it was black as pitch inside. Inching through the doorway, he felt his way along a corridor until he found another door. It was open, and someone in the room was snoring loudly—probably the Salvadoran comandante. If Elizabeth was in there, she had likely been raped. He waited. He listened. He could see nothing, but something told him the snoring man was alone.

Buddy's eyes were still unadjusted to the darkness as he again began feeling his way along the wall. The wood floor creaked beneath his boot. He froze. The snoring in the next room ceased. The man coughed, and squeaking bedsprings indicated his movement. Buddy readied his knife and waited. A moment later the snoring continued. He exhaled and again began moving until he found another open doorway. Stopping there, Buddy listened. There was no sound, but the faintest hint of a familiar scent reached his nostrils. He inhaled. It was a pleasant one, but it took a moment before he recognized it.

It was that day after Elizabeth returned from the shower, when she stood in front of the window fan brushing her hair. The scent of her shampoo had filled their room. That was it. He stepped through the doorway. With the dim contrast from an outside window, he made out the shape of an office desk.

The sound of the rainfall on the metal roof continued, but he heard her exhale. She was there, sitting against the desk.

He stepped forward, knelt beside her, and whispered in her ear. "Are you ready to blow this joint, Babe?"

Her head jerked upright, but she stared straight ahead as she gasped and mumbled something unintelligible to herself.

"Babe, do you hear me?"

She froze.

"Buddy?"

"Ssshhh, not so loud."

Slowly she turned her head.

"Are you really here?"

"I'm here, Babe."

"No. I'm dreaming."

"No! I'm really here."

He touched her face, gently drawing his thumb across her lips.

"Buddy, Buddy. It's really—"

"Sshh, not so loud!"

"My hands and feet are tied," she whispered.

He found her arm and followed it to the rope tying her wrists. Inserting the knife, he cut it. Babe threw her arms around his neck and kissed his face. Her lips found his. Buddy held her close.

"It's okay," he whispered. "We've got to go now."

"Thank you for coming for me. I thought I was going to die. Thank you—"

"Ssshhh. You're welcome," he whispered.

He cut the ropes around her ankles and helped her to her feet.

"Can you walk?"

"Yes."

Turning toward the door, he took her hand, but outside in the corridor the wood floor creaked. Elizabeth gasped.

"Sit back down and put your hands behind your back," he whispered.

He grasped her shoulders and helped her sit. A light shone out in the corridor, and he backed against the wall beside the door. The soldier stepped into the doorway and pointed a flashlight into Elizabeth's eyes. It was the comandante.

"You are making too much noise, whore, but that is okay. I am rested now and ready for you. You can make all the noise you wish in my bed."

Buddy waited until the man stepped into the room. With his knife, he made a hard, but quick and deliberate motion, drawing the razor edge across the commander's neck, slashing his throat. Shoving the soldier's head back with his left hand, Buddy reversed the knife and repeated the motion, but it wasn't necessary. A gurgling expulsion of air came from the wound as the soldier stumbled forward with his windpipe and jugular severed. The blood spurted from his neck, and he gripped his throat as he dropped to his knees. Buddy picked up the flashlight and waited until the man fell face down with a thud. Bright effervescent blood pooled around him.

"Let's go," he whispered. "Whatever you do, stay close and stay quiet."

He led Elizabeth to the outside door where he stopped to study the grounds of the compound. A misty rain was still falling, and silence permeated the compound. There was no movement anywhere. He waited. He watched. After a minute or two, he was satisfied no one was awake. He thought about the hole under the fence, but with the mines and boobytraps, the safer option was the gate.

"Come on."

Holding Elizabeth's hand, he crept out to the road where he spotted the shapes of two soldiers. They were sitting atop piles of rubble, hunched over on either side of the still open gates. With their heads beneath rain-soaked ponchos, their snores told the story. They were sleeping soundly. With his .45 at the ready, Buddy led Elizabeth by the hand and held his breath as they crept past the guards and through the gates. Silent shadows in the darkness, he and Babe disappeared into the night.

Colonel Jim Parker knew things no one else knew. His commander had given him a free rein except for one caveat. He would cover for him, but he was on his own if this thing went south. The chances of rescuing Buddy and the girl were slim, but he had to try. He would not leave his friend hanging in the wind somewhere out there in the jungle. They had been through too much together in Nam, and he knew Buddy would do the same for him.

The problem was the rapidly approaching nightfall. He had to get his team inserted without detection by the Salvadorans. This would allow him time to rendezvous with his A-team and formulate some sort of plan. After grabbing his gear, he met with his men for the pre-mission briefing. His hope was to communicate with the Salvadoran military commander and possibly negotiate the girl's release. That failing, he was left with one other option—one which his boss suggested he avoid—the use of force.

Thirty minutes later, they were airborne and in communication with the Alpha Team near the airstrip. The team leader reported an explosion in the village that apparently destroyed a Salvadoran army jeep, and later a much more massive one had occurred up at the government compound. Parker's first thought had been FMLN rebels were attacking, but Chief Foster cleared that up when he said Rider had gotten some grenades and C-4 explosive from the A-team. It figured. The sonofabitch had always been resourceful—one of his best.

The sun had set when the chopper came in low behind a nearby ridge and dropped the team on a grassy slope. The insertion apparently went undetected, and Parker ordered a quick relocation. Only at last light did he call the team to a halt and put them into a night defensive position. It would be folly to attempt further movement in unfamiliar terrain after dark. The plan was to move the remaining two klicks and rendezvous with the Alpha Team the next morning.

———————

Buddy's boots sucked loudly in the muddy road as he hurried with Elizabeth down the mountain, but after a few minutes he noticed she was having trouble keeping up. He slowed and glanced down at her feet. It was difficult to see, but it seemed she was barefoot.

"Where are your shoes?"

"That animal took them so I couldn't run away."

"We won't get far with you like that, but we've got to get off this road. We're leaving them a clear trail."

He led her into a steep ravine and removed his backpack. The rain had stopped.

"Sit down and let me have a look."

The clouds overhead left the night without a hint of light. Feeling inside the pack, he found socks, and put one on each of her feet. After pulling two thick green leaves from a nearby plant, he placed one under each foot and slipped another pair of socks on over the leaves.

"These will protect your feet for a while. Right now, we've got to put some distance between us and that compound before daylight. Let me know if you start hurting again. We can't afford for you to get lame."

He pulled her up, and they walked in the jungle paralleling the road for a half hour before Buddy stopped and cut a brushy limb. After leading her back to the road, he stopped and looked carefully in both directions. All remained quiet.

"Okay. Walk to the other side of the road and wait for me."

He backed across behind her while swirling the mud and blotting out their tracks.

"What were you doing?"

"Scrubbing our trail. Come on. Let's move."

The road followed the ridge westward down the mountain toward the village, and Buddy knew they had to head further down into the jungle. He turned north and moved down the mountain as they walked steadily for several hours. Pushing through the wet vegetation, fighting spiderwebs, and climbing in and out of ravines, they made their way deeper into the jungle. Elizabeth was a real trooper and hung with him until near dawn when she called out.

"I just can't go any more," she said. "Please. I'm freezing, my feet are hurting, and I'm exhausted."

By his calculations, Buddy figured they were well over a mile and a half down the mountain from the road. He doubted the Salvadoran troops would venture this far into the jungle because of the rebels. Despite the darkness, he was able to find a relatively flat spot in some ferns and spread the poncho on the ground.

"We'll rest here awhile. I want you to drink some water and eat one of these LRRP rations. Then we'll get some sleep."

The mountain air had cooled in the night, and they were both wet. Buddy rehydrated the ration and gave it to Elizabeth. Scooping the rice and chicken from the bag with her fingers, she ate ravenously. While she ate, he removed the tattered remains of her socks and dried each foot. When he was done, he pulled a dry pair from the pack and slipped them on her feet.

"Wrap yourself in the poncho and get some sleep. We'll start moving again when it gets light."

"Aren't you cold?" she asked.

"I'll make it. Get some sleep."

She picked up the poncho and sat beside him wrapping it around them both.

"Now we can both be warm while we sleep."

Her light brown eyes glowed in the predawn darkness and Buddy gazed into them. Elizabeth quickly turned away. Although showing more trust, she was still seemed ill at ease, and he felt a sudden remorse for not treating her better. Perhaps some more good-natured kidding would declare his attempt at détente. Wrapping his arms around her, he pulled her close as they lay back.

"Just don't snore too loud," he said.

Her elbow shot back and jabbed him in the ribs, but she immediately grasped his hand and pulled it close against her abdomen. He buried his face in her hair and closed his eyes. He had never experienced anything like this in Nam, but his exhaustion left him with only the desire for sleep.

"Buddy?"

"Yes?"

"I've never seen anyone killed before."

"He would have killed us both. Try to think about something else. We can talk about it later. Right now, you need to get some sleep."

She pulled his hand close between her breasts and within seconds she was breathing heavily as she fell into an exhausted sleep.

CHAPTER TWENTY

A Walk in The Jungle

Colonel Parker called the TOC and had them report that an El Salvadoran military compound was under attack, and that he was sending an additional team to recon the situation. It was the first step toward plausible denial of this entire affair. His CO would like his creativity. He met up with his Alpha Team at mid-morning. Two Salvadoran army vehicles had driven down from the compound and were parked on the airstrip. He studied them through binoculars for several minutes.

"I think they're waiting on someone. Let's see if we can talk to them," he said. "Spread the men out where they can be seen. We'll signal the Salvadorans, before we approach. That should keep them from getting trigger-happy but be ready. If they open up on us, I don't want any of our men hurt, but we will do what we have to do."

The colonel had a man flank him on either side as he raised his weapon over his head and signaled the government troops waiting near the vehicles. Jumping to their feet, the Salvadorans scrambled about, but soon calmed when they realized they were Americans. Parker approached with caution. According to intelligence reports, these boys were members of the El Salvador National Guard, the same bunch that had wiped out entire villages, nuns, news correspondents, and anyone else who provoked their paranoia.

"Do any of you speak English?" he called out.

One of them stepped forward. "Who are you?"

"We are United States Army Special Forces, and we were told you were under attack by rebel forces."

"Yes, our facility, it is heavily damaged by the rebels. Our commandant was murdered by a prisoner, a woman, one of the gringo nuns from the village. She escaped, and we are searching for her now."

"Did you capture or kill any of the ones who attacked your facility?"

"No, but my colonel is coming now with helicopters from San Salvador. He is bringing more men and tracking dogs. We will find them."

Buddy opened his eyes. Something had awakened him—a sound perhaps. He had slept longer than planned. The sun had climbed high into the sky, and Elizabeth was still sleeping. He scanned the surrounding jungle and listened. At first there were only the sounds of birds, but he heard it again. From far to the south on the other side of the mountain came the distant drone of helicopters. It could be Colonel Parker coming, but he doubted the Special Forces would use so many choppers. It was likely more Salvadoran troops coming to the airstrip.

He needed to wake Elizabeth and begin moving again. Softly, Buddy brushed his hand over her hair. She awakened with a start.

"It's okay. I'm sorry to wake you, but we need to get moving."

He threw the poncho off, stood, and pulled her to her feet. Only then, in the full light of day, did he see her blackened eye and the cut on her chest. Dried blood stained her bra. She self-consciously pulled her shirt together. The animal had apparently cut it open, cutting her chest in the process. He quickly unbuttoned his shirt.

"Put my shirt on and sit back down. I've got to make you some shoes."

Buddy couldn't look her in the eyes. Somehow, despite all logic, he felt responsible for letting this happen. From the very beginning he had known better. She had no idea just how dangerous a mission such as this could be. He used his knife to cut two of the outer pouches from the nylon backpack. After stripping the tie-down cords from the pack, he used them to lace a pouch around each of her feet.

"There. That should help protect them, but remember, the only way we're getting out of here is by walking. You need to take care of your feet. You ready?"

She nodded.

"Okay. Let's get moving."

"Where are we going?"

"We'll head west for a few klicks then turn south, and hopefully come back up the mountain on the western edge of the airstrip."

"What's a klick?"

"Army lingo for a kilometer. We're going to move a mile or so westward and circle the mountain, to avoid the Salvadoran troops. We should be relatively safe for now. I'm certain they won't come this deep into the jungle."

Buddy and Elizabeth walked for the remainder of the day before finding a small mountain stream. The sun had dropped low in the west and the jungle had grown quiet. It would be dark soon, but so far, luck was with them. As he figured, they had neither seen nor heard any government troops. Buddy refilled the canteen and dropped a purification tablet inside.

"We'll rest here for now—maybe stay the night. We'll see."

Elizabeth's eyes had again faded into that faraway look.

"Are you okay?"

"I'm fine. It's just...I'm tired is all—that and my jaw is aching."

"Sorry bastard beat the hell out of you, didn't he?"

"I thought he broke my jaw."

"Well, he won't be beating up any more women, leastwise not in this life."

"Do you ever think about it?"

"About what?"

"The ones you've killed."

"You never get things like that entirely out of your mind. You can't change it, so you learn to cope and move on with your life."

She gave a solemn nod.

"Do you think your friend, Colonel Parker, will try to find us?"

Buddy couldn't tell her the truth. Parker would search for them, but the odds were against them. They faced dangers not only from the Salvadoran troops, but from the rebels and the unforgiving jungle. Any of the three had the ability to end their lives.

"I'm sure he will, but he'll be taking a lot of chances when he does."

She said nothing as she gazed at him. It was clear she was trying to determine if he was telling her everything. Elizabeth was a woman of action, and Buddy figured she needed a distraction.

"Jim Parker is a friend who will not abandon us, but you've

got to remember one thing. He could get into trouble if the government discovers he was involved. It could cost him his career, maybe more. No matter what happens, if anyone ever questions you about him or the Special Forces camp, you were never there, and you've never heard of him. You never saw him, met him, or heard his name. Understood?"

"Got it," she said. "Can I ask you a question?"

"Sure, but I can't guarantee I'll answer it."

"How did you find me last night in that room? It was really dark in there."

"Dude was snoring in the first room, and I was pretty sure you weren't in there, but when I stuck my head in the next room where you were, I smelled your hair."

She wrinkled her forehead.

"My *hair*?"

"Well, I mean I smelled your shampoo."

"How did you know it was…oh, never mind. I remember now. I was drying my hair in front of the fan the other night."

"That's right. Let's split another of these rations and stay here for now. Try to get some sleep. We have a long way to go yet."

Colonel Parker pulled his men back as the Salvadoran helicopters came thundering in over the airstrip. He had learned what he needed to know. Rider and Elizabeth had apparently escaped and were somewhere in the vicinity. The problem now was to find them before the Salvadorans.

Six Hueys landed and Salvadoran soldiers wearing American-made camouflage fatigues scrambled into a perimeter around them. One group was restraining several dogs. Two were hounds, obviously used for tracking, but there were four other dogs—huge ones. They were muzzled and appeared to be crosses between Dobermans and Mastiffs. The animals strained stubbornly against their leashes, while the handlers pulled them away from the helicopters.

Parker studied the scene through his binoculars as a single soldier stepped rigidly from the last chopper and walked toward the troops from the compound. The Salvadorans all snapped to attention and saluted him. He was apparently the colonel they mentioned. After a few moments, the officer glanced toward where Parker stood at the jungle's edge, nodded, and strutted boldly toward him. The A-team commander, Captain Stark, stood beside Parker as the officer approached.

The Salvadoran wore spit-shined black Corcoran jump boots, starched camo fatigues, a burgundy beret, and wire-rimmed aviator sunglasses. He also wore the insignias of a full bird colonel on his collar and the patch of the Salvadoran National Guard on his shoulder. A finely beaded sweat hung above his carefully groomed Errol Flynn mustache.

"What do you think, sir," Stark muttered as the soldier walked their way, "hubris on steroids?"

Their eyes remained fixed on the man as he approached.

"I'd say that's an apt description," Parker muttered.

It was the Salvadoran National Guard that had raped and murdered the four missionaries in December. It was also the same National Guard that had massacred the entire populations of at least two villages—supposedly people who supported the FMLN rebels. The Salvadoran colonel stopped before them but did not offer a salute. Of course, Parker and his men were wearing neither rank nor insignia.

"So, my sergeant tells me you are United States Army Special Forces. Why are you here?"

"We were told your troops were under attack by rebel forces and we came to assist."

"Is that so?"

"Yes, and it was reported that your troops also have an American missionary in custody here. We have come to get her."

"How many men do you have here?"

One of Jungle Jim's favorite pastimes was poker. He enjoyed most facets of the game, except for bluffing. It was a tactic he seldom employed, but his current situation demanded one.

"I have about sixty men in the area—four fifteen-man teams," he said.

Despite his sunglasses, the Salvadoran Colonel's face revealed his surprise, but he quickly regained his façade of collected calm.

"I regret that I must disappoint you, but we do not have an American missionary in our custody, but there is a female rebel in the area who has murdered the commander of this facility, and we intend to find her. I must also direct you to remove your troops from this area immediately. They will cause great confusion, and my men could possibly confuse them for the enemy."

Parker set his jaw and squinted at the pompous fool. It was time to up his bet.

"That would be unfortunate, Colonel. My boys are loaded for bear, and I certainly wouldn't want to see any of your men get hurt."

The colonel's eyebrows again crept above his sunglasses, and Jungle Jim knew his bluff was successful, at least for the moment.

"I don't have the assets available to transport my men

immediately, but I can have them stand down, but I would like to suggest we work together to find the rebels."

"I do not need your help. You are supposed to be here only to train our men. I warn you again, stay clear of my troops."

The Salvadoran colonel was hiding something—likely his drug facility at the now destroyed compound.

"And Colonel, I warn you, if there are any United States citizens harmed by your men, I will see that you are personally held accountable."

"We will see about that."

With that, he whirled about and strutted back across the airstrip. Jim Parker felt Captain Stark's eyes fixed on him. The young officer realized the gamble his commander was taking and stood by in grim silence.

"Don't worry, Captain," Parker said. "I will take full responsibility for this if it goes sideways."

"Sir, with all respect, don't *you* worry. I'm glad you put that pompous ass in his place, and my men and I will stand with you, no matter what happens."

Elizabeth opened her eyes at first light. The beautiful warbling of a songbird came from somewhere high in the jungle canopy. A light fog floated above the stream. All night she had listened to its gurgling waters as they flowed over the rocks, and from somewhere further down the mountain came a subtle but mysterious roar. She felt his warmth close behind her and turned to find Buddy's bright blue eyes already open and alert.

"You slept well," he said. It wasn't a question.

She rolled over to face him.

"Well, then, did I snore?"

"Like a drunken barmaid."

She poked him with a finger.

"You liar."

Mere inches separated their faces, and Buddy winked before bending forward and kissing her lightly on the cheek. It was by no means a passionate kiss, not even one that seemed romantic—a friendly buss at best, but certainly not a kiss that should have ignited the flush of heat she now felt flooding her body.

"I don't think we're in danger for now, but we need to get moving," he said. "We have a long way to go."

But she did not want to go. The mountain jungle had grown cold during the night and Buddy's warmth had been her security blanket. She wanted to stay here, wrapped in this camouflaged poncho with this man who suddenly meant more to her than she had realized.

He was risking everything for her. He had stayed behind for her. He had killed for her. Buddy was a man most women could only dream of in their wildest fantasies. His eyes sparkled and she gripped his forearm, not wanting to let go. For the first time in her life, Elizabeth was tempted to pull a man closer and let herself go, but she froze.

"Are you okay?"

His words shook her from the momentary hypnosis.

"Oh, uh, yeah. I mean, sure." She released his arm.

Buddy had her fixed with those mesmerizing eyes, and Elizabeth knew she had just brushed close with a life-changing moment. She paused and cocked her head. "Do you hear that sound?"

He cast what was becoming a familiar sarcastic gaze at her, and she suddenly felt like an idiot. The entirety of God's jungle creation was warbling, croaking, rustling, and chirping.

"Hear what?"

"That roaring. It sounds like—"

"—a waterfall?" he said.

"Yes. That must be what it is—a waterfall."

"I think it's in the direction we're going. We'll check it out. Let's eat something first."

He pulled another LRRP ration from his backpack, opened it, and added water. Two weeks ago, if someone had told her she would scrape cold meat and vegetables from a bag and love every bite, she would have laughed. Even college dorm meals from long ago now seemed like decadent feasts. The iodine-flavored water Buddy added to the ration made no difference. It could not have tasted better had it been a hot Chicago Pizza.

"You're hungry this morning," he said.

She licked her fingers and nodded while he stuffed the poncho in the backpack.

"I think my guardian angel is taking care of us," she said.

"Your guardian angel?"

"Yes. Don't you believe everyone has a guardian angel?"

"I want you to drink more water, today. You need to stay hydrated."

"I think you and my guardian angel are working together."

"That's good. We can use all the help we can get. Let's pack up and get moving."

Forty-five minutes later they were further into the trackless jungle and standing at the foot of a falls coming off a high escarpment. The sun-drenched waters sparkled with a mist that cooled her face and brought with it the scent of jungle flowers. Elizabeth remembered Buddy's comments about smelling her hair and realized she hadn't bathed for two days—two days of sweating toil and terror.

"Do you care if I take a quick shower?" she asked.

The look on his face made it clear he did not want to stop. "Please?"

After surveying the surrounding jungle, he gave a sigh of resignation. "Okay, we're safe for now, but hurry."

"Promise me you won't look."

"I'll try. You want some soap?"

"Oh. Yes. That would be nice."

"Sorry. I'm all out."

"Buddy Rider, you are one obnoxious man. Turn around while I undress, and *don't* look."

With his back to the waterfall, Buddy glanced at his watch then looked up at the sun. Stopping for a bath was an unnecessary delay and a distraction, and the waterfall prevented him from hearing much else, but they were now miles from the nearest road. He had to admit, he was growing fond of her. This young woman had somehow snared him with his own infatuation, but he could not let it affect his judgement.

He thought of the helicopters he had heard the day before. They would probably be used by the Salvadorans to search for them, but he would hear them before they got close. He searched the surrounding jungle with his eyes. There were likely scores of Salvadoran troops scouring the areas higher up the mountain at this very moment, but the government troops probably feared rebel ambushes and would stay close to the roads. Still, he worried.

"Hurry up," he said.

He was certain the falls had drowned out his voice, and it dawned on him that there was always the chance neither of them would escape this jungle alive. And perhaps it was this thought that caused him to turn and watch Elizabeth wade into the knee-deep pool beneath the waterfall.

He drew a deep breath at the sight. Her naked female form, at its youthful peak, was mesmerizing as she raised her face into the falls. The sun caught the prism of the misty spray casting a gossamer rainbow across her back. Buddy was spellbound.

Lost in a paralysis of wonderment, he was unable to pull his eyes away. It was a private moment he was stealing from her, but his theft was not one of greed or lust. Rather it was driven by a growing endearment for this girl whom he had so disliked in the beginning. He had to admit, despite all her faults, she had many more strengths—mostly her stubborn bravery and commitment to others. Elizabeth had him to the point where he no longer wanted to push her away.

She turned and cast a glance his way. Her reaction was instantaneous as she squatted in the pool and crossed her arms over her breasts.

"I told you not to look!"

He turned away. "Sorry. I lost my head. Hurry up."

CHAPTER TWENTY-ONE

Run Through the Jungle

Many of Jim Parker's Green Berets had served in Vietnam, crossing into Cambodia, Laos, and North Vietnam, where they pulled reconnaissance in the lairs of the enemy. They were experienced in jungle warfare, and it took not only talent but a special breed of soldier for this type of duty. Parker was confident his men could ghost along with and around the Salvadoran troops undetected while they searched for Rider and the girl. The plan was to watch and listen. If the Salvadorans struck a trail with their dogs, his men could get ahead of them to confuse and impede their progress.

After sending one team up the mountain closer to the government compound, he took another and moved into the jungle west of the village. Two other three-man groups were established as mobile observation posts to follow any government troops patrolling the jungle. Yet there was still no movement by the Salvadorans.

Long after their helicopters departed, they remained clustered around the airstrip, apparently satisfied to wait until the next day to begin their search. They had formed a night perimeter at one end of the strip, built fires, and disregarded any notion of maintaining the discipline and training the U.S. military had provided them. It would be sheer luck if the rebels didn't sneak in and attack them.

The following morning the Salvadoran troops began their search, as men shouted and vehicles sped up and down the road. Several hours passed before Captain Stark called on the radio and reported the dogs trailing something down the mountain north of the road near the compound. A few minutes later, he reported a truck arriving with a dozen troops. They had gone into the jungle behind the dogs.

Buddy laced up Elizabeth's makeshift shoes, while she gazed into a tiny mirror and brushed her hair.

"Where did you get that brush?" he asked.

"You told me to put my personal items in your backpack, so I did."

He noticed she now wore only the light shirt he had given her along with the clean khaki slacks. She noticed he noticed.

"My bra is just too nasty and sweaty. Besides, it has dried blood on it, and I'm tossing it."

It was tempting to tease her about going au naturel like the other jungle inhabitants, but he resisted. He was growing to care about her feelings, and this wasn't the time or situation for crude humor. He remained silent.

"I suppose it's worth about as much as some of the things those poor nuns taught me in school. Sometimes I even wonder where God is in all this mess."

Elizabeth's eyes were suddenly filled with anger and disappointment. Buddy turned and gazed off into the jungle. She stood and with a vengeance she threw the bra into the stream. As it floated away, she blushed and seemed caught in a moment of embarrassed self-realization.

"It's just not a good time for me," she said. "I've come to

realize how much of what I thought I knew simply isn't true."

After a self-conscious glance at him, she dropped her head. It was evident she had shared something deeply personal and was now primed with self-doubt. She needed his reassurance.

"It's okay. I think we've both learned some things the last few days," he said. "Just don't give up hope. You have a lot of faith in God, and I think that's where your strength and loyalty come from. As for your bra, the only one who will see you without it is one lecherous old pilot."

Her blush remained and she continued staring down at the ground.

"You're not lecherous, and you're not old."

"Do you want to tell me the *real* truth behind this rescue mission?"

Buddy felt cruel for confronting her in this moment of weakness.

"What do you mean?"

"I think it's time we trusted one another. I don't think you've told me everything about your motivations, your sponsor, or why you're willing to sacrifice everything including your life to free those nuns. There's something more you haven't told me, isn't there—perhaps about your best friend?"

The roar of the waterfall seemed to grow in the extended silence.

"Well, I suppose I didn't tell you about her. My friend was the lay missionary who was with the nuns we rescued. She's the one who went back to the village to get the baby that was left behind. Her name is Melissa Hanahan, and yes, she's my best friend. We were college roommates. Melissa is from a well-known family in Massachusetts, and her parents are somewhat wealthy, but none of that mattered to her.

"When I volunteered for the missionary program, I invited

her to join me. Her parents pitched a fit. They wanted her to get a master's degree and go into some sort of government diplomatic service, but she volunteered for the lay missionary program with me and received the El Salvador assignment in October."

"And I assume her parents are the ones bankrolling this rescue mission?"

"Some of it, yes. I'm using five thousand dollars of my trust fund money, but her father put up the other half. He was a big supporter of President Carter and served on his election campaign committee, but when Carter lost the election and the administrations changed, Mister Hanahan felt the State Department wasn't doing enough. He was desperate and determined to save Melissa himself."

Buddy once again found his admiration for Elizabeth growing. She had put up a large sum of her own money and likely sacrificed a master's degree to save her friend.

"And you volunteered to be point-man for this mission?"

"I talked Melissa into this mess, and I wasn't going to leave her. I had to try no matter how dangerous it was."

"Well, do you regret it now?"

"No. I would do it again, no matter how all this turns out."

Buddy took her by the hand. "You're a brave woman, Elizabeth Anderson. Come on. Let's get moving."

Within minutes they were again moving around the base of the escarpment, searching for a trail to take them southward, but the jungle was trackless. Several hours passed, and their progress was slowed as Elizabeth continually fell behind. Buddy stopped to allow her to catch up. Panting, she swiped her arm across her forehead and bent over, putting her hands on her knees.

"You're really walking fast. Is something wrong?"

His first inclination was to tell her everything was great, but she needed to understand the danger they faced if they didn't reach the airstrip soon.

"I'm pretty sure those helicopters we heard yesterday were bringing in more Salvadoran troops to search for us. We need to keep moving. Are you okay?"

"Yes. I'm just winded."

He pulled the canteen from the backpack.

"Drink some water."

She took a quick gulp and wiped a dribble from her chin.

"Drink some more."

"You aren't going to complain when I have to stop to pee, are you?"

He wanted to laugh, but he heard something in the distance—something that made his blood run cold.

"Did you hear that?" he asked.

She recapped the canteen.

"Hear what?"

He heard it again—dogs howling.

"That."

"Yes!" she said. "It sounds like dogs barking. We must have passed a village somewhere back there."

Buddy knelt and removed the canister of powdered CS from the backpack.

"I'm afraid not. Those are tracker dogs, and they're on our trail. I'm an idiot for not thinking about this sooner."

Elizabeth's face paled.

"Walk up farther while I put this stuff out."

Buddy began scattering the powder across their trail. When he was done, he moved out at a trot.

"Let's go."

"What were you doing back there?"

"That's a powdered form of tear gas. When the dogs hit it, the chemical will burn their noses and they won't be able to track us. It should buy us some time."

After nearly a mile of moving non-stop, Buddy noticed the escarpment had given way to a steep slope, but he stayed with the contour as he circled southward around the mountain. Glancing back, he saw Elizabeth was again struggling to keep up. He stopped to wait for her. As before, her breathing was labored, but this time there was something more. She was limping.

"I'm doing all I can, but I'm really hurting," she said, her voice cracking with emotion.

He took her in his arms. "It's okay. You've already done better than most men could do. Sit down and let me take a look at your feet."

He unlaced the nylon booties to find both feet blistered and bloody. Reaching the airstrip by nightfall was not going to happen. Elizabeth had gone as far as she could on her own. He sat a moment and gazed from the mountainside out over the jumble of ridges and mountains. They stretched for miles out to the far horizon and the Pacific Ocean. To continue in that direction would be folly. He had to stick to his plan, but that meant they would have to climb the mountain again when they neared the airstrip.

His only option was now apparent. He would have to carry Elizabeth if they were going to escape this jungle. It reminded him of his last tour of duty in Nam when he crashed in the mountains above the A Shau Valley. Buck had carried him on his back for miles while they dodged NVA patrols. It was a feat of stamina he would have said was impossible if the roles were reversed, but here he was facing the same challenge. At least Elizabeth was lighter.

"If they get close to catching us," she said, "I can stay behind and surrender. They are less likely to harm me than you."

Buddy shook his head. She knew better. This was the sort of thing that was steadily increasing his respect for this woman. She may have been young and ignorant in many ways, but she possessed unselfish courage.

"Elizabeth, don't you understand that as far as the Salvadorans know, you were the only one there when their commander got his throat cut? They think you did it, and if they catch you, what they will do won't be pretty."

It was something he immediately regretted saying because the bellowing howls grew suddenly louder in the jungle behind them. These were the throaty howls of bigger dogs—animals bred to hunt down and kill their prey. They had gotten past the first line of CS. Elizabeth stood white-faced and frozen in place.

"Okay, don't panic. I have a plan, but we need to work quickly."

She nodded, but gave him a puzzled look as he removed the backpack and again dug out the powdered CS. After sprinkling it all around, he gave her the canister.

"If they get after you, shake the powder on your clothes and in their faces. Now go."

She stood staring at him. "What are you going to do?"

"I don't have time to explain. Go. I'll catch up."

She limped away as Buddy pulled the tripwire and two frags from the bag. Unscrewing the fuses, he cut them. After screwing the shortened fuses back in place, he wired the grenades to trees on either side of the trail and attached more wire to the rings as he stretched it across the trail.

The howling was now growing closer. It sounded like several dogs, and they were coming fast. He turned to see Elizabeth still standing only twenty yards away.

"Go!" he said, motioning with his hand. "I'll catch up in a minute."

Carefully but quickly, he straightened the pins on the grenades. He caught sight of the dogs. There were four of them—huge animals barely a hundred yards away. Pulling the .45 from his belt, he turned and ran. Buddy made it fifty yards before the grenades exploded simultaneously. A scattered drizzle of shrapnel fell around him, but he refused to stop until he nearly ran over Elizabeth. She was sitting with her head in her hands.

Spinning about, he looked back while holding the .45 at the ready. He waited. The dogs were no longer barking. After a minute he relaxed.

"I'm sorry," Elizabeth said. "I just can't go anymore. My feet hurt too much."

He turned and knelt beside her, pulling her close.

"It's okay. I think we stopped them. You need to stay strong. You've done a hell of a job up to now."

She looked up at him. Her eyes were bloodshot and desperate. She needed encouragement.

"Hell, I thought you were just a hot-shot college grad with a lot of spunk and no sense, but you've proven to me you're a woman with a lot of courage and a good heart."

Elizabeth wrapped her arms around his neck and pulled him closer as their lips met in a passionate kiss. After several seconds, Buddy knew this woman had him. He needed to break away lest he lose control. After gently pushing her back, he stood and gave her the backpack.

"Put it on," he said.

"But...what are we going to do? I'm telling you. I mean it. I really can't walk and—"

"Stop! Do you remember me telling you how Buck Marino carried me out of the jungle?"

"Yeah?"

"Well, I'm carrying you out of here. When you're ready, climb on. Wrap your legs around my waist and hold on tight."

With Elizabeth on his back, Buddy began walking. She felt incredibly light—at least for the first hundred yards. The second hundred yards were somewhat tougher, but he was determined. He continued walking—three hundred, four hundred yards, through ravines, across streams, briars, sharp rocky slopes. Soon, he found agony in every step taken. The only thing that prevented him from stopping was her soft breath in his ear. He was an old fool inspired by this young jockey to run till his heart burst.

He walked, one step at a time, one foot in front of the other, refusing to stop. He walked slowly, deliberately, but he covered ground, and eventually the sun dropped into the hills to the west. A foggy haze settled into the jungle around them, but his instincts drove him onward. The clock was running, and their survival depended on reaching the airstrip before the Green Berets were ordered out of the area.

The hours slipped by as he doggedly ignored the screaming pain in his back and legs. There was no acceptable alternative. He had to walk out of here with Elizabeth, but they had to find help soon, because the longer they remained in the jungle, the more likely they would be given up for dead.

"Buddy," she whispered. "You need to stop. Please. You're killing yourself. You need to save something for later."

She was right. He had pushed himself to the limit. She unclasped her legs from his waist and let her feet reach the ground. He instantly dropped to his knees.

"Buddy!"

"I'm okay."

She pulled his head into her breasts, and he would have died happily at that moment had he smothered in them. That was not to be, but he reveled in their tender softness and warmth.

"What are we going to do?" she asked.

"Give me a few minutes to catch my breath."

He felt a wonderful heat from her body as she snuggled closer against him, and he lay back, closed his eyes, and tried to come up with an answer. Too exhausted to even think, he decided to rest his eyes a few moments before giving her an answer. He needed rest. He needed a minute or two to gather his wits.

CHAPTER TWENTY-TWO

Using the SWAG

From somewhere deep in his subconscious, he heard her voice. "Buddy. Wake up, Buddy. You need to eat this."

He opened his eyes and stared up into a purple-black night sky filled with a trillion stars. The realization was startling. He'd been asleep for a long while.

"How long have I been sleeping?" Buddy asked.

"I'm not sure. I fell asleep too, but it's been several hours. I've been listening. I don't think anyone is following us. Come on. Eat this."

Despite their desperate situation, her voice was a warm blanket that brought him some element of security.

"We'll split it," he said. "It's the last one."

"No, you're going to eat it all. Now, be quiet and eat."

She scraped the beef stew from the bag with her fingers and fed him. Only then did he realize the degree of his hunger. He chewed and swallowed, and she couldn't feed him fast enough. When the bag was empty, she pressed the canteen to his lips, and he drank. After a while he felt somewhat revived and remembered her question. He tried to think through their situation. The first quarter of the new moon had risen above the mountain in the east.

"Buddy?"

"What is it, Babe?"

"What do you think? Are we going to make it?"

She needed to be told the truth.

"I don't know. We really need some help."

"Yes, but from who?"

Her voice betrayed her. Her desperation was graduating to hopelessness, and he had to keep her spirits up. Their situation wasn't yet hopeless—close perhaps—but he wouldn't allow her to give up—not now after they had made it so far. It reminded him of another time when things seemed this bad.

"You know, we may not get help from someone. We may have to get it from a place you don't know about yet."

"I'm not sure what you mean."

"Back when I crashed my plane that last time in Nam and broke my ankle, I figured I was done for. It was nightfall, and there were North Vietnamese soldiers everywhere in the jungle searching for me. I could hardly walk. Hell, half the time I was crawling on my hands and knees, and the enemy patrols were constantly passing, but I didn't give up. I forced myself to keep moving.

"I was stumbling down this trail just after another enemy patrol had gone by, and I stopped to catch my breath. I was leaning against a tree and thinking I was going to end up being a POW when I heard this voice in the darkness. It was as if God was whispering in my ear and calling my name—*Captain Rider*. In fact, I was hallucinating because I really did think it was God calling."

"It was your friend Buck Marino, wasn't it?"

"That's right. He stepped from behind the tree I was leaning against. He was so close I reached out and touched him. I mean I wasn't sure he was even really there. His face was black with camouflaged paint, but believe me, that did not keep me from wanting to kiss him."

"How did you guys escape?"

Buddy remembered that night and the morning several days later when they were rescued. Buck refused to give up. He was using a small mirror to signal a searching bird dog aircraft. The plane was over a mile away, and Buddy was certain the young army ranger's desperate attempts were wasted, until several minutes later when the aircraft broke from its search pattern and flew their way. It was a lesson he had never forgotten.

"We escaped because Buck found help in that place we all have in our souls. When every bit of reason said we were done for, he never, ever gave up. Even when the enemy troops were everywhere around us and he was so exhausted he could hardly walk, Buck Marino refused to give up. He carried me out of that jungle on his back, the same way I'm going to carry you out of this one."

A cool breeze came up the mountain from the south—bringing with it the salty odor of the Pacific. It also brought new strength to his spirits.

"I believe that place in our souls is also blessed with the grace of God," Elizabeth said, "and you were right about not giving up on him."

Buddy reached out and took her hand.

"Let's rest and wait for daylight. We'll turn and start our climb up the mountain when we can see."

"Do you think we're near the airstrip?"

"Using my best SWAG, I'd say it's up the mountain east of us."

"What's a SWAG?" she asked.

"SWAG is a military term—an acronym actually. It stands for scientific wild ass guess."

Her eyes were sad in the moonlight, but the corners of her mouth were turned upward.

"You're really something, Buddy Rider."

"I'll take that as a compliment."

She leaned her head against his chest and snuggled close.

"You should. All my trust is in that special place in your soul."

Buddy felt something he had not felt in years. The word trust—at least as far as the opposite sex was concerned—had become anathema to him. Yet, it was Elizabeth who was putting hers in him. He would not let her down.

CHAPTER TWENTY-THREE

Meeting the FMLN

Farabundo Martí National Liberation Front

Jim Parker thought through the situation. His men had followed the progress of the tracker dogs and reported how they had suddenly lost the scent. This was probably because Buddy had used the powdered CS. But the Salvadoran troops seemed convinced the trail was that of their fugitives and hadn't given up the chase. They turned loose the four bellowing bull mastiffs on the trail. Parker felt sorry for the dogs.

The animals quickly ran beyond hearing range, but a while later what sounded like simultaneous grenade explosions occurred far down the mountain to the west. Parker's men reported two of the dogs had returned to their handlers—bloody, limping, and cowed. It was as he knew it would be. Rider was putting his old S.F. escape and evasion skills to good use. Parker's only hope now was that the Salvadorans didn't catch up with his old friend, because he was certain the results would be the same for them.

The Salvadoran colonel moved his patrols west of the village. Parker had to play his hand carefully to avoid them, but he did the same with his men. He was certain now that Buddy was circling, trying to reach the airstrip. Radioing the TOC, he ordered the choppers to begin a search grid at first light and for Stein Foster to get the Lear Jet airborne and fly over the area as well. It was the classic needle in a haystack search, but Jim Parker intended to use every means possible to find Rider and the girl.

So far, the Special Forces teams had avoided the Salvadorans, but the biggest problem Parker now faced was time. It was not on his side. A standdown order was likely coming at any time. It was an order that would come only through his boss from the highest levels, and one he would have to obey. If he left them behind, Buddy and Elizabeth would probably fall into the hands of the Salvadoran troops—an almost certain death sentence. If the Salvadorans didn't capture them, the rebels probably would, and there was always the unforgiving jungle. It had swallowed many a man without a trace.

It was still dark and just before dawn when Buddy awakened. Elizabeth was still snuggled in his arms and sleeping soundly.

The moon had drifted into the western sky and the jungle vegetation glowed in its soft light. The Pacific breeze had faded, and the mountain jungle had grown silent. Only the occasional call of a night bird came from somewhere down the mountain. Elizabeth stirred.

"You awake?" he whispered.

"Mmm, yeah, but I don't want to move."

She snuggled closer.

"Buddy?"

"Yeah?"

Several seconds of silence passed before she sat up. The moonlight reflected in her face, and her teeth glowed white. Despite all that they faced she was smiling.

"I just want to tell you something—something important—something that I—"

"Ssshh."

He pressed his fingers across her lips. Her eyes glowed wide in the moonlight.

"What is it?"

"Ssshhh."

There was something strange, but it wasn't a sound. It was an odor.

"You smell that?" he whispered.

She raised her head and drew a deep breath. "Yes. It's something burning. It smells like—"

"Marijuana," Buddy said.

"Yes."

Buddy placed his finger across her lips. "Listen."

"What do you hear?" she whispered.

"Just listen."

After a moment he pressed his mouth against her ear. "It's voices, and they're close."

"Where?"

"I'm not sure, but I need to go take a look."

She grabbed him. "No! Please don't leave me."

"Ssshhh." He pulled her close and whispered in her ear. "It's okay. Just stay here while I check it out. I'll be back in a minute."

The odor of the pot was strong, and whoever was smoking it was not far away. He put the last fragmentation grenade in his pocket and pulled the .45 from the backpack. After shoving it under his belt, he dropped the two extra ammo magazines into his pocket. He stood and faced into the wind. The odor grew even stronger.

Buddy had no delusions of being as efficient or talented as he once was. He had lost his edge, but he had to do this recon in the dark and not get caught. He had to sneak into the undergrowth and find them. Someone was smoking pot, and enjoying their night in the jungle, probably FMLN rebels—campesinos who would take great pleasure in torturing a couple of lost Americans. The sky in the east had developed a faint glow. Dawn was coming, and the Pacific breeze again began filtering up the mountainside and rustling the surrounding trees.

Scattered clouds came and went, covering and uncovering the moon. That along with the breeze coming in from the ocean caused the jungle shadows to dance ghostlike amongst the trees. It reminded him of those nights in the A Shau Valley when Buck had saved his butt. Buck was an absolute freaking hero—his hero. He wished he were here now.

Buddy glanced back. Elizabeth's trusting eyes still shone in the moonlight, and only then did he realize she must feel the same about him as he did Buck. He began slowly pushing through the thick wall of vegetation. Elizabeth remained still and quiet as he left her behind. Limb by limb, leaf by leaf, he slipped silently through the undergrowth, careful not to create the slightest rustle.

He had moved only twenty yards, when he stopped and drew another breath through his nostrils. The intensity of the pot odor had increased. He waited, he listened, and there came on the breeze the low murmurs of men—men who were close, men who knew their lives depended on remaining undetected. Buddy dropped to his knees.

With his knife in one hand and the .45 in his other, he crawled toward the voices. Only when he saw the glow of their cigarettes did he realize just how close he had gotten. They were little more than twelve feet away—close enough that he now smelled their body odor. He had gotten too close, yet it was less than forty yards back to where Elizabeth was waiting. They were in grave danger.

His first inclination was to crawl back to her and flee, but he remembered the times when he lay beside a jungle trail within a few feet of passing North Vietnamese patrols. One by one, scores of soldiers passed nearly within arm's reach, while he and his A-team counted them and noted the weapons they carried. It was important to know how many were, and he and his men always maintained their position while attempting an accurate count.

The rebels spoke with subdued voices. There were at least five of them gathered in a circle, passing multiple joints. He understood little of what they were saying, but their confidence was undeniable, and he was able to interpolate their ruminations into some form of logic and understanding. It seemed subtle laughter expressed their opinions of the government troops, but when one said "boinas verdes yanquis" the others grunted and nodded, giving guttural expressions of respect for the Yankee Green Berets.

The moon came from behind a cloud, lighting the clearing below, and Buddy saw what he already suspected. The men smoking the marijuana were not alone. There at least twenty others wrapped in blankets, sleeping, with the glint of their weapons at their sides, while their comrades got stoned and guarded the camp. Slowly, inches at a time, he backed away, and when he was twenty feet from the men, he turned and crawled back to Elizabeth.

Jungle Jim had said the military coup and subsequent insurrection had become a full-blown civil war, and it now seemed Buddy and Elizabeth had nearly stumbled into the camp of another of the major factions. Quickly he pressed his index finger across her lips as he bent close to whisper in her ear. Cheek to cheek with her, he could hear the thump of her heart as he explained how the rebel troops were less than forty yards away.

"We have to go, now. Put the pack on your back and climb on."

The previous day he had walked for hours and lost track of how far he had come around the mountain, but it made sense that they were west of the airstrip—or so he hoped. Regardless, it wasn't long before dawn would come. They had to move quickly.

With Elizabeth on his back, Buddy turned up the mountain and began climbing. Hand over hand, he pulled himself and Elizabeth upward through the thick undercover. Silently, he picked his way so as not to disturb a single stone nor break a single limb. He climbed toward what he hoped might be the airstrip, but his primary goal was to get as far away as possible from the rebels.

After a while, a gray light fell across the mountainside as dawn broke. They had reached several acres of open ground covered with nearly chest-high green grass. Dew-soaked and lush, it was an inviting bed. Buddy paused.

Elizabeth wasn't a big person. She was actually thin and shapely and should not have felt quite so heavy, but it no longer mattered. His legs were jelly. The few hours rest he had gotten that night had not been enough to recuperate. Even a few minutes respite might help.

"I need to stop," he said.

Elizabeth let her feet down, and Buddy dropped to the ground without looking for a dry spot, but he noticed something. The ground here was bare. They had somehow found a well-trodden trail. This was a good thing. It probably led either to the village or the airstrip. Elizabeth sat beside him, but she seemed distracted as she looked back.

"Did you hear that?"

He had heard something, but his senses were dulled by exhaustion. He heard it again. There were men coming—the scuff of their boots, their heavy breathing, and the quiet rattle of their weapons said they were terribly close. Taking Elizabeth's hand, he pulled her to her feet.

"Come on. We've got to get off this trail."

His legs were numb, but he led Elizabeth into the deep grass. They had moved only a few yards when he heard the murmur of voices coming from just down the mountain. It had to be the same rebels he had seen earlier. They were coming.

His eyes met Elizabeth's. "Ssshhh," he whispered, crossing her lips with his finger. "Lay down, and they'll walk past. We'll be fine."

They lay silently in the wet grass as the full morning light fell across the slope and the line of men began passing. It was as he thought, the rebels—young men, burnt brown by the tropical sun, each carrying an AK-47 with bandoliers of ammunition slung across their chests. Their jaws were set with determination, and they were clearly hell-bent for a fight with the government troops. Their heavy breathing was as clear as the thump of their boots on the trail as they climbed the steep mountainside.

Buddy felt Elizabeth's fingers digging deep into his arm, a death-grip of fear, and only then did he hear something else. It was the same as it had been that day back in the A Shau Valley when the rescue choppers came. He was again hearing the rhythmic thump of rotors somewhere in the distance—the sound of an approaching Huey helicopter. Perhaps it would come save him from another impossible situation.

Muted shouts of alarm came from the rebels as they broke and ran into the undergrowth. The guerillas dove into the high grass all around, freezing and staring up at the sky with fear. The chopper passed slowly overhead—apparently flying a search pattern. It was one of the black Special Forces UH1H helicopters. Buddy had removed the little mirror from is pocket and was about to signal it when he realized this was not an option. He was staring into the startled eyes of a young rebel.

"I sure wish I spoke Spanish," he said.

"I do," Elizabeth replied.

The young soldier's mouth fell open only a moment before he sprang to his feet and pointed his AK-47 at them. "Compañeros, yanquis! Hay yanquis aquí."

Buddy and Elizabeth raised their hands above their heads. For a moment there was only silence, and no one moved.

"Yanquis!" the boy shouted again.

It seemed the others thought the boy was loco.

"Está bien, te creemos, Miguel. ¿Dónde están?" another man shouted.

"Ellos están aquí delante de mí. Ven rápido."

The chopper had passed, and several men pushed through the high grass to where the boy stood with his weapon trained on his captives. After everything they had been through, Buddy was certain it was going to end here. These men had no reason to spare them and every reason to kill them. It could be over in seconds.

CHAPTER TWENTY-FOUR

When Death No Longer Matters

A fter dispatching his teams along the trails leading to the village and airstrip, Colonel Jim Parker waited. He still hoped to save Buddy and the young missionary without mixing it up with the Salvadoran troops. The Salvadorans were blundering about everywhere around the mountain, and rebels had been spotted as well. At first light, one of the search choppers reported a column of them moving up the mountain from the west.

The latest intelligence said that despite counterinsurgency progress in other Central American countries, the Salvadoran civil war had become a bloodbath. The U.S. was backing a government dictatorship as ruthless as the one it had overthrown. Although somewhat aligned with American political interests, the new government junta was rife with corruption—another of the unforeseen consequences that arose when choosing sides in a civil war.

The conundrum facing the Americans was an impoverished population that was sold a Trojan Horse by the Communists— one promising the free bubble-up and rainbow pie of Utopia. The country—now divided into several warring factions—had become a free-fire zone with no regard for the lives of innocents. The State Department ordered U.S. forces to temporarily standdown while the Salvadoran troops they had trained were massacring peasants and the opposition. Jim and his men were stuck in the middle of this failed strategy.

Parker knew if it were Buddy alone out there, the former Special Forces soldier would probably make it, but the young woman with him was a wildcard. Buddy would not leave her behind and this would put him at a disadvantage. Time was not on their side.

———————————

At that moment Buddy needed to think faster than his exhausted body and mind would allow. With a dozen AK-47s trained on him and Elizabeth, he needed to make these Salvadoran rebels understand he was not their enemy, but the situation seemed hopeless. He was out of ideas and in need of a miracle.

"I'm going to tell them I'm a missionary from the village orphanage," Elizabeth said.

"Do you really speak Spanish?" Buddy asked.

"You should be happy I insisted on coming along." She turned to the rebel. "Soy una misionera del pueblo."

The rebels gazed at her with skepticism—rightly so. Elizabeth's eyes were wide with fear, and her amber brown hair was scattered wildly. Her shirt, now soaked by the dew laden grass, did little to disguise her breasts. No doubt she was unlike any missionary they had ever seen.

"¿Quién es él?"

The rebel motioned with his rifle toward Buddy.

"He wants to know who you are," she said. "Vino a rescatar a los misioneros y huérfanos de las tropas del gobierno."

"What did you say?"

"I told him the truth—that you are the man who came to rescue the missionaries and orphans."

Buddy was beginning to believe her fable about guardian angels. Even while staring into the barrels of their automatic weapons, she remained calm and spoke with poise and confidence. Elizabeth was the miracle he had hoped for. The rebel to whom she was speaking was an older man, likely their leader. He looked to be in his forties. The others were much younger, some barely in their teens.

The rebel leader reached over and snatched Buddy's canvas satchel from him. Opening it, he took out the remaining fragmentation grenade and held it up for the others to see. They cast knowing nods back at their two captives.

"¿Vino a rescatarte con granadas?"

Buddy didn't need Elizabeth to translate. The man thought she was lying and wanted to know about the grenade. Their situation was growing more precarious by the moment.

"Tell him how I destroyed the government compound and killed the commandant there. Tell him how we have already rescued the nuns, old people and the children. Tell him before he decides to kill us."

Buddy locked eyes with the rebel, and only then did he realize the man understood everything he was saying.

"So, you say you have destroyed the government's compound. How did you do that?"

Buddy motioned to the bag. "Look in there."

The man reached inside and pulled out one of the remaining blocks of C-4. For a moment his eyes grew with amazement, but they quickly narrowed as he turned to face him.

"And you have this explosive to go with your hand grenade, so how am I to believe you are not one of the American soldiers?"

"The American soldiers have helped us, but I am not one."

"No!" the rebel said. "The Americans would not support you. They support the ruling Junta. Why would they allow you to destroy their drug operations?"

"They didn't. They only wanted us to rescue the nuns and children, but they didn't know I would destroy the government compound."

The old rebel seemed perplexed as he contemplated his next response. "So, you will accompany me and my men? We are going to the government compound and kill the soldiers there."

"You will never reach the compound."

"Why do you say that?"

"Because when I blew it up, many more government soldiers came in from San Salvador. They are searching for whoever destroyed their processing facility."

The rebel—obviously vexed by these revelations—slowly shook his head. Buddy had to convince him he was telling the truth. He started from the beginning, explaining how the missionaries and villagers had been rescued, and how Elizabeth had been captured. He told the man how the entire mission had evolved up to now. When he was done, he reiterated, "I am working with people who only want to see the missionaries and the villagers rescued."

The rebel's silence was long and hollow, as if begging for additional information—something that might confirm Buddy's story.

"Why are you going back to the landing strip, if you are trying to avoid the soldiers?"

"There are United States soldiers there trying to find us. The Revolutionary Government Junta refused to allow the nuns and people in the village to leave, because they had witnessed their drug operation and the murders of others from the village. We felt the missionaries might also be killed by the Salvadoran National Guard, so we disobeyed our own government by rescuing them. When this lady and I were left behind, our army sent men here to find us."

The rebel slowly shook his head. "Madre Santa! Dime qué creer!"

After staring at Buddy for several seconds, the rebel turned and walked across the slope, motioning for the others to follow. A discussion ensued as sharp whispers and subdued voices clashed. The men cast wary glances their way while they talked. After several minutes, their leader stood and walked back to where Buddy and Elizabeth sat in the grass.

"Some of my men do not believe you, but I do. Because you have saved our old people and children, we have decided to set you free. Go now, before we change our minds."

Buddy motioned to his .45, the knife, and the contents of his backpack now scattered on the ground.

"What about my supplies? I need them."

"No, you do not need them as much as we do."

"We might die without them," Buddy said.

"When a man takes such desperate actions to protect others, death no longer matters to him. I believe you are one of those men, and I respect you for that, but we too are desperate and in need of your supplies. Now, go."

Buddy stood and pulled Elizabeth to her feet. Taking her hand, he led her through the tall grass back to the trail. She limped along beside him until they were a safe distance up the mountain. There he stopped and examined her feet. Cracked and swollen, they remained caked with dried mud and blood.

"Come on," he said. "Climb on my back so I can carry you."

"No. I can walk for now."

He would have insisted, but he was exhausted and doubted he could climb the slope with her on his back.

"Are you sure?"

"We will see."

"You are one tough little lady, and I guess you know you saved our butts back there. Thanks."

Elizabeth stared at him several seconds before nodding. After all those years in college when she dated different men, there had never been one like Buddy Rider. Those boys could only dream of someday becoming the man he was. She could not believe she had thought of him as the devil incarnate. If he was the devil, she was now ready to sell her soul. Only at that moment did Elizabeth realize she did not even know his full name.

Buddy was probably six or seven years her senior, a strong but lean man, probably not more than five feet ten inches tall with sandy blond hair. His blue eyes were surrounded by the slight hints of crowfoot lines that lent themselves to his handsome looks. His heart and soul seemed equally attractive, and it made her all the more determined to show him she had been wrong. Her prayer was that she hadn't already driven the wedge too deeply between them.

"Just don't walk too fast," she said. "I'll keep up."

"Okay. I'm not sure where this trail goes, but it leads either to the village or the airstrip. That means we could meet a patrol at any moment. Keep your eyes on me. Stay about ten or twelve feet behind me. If I stop, you stop. If I dive off the path, you dive too and crawl as far as it takes to hide from anyone passing by."

Buddy must have read the fear in her eyes because he grinned. "Don't you worry none, little lady, Ranger Buddy will have you fully trained in jungle survival tactics by the time we get home."

He said it imitating a John Wayne voice, and that was it, or at least one of many "its" that made him so attractive. He saw her fear and tried to distract her with his self-effacing humor. And the strangest thing was that it worked. He had put her at ease, even in these direst of circumstances.

"How far do you think it is to the airstrip?"

"Do you see that ridge stretching to the south up there about a half-mile away?"

"Yeah?"

"I think that's where it is. It's a pretty steep climb, but we should make it before dark."

And that was another thing—another "it" in his repertoire of talents. Perhaps it was his military training, but it seemed Buddy had an innate ability for navigating in places and conditions where she felt totally disoriented. Most of the boys she dated in college got lost trying to find the pizza places in Chicago.

They began walking, sometimes nearly crawling, as they climbed a mountain trail so steep in places, they were using saplings to pull themselves upward. Buddy stopped continuously, patiently coming back to pull her up some of the steeper sections. After hours of hiking, he again stopped, and they rested. She stared up at the ridge. They had climbed most of the day, but it seemed they were getting no closer.

Buddy too was gazing up that way. The look in his eyes said it all. He had reached the limit of his endurance. Like her, he too was winded and beyond exhaustion. Back to the west, the sun was sinking into a flaming bank of clouds above the hills. Long shadows stretched across the mountainside, and it seemed they were destined to spend yet another night in the jungle.

"I'm sorry I talked you into this, Buddy."

Her hand was braced on a flat rock in the trail, and he reached over and placed his atop hers. His palm was callused and rough but warm. The roughness reassured her of his strength. He winked at her.

"Don't worry. I'm not."

"Why?"

"Babe," he said. He paused. "Do you mind if I call you—"

She quickly raised her hand to silence him and shook her head slowly side to side.

"You know you don't have to ask."

"Okay. It's been ten years since I got home from Vietnam, and I've had several girlfriends, but I pushed them all away. I'm not sure why. I reckon there were too many of my buddies who never came home, and I was pretty much done with life. I only wanted my airplanes and nothing or nobody else. You've changed that."

Elizabeth could not help herself as she pushed herself into his arms. Pulling him close, she found his lips and surrendered herself to him. Raising her shirt, she pressed her breasts gently against his body. It was a passion unlike anything she had ever experienced. His hands dropped and grasped her hips pulling her tightly against him. She wrapped her leg behind his and found the heat of his body overwhelming. This was not how she imagined her first time would happen, but she did not care. She wanted him, and she wanted him now. She could wait no longer.

CHAPTER TWENTY-FIVE

An Inconvenient Interruption

I t was dusk and the jungle was rapidly fading to black when Colonel Jim Parker's RTO tapped his shoulder. He had the radio handset pressed to his ear.

"Roger, Black Shadow Three. Standby. Over," he whispered.

"Black Shadow Three has spotted them, sir."

"Rider and the woman?" Parker asked.

"Yes, sir. They're only seventy meters below them on the trail and the team is moving their way."

"Thank God," the colonel said. "Tell the team leader to send me a sit-rep as soon as they reach them."

"Roger that, sir."

———————

Despite near exhaustion, Buddy realized he and Babe were about to consummate their love in a very real way. Lying atop him, she had unbuttoned her khaki trousers and he had locked his thumbs inside her waistband, about to push them over her hips. Her quiet groans of anticipation wiped away all his inhibitions and her hot breath on his neck pushed him over the edge. He wanted her as much as she seemed to want him.

But he heard something—as if someone were clearing their throat. He hesitated.

"Uh, sir?"

It was a voice.

Babe's breaths were coming in rapid gasps, and she seemed oblivious. Buddy reached up and pulled her shirt down to cover her back.

"Sir, uh," the man's voice came again.

Babe heard it and drew a loud gasp as she rolled on her back. Buddy gazed into the gathering darkness at what he quickly realized was the shadow of a camouflage-clad Green Beret standing in the trail above them.

He pulled Babe close. "It's okay. They're Americans." Her heavy breathing gave way to sobs.

"Do you have some water? We haven't had any all day."

Within seconds they were surrounded by a protective perimeter of Special Forces soldiers. Buddy held a canteen to Elizabeth's lips while she slurped greedily.

"Slow down, Babe. Don't drink too much."

"Sir, I have to report back to my commander. Are you folks okay? Do you have any wounds?"

"Who is your commander, Sergeant?"

"Right now, I'm communicating directly with my colonel."

"Jungle Jim?"

"Yes, sir. That's right."

"Tell him I said, thanks to him we're going to be okay. Her feet are in bad shape and in need of medical attention. We'll have to carry her. Outside of that, we've been fortunate."

A minute later the sergeant returned. "Black Shadow Six ordered us to lagger in place tonight, sir. He is going to move the rest of the teams to an extraction point where we will meet tomorrow."

"Right, but I'm going to recommend you relocate your team at least a hundred meters off this trail. We ran into a large group of FMLN rebels this morning—twenty-five or more."

"Shit," the sergeant muttered. "Sorry, ma'am."

Thirty minutes later, they were in their alternate night defensive position. "What can we do to make you and the lady more comfortable?" the sergeant whispered.

"Do you have a couple extra rations?" Buddy asked. "We haven't had anything to eat since yesterday evening."

A few minutes later a soldier showed up with two bags of chili-mac. He gave them both plastic spoons. "Sorry, they're cold, sir. Maybe these will help." He pushed two poncho liners into Buddy's arms.

"Thanks. We were getting cold."

"You're welcome, sir. The sergeant told me to look at the lady's feet. I'm going to put a poncho over them and get under there with a flashlight. Do you mind, ma'am?"

"No," Elizabeth said.

"I'm going to wash your feet, then clean them with alcohol. I'll try not to hurt you, but it will burn, and you must remain quiet. I have this packet of antibiotic to apply after we get them clean. Then I'm going to put these special socks on you."

Elizabeth laid her head back in Buddy's lap and closed her eyes while the soldier worked on her feet. Several minutes later, when he was done, he came from beneath the poncho.

"How do your feet feel now?" the soldier whispered.

Elizabeth was breathing heavily and did not answer.

"They must feel pretty good," Buddy said. "I think she fell asleep."

"I'll check them again after daylight. I'll be right here if you need me."

"Thanks."

Buddy pulled his poncho over his shoulders and held Babe's head close as he closed his eyes.

———————————

Elizabeth awoke to a new day as the soldiers carried her in a poncho litter. Buddy followed close behind. She watched him, but he said little, and their eyes met only occasionally as the team made the climb up the mountainside to the extraction point. She could not help but wonder what was going through his mind and what he thought about the evening before.

Overcome with passion and having lost all inhibition, she had wanted to give herself to him, but the rescuers interrupted them. Now, she was likely going home, and she wondered if this would change things. Buddy had not spoken to her the remainder of the morning. His silence was unsettling.

They reached a flat clearing around noon, where the group rendezvoused with the colonel and the rest of his men. The thumping rotors of approaching helicopters were a music not unlike that of an alleluia choir, and the wash of the rotors were as if heaven itself had opened its doors to cool the midday heat. Buddy crawled in beside her and closed his eyes. She wanted to reach over and take his hand, but with the soldiers around them, she didn't want to put him in any more of an awkward position.

By early afternoon they were back at the Special Forces Base in Honduras. After Elizabeth celebrated a tearful reunion with Melissa and the other missionaries, showers were taken, and they joined Buddy for their first hot meal in days. Later they celebrated with drinks, but there was no opportunity for her to be alone with him.

When Buddy went to the TOC for what he called a mission debriefing, Elizabeth returned to the little building that housed their room. She crawled under the mosquito net to nap. It was much warmer here than in the Salvadoran mountains, and she sweated while dreaming of her recent days in the jungle with this man she had grown to love.

Sometime later she awakened. The room was dark, and the night sounds of the jungle came from outside the window. She squinted across the room. A vague hint of moonlight came from outside the window, revealing Buddy asleep on his cot. He breathed heavily in his sleep—no doubt exhausted from their ordeal.

Propped on one elbow, she listened to him sleeping, and so badly she wanted to go to his cot and slip beneath the mosquito net to be with him. She wanted to sleep beside him as she had in the jungle, but he had hardly spoken since their rescue. Now that they no longer faced imminent danger, it seemed things had changed.

Even while they were eating and drinking that evening, he had said little. She lay awake for hours listening to the geckos, the night birds, and the drone of the insects. Buddy was a true gentleman, and even though he espoused little use for religion, he was a devout believer in God. He was also the first man who had ever so totally captured her heart this way. Sleep came, but only after hours of anxious second-guessing.

Buddy grabbed his boots and slipped from the room at first light. The plans were already in progress for their return to the U.S. The January weather was crisp and clear all the way to South Texas where they would land on a remote airstrip near

San Benito. Jim Parker had used a classified satellite telephone to make contact with the person Elizabeth identified as her sponsor. If all went as planned, a bus would meet them to take the missionaries, nuns, and orphans to an undisclosed safehouse somewhere up north.

Stein Foster again agreed to fly copilot with him, and the aircraft was prepped by the Special Forces ground crew. Buddy walked around and checked the old girl's control surfaces. Only then did he notice the aircraft tail number had once again been stenciled on the fuselage. It looked even better than the original. Jungle Jim had not missed a single detail. Buddy made his way over to the TOC where he found the colonel drinking coffee with Chief Foster.

"Are you ready to head home?" Jim asked.

Buddy poured himself some coffee.

"Yes, sir, I am."

"That's good. I wish you Godspeed, and please, don't be calling me for any more favors."

Jim was giving him some well-deserved smashmouth humor, but there was something else Buddy wanted to say. An uncomfortable moment of silence ensued before he drew a deep breath and looked his friend in the eyes.

"Jim, I don't know how I can ever repay you."

"I'll tell you how. You know that place you told me about that your friend Marino owns called Bayou Bois de Arc? You said it was the best duck hunting hole in all of Mississippi."

"Yeah?" Buddy said.

"Well, when I retire, I want you to take me duck hunting there, and when we're done, I want you to cook me a pot of that duck gumbo you were always bragging about."

"You come hunt there anytime you want. I'll be your personal guide, chief cook, and bottle washer."

"Go wake Elizabeth. They're feeding her refugees now, and when they're done, the mess sergeant is bringing us some hot breakfast, too. After that, you'll be on your way home."

Buddy tapped lightly on the room door.

"Buddy?"

"Yeah."

"Come on in."

Elizabeth was already dressed and sitting at the desk.

"Are those the clothes you plan to wear for the trip home?" he asked.

"We're leaving *today*?"

"Probably within an hour. Pack your bag and we'll go get some coffee and hot breakfast at the TOC."

"Was the colonel able to contact Melissa's parents?"

"They're having someone meet us with a chartered bus this evening at an airstrip near San Benito, Texas. Chief Foster is flying copilot for us again and the weather is clear all the way. The only drama we may face is getting the people off the plane and out of there before the DEA or other fed types catch up with us."

"Do you think they'll show up?"

"It's like everything else we've done up to now—a crap shoot. Stop your worrying. It won't change things."

When she was packed, Buddy carried her bag as they walked to the TOC. He wanted to hold her hand, but it seemed suddenly inappropriate—perhaps unwanted. She was too quiet, and it was as if she had reverted from Babe back to Elizabeth. What had changed he didn't know, but something about her was different. She had become suddenly distant, and he wanted to ask if she was having second thoughts, but the time wasn't right. The flight would take eight hours or more. Perhaps they would have a chance to talk then.

They ate breakfast in silence, and when it was done, there were thanks and hugs all around. Afterward, they went to help the passengers board the aircraft. Buddy helped get everyone strapped in, but Babe said little—probably because of the people around them. The uncomfortable silence between them continued.

CHAPTER TWENTY-SIX

A Quick Goodbye

The familiar electrical odor of the warming instruments filled the cockpit, while Buddy ran through the preflight checklist with Stein Foster. The engines were running strong when Jungle Jim—always the wise one—showed up at the last minute with two five-gallon pails—extra chamber pots, he explained. Elizabeth took them through the cargo door and latched it shut. Buddy eased the throttles open and glanced over at Stein Foster as they taxied the aircraft onto the strip.

"No offense," Buddy said, "but I am *so* ready to get out of this place."

Stein merely grinned as Buddy pushed the throttles forward and the old plane trundled lethargically down the runway. After a while when the speed indicator said they were ready to fly, he pulled back on the yoke, and Miss Molly rose into the air as they shot out over the jungle. They climbed and banked toward the Gulf of Mexico. The jungle below grew more distant, and the sparkling blue waters of the Gulf appeared on the horizon.

A strange déjà vu came over him, and Buddy realized he had felt this way once before. It was the day he departed Vietnam, riding the freedom bird out over the South China Sea, bound for the United States and home. The soldiers aboard had cheered mightily—some even coming to tears. It was as if they had broken free and were soaring out through the gates of hell to a new life back home.

He glanced over at Stein. The Chief Warrant officer gave him a nod. "It feels good, doesn't it?" Stein knew exactly what Buddy was thinking because he too had experienced it.

The flight was a thing of beauty. With the perpetual thrum of the engines and clear skies, it was almost boring, but there would be no complaints on his part. Buddy had seen times when he prayed fervently for such conditions, but there was little relief from the ache he now felt in his heart. He wanted to talk to Elizabeth—not to change her mind, if she was having second thoughts—but at least to better understand what she was thinking.

They were six hours into the flight when for the second time he turned the flight deck over to Stein and walked to the rear. The first time he had done this was three hours ago, and Elizabeth had scarcely acknowledged him as she rocked a crying baby. This time she was holding another orphan, a boy who was sleeping soundly. Their eyes met, and Buddy thought for a moment she might talk, but she looked down at the boy. The nuns and old people were watching them intently. It was probably not a good time to start the discussion.

"I'll check on you later," he said.

She nodded but didn't look up. He wanted to kneel beside her and tell her everything would be okay, no matter what she chose to do. She deserved as much, but he didn't want to make her the object of speculation by the others. He turned instead and walked back to the cockpit where he slid into his seat.

"We've got a visitor," Stein said. He motioned with his chin. "Out there at nine o'clock."

The plane was a half mile away, flying parallel with them at the same altitude.

"DEA?" Buddy said.

"That would be my guess," Stein said.

Buddy studied the little aircraft. It would likely follow them all the way to Texas, and he had no idea how to escape them discovering his planeload of passengers. He had come too far to lose it all now, but he was out of ideas.

"You got any suggestions?" he asked Stein.

"I don't think they would have let us see them if they thought we were drug runners. They aren't sure what we're doing, but my guess is they're just curious about your old gooney bird. I mean you've got her painted up real nice. But to answer your question—I suggest we maintain zero-nine thousand and don't descend until we're past Brownsville. I think they'll lose interest and go off to find another rabbit to chase."

"If they follow us, all these people will likely be deported," Buddy said, "and I'll be sent up to the big house to be a bitch for the booty boys."

Stein laughed aloud.

"I'm beginning to understand why Jungle Jim says you're one of his closest friends."

"I'm not sure how to take that."

"Believe me, sir, it's an absolute compliment. I think you and that old hard ass were poured from the same mold. I'd feel sorry for the dumb bastard who tries to mess with you."

"Thanks, Chief. Let's pick up a VOR radial for Brownsville. We'll start our descent after we pick up the highway to San Benito. Once we spot the big grain bins north of town, we can circle and set up to land on the crop duster strip."

"Sounds like a plan. Let's just hope Elizabeth's people are there with the bus."

"What if they aren't?" Buddy asked.

"You're not going to like what I have to say."

"What's that?"

"If that bus isn't there, we have to leave them on the ground and get back in the air."

Buddy did not reply. Stein was right. It was the reality of the situation, and if he did that, he could probably bid Babe farewell forever.

"How about going back there and getting everyone strapped down?" Buddy said. "And tell them as soon as we land to move fast. Tell them we'll probably have less than ten minutes to get them off the plane, on that bus, and gone."

Stein slipped from his seat, but he stopped and looked back.

"We'll make it, sir. I'm going to stick with you as long as I can."

A few minutes later, Stein returned to the cockpit and buckled his seatbelt. As they passed by Brownsville, the two pilots searched the sky for the aircraft that had been tailing them. It was nowhere in sight. It seemed Elizabeth's guardian angel was still riding shotgun for them.

"We must be doing something right," Buddy said.

"Except for Elizabeth," Stein said. "She was crying when I went back there. I asked her if she was okay, but she wouldn't say. You guys okay?"

Buddy knew why she was upset, but he couldn't leave the cockpit to talk with her. Hopefully, she would come to him while the orphans were being transferred to the bus.

"We had a tough time out there in the jungle, and I think

she's a little confused." He pointed toward the right-side window. "That's the airstrip over there to the northwest."

Buddy banked toward the little airstrip and lowered the flaps and landing gear. Just off the airstrip he spotted a large silver and blue charter bus. He breathed a sigh of relief. This whole affair might end well after all. He checked his altitude and airspeed. All was good. Elizabeth's guardian angel was still on the job.

"When we've offloaded the passengers are you flying back to Brownsville for fuel?"

Buddy glanced at the fuel gauges. "I figure the federal boys might be waiting there for me, in which case I'll have to answer a million questions. I need time to get my story together, and with that tailwind, we're still running pretty fat on fuel. I'm going to try to make Jack Brooks up at Beaumont."

"Stretching it a bit, aren't you?"

"Maybe, we'll see. When we land, I'll taxi to the bus and stop where they have to run toward the tail to reach it but warn them all to stay the hell away from the props."

"Will do."

The landing was smooth, and Buddy taxied the aircraft to within a few yards of the bus. Stein had the cargo door open before they stopped. Within minutes all the children, old people, and missionaries had deplaned and were on board the bus. Buddy waited and hoped. Surely, she would come to the cockpit for a final goodbye. Opening his side cockpit window, he looked back toward the bus. She was standing there in the doorway waving him goodbye.

His heart sank, and a lump rose in his throat. He had been a fool. The emotion was nearly overwhelming, but he hadn't shed a tear for the friends he lost in Nam and crying for this confused woman would only desecrate their memory. He sucked down a deep breath and swallowed the emotion as the cargo door slammed shut in back. Stein came up to the cockpit.

"Are you going with me?" Buddy asked.

Stein sat and buckled in. "I told Colonel Parker I would make sure you got home safely. That means I'm going as far as Mississippi with you."

Buddy watched as the bus turned onto the highway and sped away. Just like that, it was gone. She was gone.

"Thanks. Let's get the hell out of here."

With that, he reset the flaps and pushed the throttles forward.

CHAPTER TWENTY-SEVEN

Crop Dusting the Memories Away

B y early March Buddy was well into his springtime crop
dusting chores. There was a lot to be said for the
therapeutic hum of an aircraft engine and the feel of air
under your wings. As he figured, the feds came around and
asked some questions, but it was clear they were fishing. They
knew absolutely nothing, and his vacation time at the resort in
Mexico had been well documented by Jim Parker. They
attempted their usual admonishments and warnings, except
Buddy's fuse was burning short of late. He sent them away like
coyotes with their tails between their legs. It would have been
satisfying had it not been for his thoughts of Elizabeth.

It was a quiet Friday evening, and he was at the Clarksdale
hangar. After a long day in the air, he had poured himself a
glass of bourbon and was walking around Miss Molly. The old
C-47 had sat in the hangar since his return from Central
America. She had done everything asked of her and more, but
something changed. Running his hand along her fuselage,
Buddy gazed up at the big radial motors. Her metal surfaces
were as cold as his heart. He had come to realize this old
airplane no longer meant as much to him. Everything had
changed since his return.

February had been one of the longest months of his life, but he had heard nothing more from Babe. Where she was, what she was doing, was anyone's guess. With no idea how to reach her, he was left to wait and wonder what went wrong. It was clear the days they spent together in the jungle were an anomaly that meant little or nothing—at least to her. She had moved on, and he was left feeling like a swooning idiot—a high school kid with a crush on the best-looking girl in the class.

He was a thirty-one-year-old man who had fought and survived two tours in Vietnam, two plane crashes and now a revolution. Letting infatuation and lost love cloud his mind was something he could ill afford while flying close to the ground every day. Crop dusting wasn't a job of daring or risk taking. It was a job of focus and concentration. Nighttime was a different matter, and he found himself slipping into a bad habit much as his old friend Buck Marino had when he first returned from Vietnam. He was knocking down several shots of bourbon every evening.

Buddy realized he was stupid—really stupid—for letting that woman get under his skin. He paused and nearly laughed aloud at the thought. A girl six years his junior had stolen his heart and calling her "that woman" was his only means of getting past Babe Anderson. Were it not for all the farmers who depended on him he would have parked the Ag-Cat in the hangar and gone on a six-month drunk.

The air in the hangar was chilly, and he sipped the bourbon while gazing at Miss Molly. This would be their last evening together because a wealthy buyer from Texas had called saying he wanted to purchase her sight unseen. The man said he had heard of Miss Molly—a painstakingly restored veteran of the D-minus drop of 82nd Airborne paratroops over Sainte-Mère-Église before D-Day. Buddy didn't have a second thought. He knew the day he returned from Central America that his life had changed.

The offer made over the phone was for a small fortune—far more money than he had spent purchasing and restoring her. Buddy agreed, and the money was deposited in his account. The man was supposed to arrive with another pilot anytime now, and from outside came the sound of an airplane circling the field.

Buddy could not help but wonder if that was it—love could be bought and sold by the highest bidder. And what or who was the higher bidder in Babe's life—a job, a calling, or was there someone else? It no longer mattered. He had to move on. He signed the papers and an hour later watched one last time as Miss Molly lumbered into the sky and banked into the setting sun toward Texas.

The week had been a long one, and he was tired. When he got home, JD was curled up on the rug in front of the fireplace. That seemed like a good idea, but there was no fire. Buddy piled kindling and struck a match, building his faithful companion a fire. While the flames grew, he poured another glass of bourbon and dropped into his recliner. The light on the phone was blinking indicating a waiting message. He punched the button.

"You have one new message," the voice said. Buddy sipped from his glass while he listened. "Hey Buddy, this is Buck." There were kids shouting and a baby crying in the background. "Call me when you can. I need a favor."

His voice was replaced by the dial tone, and Buddy wished Buck were here now. He needed someone to talk to. Patrick "Buck" Marino was his closest friend and a man who had found peace and purpose in his life since the war. Buck deserved it, and Buddy was ready for the same kind of life for himself. He wouldn't mind having a couple of kids to take for rides in his airplane. After glancing up at the clock, he picked up the phone and dialed Buck's number.

"Hello?" It was Janie's warm voice.

She was the army nurse who had never given up on her man.

"Hey, beautiful, this is Buddy. Is your old man around?"

A television was playing in the background.

"Well, hey Buddy! Yes. Hang on. I'll get him."

There wasn't much he could share with Buck—at least on the phone—but when he told him he had sold Miss Molly, the silence was deafening. Buddy listened, but there now wasn't even the sound of a kid screaming in the background—nothing.

"Are you still there?"

The silence continued for several more seconds before Buck spoke.

"You've been working on that old plane for what—four, five years? I mean—what's going on? Are you okay?"

The truth was something Buddy wasn't quite ready to share.

"I reckon the guy who bought her wanted her more than I did. Believe me, he paid a handsome price."

"Well, I didn't see that one coming. I thought you were madly in love with that old pile of scrap metal."

"I reckon my love got trumped by too many greenbacks. So, what's this favor you're needing?"

"I got a call this morning from someone down there. They saw the rental sign on the old home place and wanted to move in immediately. I told them where the key was and that you would come by to pick up the first month's rent. If you don't mind, I would appreciate you going by there tomorrow to make sure they're legit and not loading the furniture in a U-Haul."

"No worries. I've got you covered."

"Oh, and you may have to help them turn on the power and check the water heater. I spoke with some woman and tried to tell her where the breaker box was located, but she seemed a little confused."

"No problem. I'll take my tools and head over there in the morning. So, when are you coming down for a visit? They say the fish are biting good up at Moon Lake."

"Winter's still hanging on up here, and we're still feeding the cattle on the lot. I've got to help Janie's dad move a truckload of hay this week and repair some fence in the high pasture before the cattle get up there. It'll probably be April before we can get away."

"I'll call you tomorrow after I meet with your new tenants."

Buddy had taken the day off but was still up at first light. He cooked up a half-dozen sausage and biscuits and filled his thermos with hot coffee. If Buck's new tenants hadn't figured out how to turn on the power, they would likely appreciate his breakfast offering. He loaded JD into the back of the pickup and twenty minutes later arrived at Buck's place in Bois de Arc. He was reaching for the bag of biscuits when JD gave a yelp and leapt from the back of the truck.

"JD!" he shouted but to no avail.

The big lab was on a mission as a yellow cat with a pink collar streaked across the yard, barely making it into the limbs of a mimosa before JD got there. With no houses in the immediate vicinity, Buddy figured the cat probably belonged to the new tenants. They would be none too happy if JD ate their pet. After a scolding, the dog hung his head, and Buddy ordered him back to the truck.

There was a small car parked in the drive, but no one had yet come to the door. He decided the better part of being a good neighbor was to climb the damned mimosa and retrieve the terrified cat. It was a fairly easy climb, and the cat seemed to have calmed as he stretched out on a limb eight feet off the ground. The cat mewed and whined but refused to come any closer. The limb sank under his weight as Buddy inched further out.

"Buddy?"

It was a woman's voice, and he looked under his arm to see her staring up at him from below. It was Babe. His grip failed and he flipped off the tree limb, hitting the ground with a thud. She was there in an instant, kneeling beside him. The shock of the fall was nothing compared to seeing Babe. Slowly, he sat up.

"Babe?"

She said nothing.

"What are you doing here?" he asked.

"I—uh—I wanted to come…here…to be near you. I mean… I couldn't just invite myself to stay at your house. I mean…I didn't know if…."

She sucked down a deep breath and her voice quavered as tears welled in her eyes.

"I didn't know if you wanted me, Buddy."

"You what? Why would you think—"

"I'm sorry. Please, don't be angry. I didn't think you would mind."

"I don't! I don't mind. No, I'm glad you came back. Why would you think I didn't want you?"

She cocked her head to one side as her eyes seemed to reflect a growing realization.

"It was because of what happened the day when we were rescued and when we got back to the Green Berets' base camp. You—you seemed so—I don't know. I thought you had second thoughts and—"

"But why? Why would you think that?"

She took his hand in hers. Her touch alone was electrifying.

"That's the same thing my friend Melissa said. She said I was crazy for not coming after you. Buddy, please believe me. If you had given me even the slightest hint, I would have slept with you in your cot that night."

He held her hand—afraid to let go.

"I suppose I'm just a stupid guy, but in all honesty, I didn't know what you were thinking, and I thought *you* were the one having second thoughts. I thought our last evening in the jungle was just a moment you got caught up in when you thought we might die."

"I've had a month to think about this, Buddy—the longest month of my entire life, and I can tell you with no doubt whatsoever that it wasn't something I got caught up in. It was because I love you."

"And you still feel that way?" he said.

She wrapped her arms around his neck, and their lips met in a kiss as passionate as the one he experienced that day in the Salvadoran jungle. When they parted, he was on fire.

Babe drew a quavering breath. "Maybe you can take me for a ride later in Miss Molly. I'd like that."

Buddy felt a sudden coldness deep within as he looked away and refused to make eye contact with her.

"What is it?" she asked.

"Well…" he paused. "That can't happen."

"Why?"

"I sold her."

Babe's face paled. "You what? I can't believe.... I thought you loved that old airplane."

"I did, but I realized Miss Molly had flown her final mission when we returned from El Salvador. She, or perhaps it was you, made me realize that she was filling a role that only a good woman like you could satisfy."

Babe remained dumbstruck.

"Don't worry. Miss Molly went to a good home. A wealthy oilman from Texas bought her for a World War Two museum that's in the works."

Babe lay her head against his chest. "Oh, Buddy. Don't you worry, either. I will always be here for you. I promise."

He looked up at the cat. It was still stretched out on the tree limb, now gazing down at them with typical cat-like curiosity.

"Is that your cotton-pickin' cat?"

Raising her head, Babe gazed up at it. "Yes. That is my *cotton-picking* cat."

Babe's face glowed with a happiness the likes of which Buddy had never seen.

"Well, it better get used to living with JD, 'cause they're going to be together for a long time."

"JD?"

Buddy pointed to the big yellow lab sitting in the back of his truck, tongue lolling and tail wagging.

"JD, do you remember Babe?"

Several hours later when she awakened from her nap, Babe lay staring up at nothing in particular, but dreaming that this day had to be really close to heaven. She sighed and turned to find Buddy fully awake and watching her. It reminded her of their days in the jungle when he was always there, always awake, and always watching over her.

"What are you thinking about?" he asked.

That morning had been her first time. And that afternoon had been her second time, and she never imagined it could be quite as good as it was—so close to another human, a man—a man she so loved. She wanted to tell him as much, but her inhibitions held her hostage.

"I've never, ever felt so.…"

She paused and blushed.

"So, you're saying Buddy Rider be much man?" He pounded his chest and pooched out his lips.

"You're so silly."

She rolled toward him, tickling his ribs with both hands. They wrestled beneath the sheet before she once again fell under the spell of this man's masculinity. He kissed her lips, her neck, and slid lower as her body again became a bonfire of burning passion. Later they stood together in the shower and washed one another. Afterward, she stood in front of a space heater while he dried her with a towel.

"Are you hungry?" he asked.

"Starved."

"We can ride down to Cleveland. It's a thirty-minute drive, but I want to take you to a restaurant there. It's got the best crawfish etouffee anywhere and the coldest beer in all of Mississippi."

She shrugged. "Works for me."

"I need to ask you something," he said. "Something important."

She wrapped the towel around her torso and began combing out her hair while looking into the mirror. Buddy pulled on his jeans and began buttoning them. When he was done, their eyes met in the mirror. The comb stopped halfway through her hair and her heart was suddenly thumping. It was the look in his eyes. They seemed suddenly somber. Something wasn't right. She turned to face him. It was clear he was struggling, but the knot in her throat rendered her mute.

"I need to know if this is—well, what I mean is—I reckon I'm sort of old fashioned about things, but I want to make sure we're both ready for this."

Her heart fell into the pit of her stomach, and she bowed her head. She should have known. He still had doubts. It was her fault. She had been too judgmental and skeptical when they first met. The wedge she created remained.

"What do you mean?" She could barely speak.

"No!" he said. "You're misunderstanding me. What I mean is, I want you to come with me to my place to live for a while. I know my feelings, but I want you to know for certain that this is the life you want."

Once again, her heart skyrocketed with joy. Exhaling, she wrapped her arms around his neck and looked up into his eyes.

"Buddy Rider, I may be a young and dumb woman who made a lot of mistakes when we first met, but I now know one thing with an absolute certainty. As long as you will have me, I will follow you to the ends of the earth, or we can stay right here in the Mississippi Delta. I will be happy as long as I am with you."

"So, if I were to ask you to marry me, what would you say?"

She paused and studied him.

"I would say that sounds a bit like a hypothetical proposal. Are you asking?"

"Okay, what I mean is, yes, I want to marry you, but I want us to get engaged first—will you…I mean…marry me, that is?"

She pulled his head down to hers. Their lips met, and when

they parted, she gazed into those crystalline blue pilot's eyes of his.

"Yes, Buddy. I want to be your wife."

The phone in the next room began ringing.

"Your phone's ringing," he said.

"My phone?"

"You're the one who lives here," he said.

———————————

Babe was still wrapped in the bath towel, and Buddy couldn't help but admire her figure as she walked across the room and picked up the phone.

"Hello? Oh, oh, yes. Yes, Mr. Marino. Yes, he did. He's standing right here. Oh, no. Everything is fine. We just—"

Buddy held out his hand. "If you don't mind, I'll talk to him."

"Hang on a second. He wants to talk to you."

She gave him the phone and stood in the bedroom door, where she dropped the towel and began dressing. Buddy watched her while he talked on the phone.

"Buck, hey. Yeah. Yeah, everything is fine. I was just fixin' to discuss wedding plans with my fiancée. Yes, my fiancée. That's right—yeah, your new tenant—well, for a week or so, until she moves into my place."

There was a pause and Buddy winked at her while she buttoned her jeans. She was beautiful, but more importantly, she was a woman he could grow old with.

"You still there? Yes. Yes. That's right, Elizabeth, except her friends call her Babe. It's a long story, my friend—one I can't discuss right now. I'll have to tell you the next time we're together. No. No. Nothing like that, but I hope to sometime in the future, maybe two or three of them. We'll see."

Buck now seemed stuck on mute.

"By the way. I'll let you know when we set a date. I'll expect you to be my best man."

I n September of 1981, Buddy and Babe married. It was a small wedding held at a friend's beach house near Perdido Key, Florida. Her bridesmaids included Melissa Hanahan, whose parents were also in attendance. Buddy's best man was Buck Marino. Jim Parker was still in Central America and could not attend, but he sent Stein Foster as his stand-in.

With Babe, Buddy found the peace and trust that had eluded him since his years in Vietnam. A year later Patrick James Rider was born. Two years later, Melissa Elizabeth Rider came into the world.

Babe joined with a local preacher named Son Freeman to provide community assistance for the people of Coahoma, Tallahatchie, and Sunflower Counties. She also worked as a counselor at a nearby prison. When she wasn't working, she did the things she had missed while growing up, including planting a vegetable garden, fishing with Buddy, and duck hunting with him during the winter. They kayaked on Moon Lake and slept on a sandbar beside the Mississippi River. And when he wasn't working, he took her high among the towers of white nimbus in his crop duster where she felt the cool wind blowing in her face.

Buddy and Babe found common ground, but she never abandoned her religion nor her liberal beliefs. Jesus, she told

Buddy, was the first liberal, but her Salvadoran experiences, along with those at the prison, gave her a somewhat broader perspective and a better understanding of both points of view. For her, Buddy was a work in progress, but one who she believed was already pretty close to perfect.

Buddy had changed the way Elizabeth now viewed the world. She still believed the meek would inherit the earth, but it would be after the Buddy Riders, Jim Parkers, Buck Marinos, Curtis Teagues, and so many other warriors laid it at their feet. Babe found a new respect for veterans, and Buddy had grown to better understand those like Babe who wanted a better world.

If you enjoyed this story

Please leave your written review for
Miss Molly's Final Mission at
www.amazon.com/review/create-review?asin=B09DMF7953

The author and other readers will appreciate your comments. Post your review now and tell others what you liked about this book.

Keep reading for a preview of Book #4 of the Vietnam War Series, *Raeford's MVP*, a humorous but very serious story about Vietnam War Veteran Billy Coker's battle with Post Traumatic Stress and a wasted past, as he finds the love of his life and seeks a meaningful future.

Excerpt from

Raeford's MVP

RICK
DESTEFANIS

CHAPTER ONE

Put a Candle in the Window

Central Highlands, Republic of Vietnam, 1970

Billy Coker sat on a sandbag, smoking a cigarette, and staring out at the fog-shrouded mountains of Vietnam. It was another dripping wet afternoon—quiet, except for the muffled voices of his men, playing cards in the bunker below. The rain had passed, and somewhere on the firebase behind him a radio played Credence Clearwater Revival. John Fogerty's plaintive voice came from the outside world, "Put a candle in the window." It was Billy's invitation to become human again, because in less than thirty days the freedom bird was taking him home. He'd have a real bath, sleep in a real bed and no longer worry about dying or watching others die. He was happy to be leaving Vietnam alive and unscathed, but without a clue as to why. It was as if somewhere along the way his life had ended, and he didn't even know when it happened.

He dropped the cigarette into a puddle and fished another from the pack in his pocket. Other than escaping his current predicament, a total lack of anticipation had him teetering on the finest edge between happiness and despair. Those years in high school when he thought he was on top of the world now came back to haunt him with guilt and regret. And the strangest part of it all—he wasn't even thinking about the last eleven months in Nam. His thoughts weren't about the futility of the war or any of the recent events that should have culminated as the defining experiences of his life. He wasn't thinking about the man he'd become, or the men he'd seen die in the mud and rain—men like Butch and Danny, men closer to him than his own brother.

He absentmindedly rubbed his thumb over the Saint Sebastian medal hanging around his neck. He rubbed it as he had a thousand times in the last eleven months. He had clung to the silly medal like a raft in a storm. It was a gift from Bonnie Jo Parker. He smiled at the thought.

Where she given the chance, Bonnie Jo probably could have charmed the pants off of most men, but she wasn't that kind of girl. She was one of the fat girls at Raeford High who wore glasses and laughed too much. She laughed, not because she was silly, but because she was happy. Billy had spent time talking to her when he could—just to be nice—but Bonnie Jo wasn't his type. Perhaps, this was why he thought about her so much. Seems the fat girls never got a break, and he sure as hell never gave Bonnie Jo one.

Of course, they hadn't been *close* friends—only buddies of a sort—but he'd seen her almost every day. He ran cross-country track, and he was good at it. Back then he was skinny as a rail, and he liked the running. It was a way to clear his mind, not that there was much to clear. But cross-country track was the only thing he did well, besides chasing girls. Billy lit another cigarette as he thought about his after-school runs. Crossing the pasture behind the school, he took the same course every day, down the hill to the creek and up through the woods. Skirting the back of town, he went behind the drive-in and around the old gravel pits, making a six-mile circuit. And Bonnie Jo was almost always there sitting at the tables behind the Dairy Queen with a couple other girls. When he passed on the trail in the woods, they waved, but he seldom did more than raise a finger in acknowledgment.

They had been in school together since their freshman year. He'd passed her in the halls almost every day, but the first time they spoke more than two words was at the beginning of their senior year. It was a Saturday in September when she walked out of the dollar store in Raeford. Billy was staring at the sale sign in the window, "Women's Summer Clothes 50% Off", thinking of—what else? —a girl with half her clothes off.

"Hey, Billy."

Bonnie Jo stopped and smiled, but he was daydreaming his way into Sissy Conroy's pants, and several seconds passed before he realized she had spoken. She started to turn away, but he snapped out of his trance.

"Oh, hey, Bonnie Jo."

She turned back. "What's up?"

He cast another glance back at the sale sign and lingered a moment before giving up on his daydream.

"Oh, nothing. Just trying to figure out how I'm gonna pass natural science this year. I failed the first test."

Billy began walking toward his truck. It was parked down by the Laundromat. Bonnie Jo tagged along.

"The way the football players talk, I thought you helped them with their studies."

"I only help those assholes with English," he said. "Grammar and comp are easy, but I'm not worth a crap with math and science. I missed all the test questions on population statistics."

"Why do you call them assholes?"

"'Cause they are—and so are most of the cheerleaders and the rest of their cliquey friends."

"Hmmm," she said. "I thought you were part of their group."

"Not really. I just run cross-country and try to survive in their world. All I want to do is graduate and get the hell out of here."

"I can probably help you if you want."

"You think?"

"Sure."

Climbing in, he cranked the truck and rolled down the window.

"Need a ride?"

"You don't mind?"

He glanced over his shoulder to see if anyone was around. Giving a fat girl a ride in Raeford, Mississippi got you permanently stigmatized by the Lizards. The name was his personal invention—one he was proud of. They all wore shirts with little Alligators on them—but he figured they were more like lizards.

"Get in," he said.

"My house is out that way, off the highway." She pointed up the street then glanced down at the schoolbooks on the seat. "So, let's start with what you know."

She picked up the science book and opened it.

"That won't be hard. I don't know shit about natural science."

Bonnie Jo giggled but stared straight ahead down the road.

"What's so funny?" he asked.

"Nothing," she said, "except that's not what I've heard."

"Huh?"

"Never mind. I was just kidding."

It finally dawned on him what she was implying.

"You can't believe the crap you hear," he said.

It was better to lie than to be like the jocks who bragged

about their sexual conquests, most of which Billy was pretty sure were with their hands and not with the girls they claimed. He continued driving past the traffic light and headed east out the highway. The roadway narrowed just outside of town passing a pasture ripe with the odor of cattle manure. White cattle egrets roosted on the backs of Black Angus that grazed in scattered groups all the way to a distant tree line.

"Oh, well, I'm glad it's not true," she said.

The tone of her voice was patronizing, but he let it pass as she thumbed through the first chapter.

"So, tell me," she said. "What do you consider the best relationship for humans to have with their environment?"

"What the hell does that have to do with anything?" he asked.

"It's the first chapter, dummy—Humans and Their Relationship with the Environment."

"You mean like what's my idea of a perfect world?"

"Okay, what's your idea of a perfect world?"

"Are you sure you want to know?"

"Sure," she said. "Tell me about your Utopia."

It was time to give goody-two-shoes a dose of reality—show her what really matters.

"Okay," he said. "In a perfect world there's a high school called Beaver Valley High, and all the girls have perfect bodies and wear cheerleader outfits year-round. And on weekends they're barrel riders in the local rodeo, crouching low on their quarter-horses with their perfect little butts bouncing high in the air as they whip around the barrels with auburn, blond and chestnut hair flowing from beneath their lady Stetsons."

She laughed. "Like I said, I've heard this about you, Coker."

"Heard what?"

"That you have a one-track mind."

242 | RICK DESTEFANIS

She seemed so self-assured. It was time to turn up the heat.

"Hell," he replied, "You just don't know what *really* makes the world go 'round. Do you have a clue about the power women have over men?"

"Power?" she said.

"Yeah. If women could find a way to make men mainline that stuff, they could rule the world with a syringe. I mean they practically own it anyway, but they can't disengage their hearts long enough to really take charge."

She rolled her eyes. "You're confusing 'means' with 'motivation'."

"Means and motivation?"

"Yeah, most girls just don't think that way."

He turned and looked at her. "You think I'm crazy, don't you?"

Bonnie Jo pointed to a blacktop road up ahead. "Turn up there on that road," she said. "No, you're not crazy. Your hormonal overload isn't any worse than most guys your age. That house down there on the right."

"So, you think it's only the guys that are crazy, huh?"

He slowed his old truck and turned into her drive. A long gentle curve of pavement took them through mature oak trees and up to the house. One of the nicer places around Raeford, the house had large gables and a big front porch.

"You want to come in?" she asked.

He shook his head. "I can't. I gotta get home to check on Mom."

"Is she sick?"

"No, not really—I mean, I don't know. It's just—she hasn't been doing so well since dad got killed last winter. Too much nerve medicine, I reckon."

Bonnie Jo looked off to the side and squinted. "I read about it in the paper," she said. "I mean, when your dad died."

"What's done is done," Billy said. "So, when do we have our first tutoring session?"

She gave him a sad smile and shrugged. "What's a good time for you?"

"How about Monday after I run?"

"Where?"

This was something he hadn't considered. The tables behind the Dairy Queen came to mind, but if he was seen hanging around town with her, the Lizards would harass the hell out of him, and it would definitely cost him some popularity points. He noticed a wooden swing hanging from a huge oak in her front yard.

"How about over there?" he said.

She shrugged.

"Weather permitting, it works for me."

"Sergeant Coker!"

Jarred back to reality—such as it was in Nam—Billy realized someone was calling him from somewhere in the warren of sandbagged bunkers encircling the firebase. Firebase Echo had been home as of late for his airborne infantry battalion. They'd been holed-up there for a month overlooking a road crossing near the A Shau Valley—'interdiction and pacification' they called it. George Custer tried the same thing with the Sioux. Billy almost laughed at the thought.

The surrounding mountains were crawling with North Vietnamese regulars, and the battalion had been whittled down to the equivalent of three lean companies of men. This was bad-guy territory, and the enemy called most of the shots. They even had anti-aircraft guns somewhere in the surrounding hills, which made re-supply choppers few and far between.

Again, someone call his name. Martin, one of Billy's men, stuck his head out of the bunker below. "It's one of the cherries," he said. "You want me to go get him, Sarge?"

"Yeah, if you don't mind. Go get him before a sniper takes his dumb ass head off. And stay down."

They'd made him squad leader, probably by default, because had there been any competition, Billy was pretty sure he'd still be a buck private. Instead, he had spent the last three months trying to keep his men all in one piece. He figured that was the most important thing, because nothing else about this war made sense. He remembered how Bonnie Jo always said he was too cynical—especially when he called the Lizards egotistical jerks. If only she could see him now. He'd perfected cynicism in Nam. It was his forte, and he'd raised it to its highest form.

Martin crouched as he trotted back down to the bunker with the cherry. "Cherry here says Bugsy wants you up at the CP. Says it's real important."

Billy turned to the cherry. Dumbass nodded earnestly as if his role as messenger gave him some kind of authority. "If you don't stop wandering around in the wide-ass open, you ain't gonna live long enough to really enjoy this war."

"But Sarge."

"No 'but' to it, dumb-ass. If you want to stay alive, start thinking like a soldier. These goddamn hills are crawling with NVA snipers, and they *will* put a round through that thick head of yours if you don't start using it for something besides a helmet holder."

Lieutenant Busby—or 'Bugsy' as the men called him—was the platoon leader. Billy decided to finish his cigarette. Sitting back down on the sandbag, he looked out across the mountains, wondering who he had become and where he was going when he left this godforsaken place. Other than eight weeks of Basic, nine weeks of Advanced Infantry Training and Airborne school, his resume before getting to Nam would say he'd read a few books and did a focused study on female anatomy. It was a damned shame. Here he was just nineteen years old and CMFIC of a combat infantry squad.

The CMFIC—that's who they ask for when they want to talk to the person in charge. People often thought it was an official military acronym, an understandable assumption, but an incorrect one. Billy exhaled a cloud of smoke into the stagnant afternoon air. CMFIC was an *unofficial* military acronym, that stood for Chief Mother Fucker In Charge. The real kicker was that his men actually thought he knew what he was doing. He was their squad leader, and they watched his every move, hoping he could show them something that would keep them alive just one more day. It would have been laughable had it not been so serious.

It was simply a matter of the one who'd been here longest leading the ones who'd just shown up. If it wasn't for the war, most of them, himself included, would have been down at a McDonalds by nightfall, trying to pick up chicks, drinking Old Milwaukee talls and listening to Hendrix or Steppenwolf. Instead, they were here on this godforsaken firebase, and Billy only hoped he could make a difference whenever the shit hit the fan.

Actually, he'd been fairly successful as a squad leader. He thought about it. Perhaps it was his ability to use their vices to motivate people. God knows, he had a few. And the cherry was just a big dumb oaf—kind of reminded him of Raymond Hokes, another old Raeford High classmate. Like Ray, the cherry wasn't too bright, and Billy realized he had to find a way to motivate him—give him something to think about beside the rain, rats and mosquitoes. He figured the best way was to find something he desired, perhaps tell him about the whores in Phu Bai, or the navy nurses on R&R down at China Beach. And if his experience with Raymond Hokes had any relevance, the theory might just work.

Sex was always his prime choice as a motivator, and it was with Ray that he first tested the theory. The way Billy had it figured, there wasn't a red-blooded boy anywhere in Raeford who wouldn't sell his soul for a few hours with the right woman—his reasoning being based on his own experiences since puberty. Women ruled the world, and he, Billy Coker was their slave. Albeit a willing one, he wasn't the only one enslaved by feminine charms, and his strategy for dealing with Ray Hokes greatly depended on that assumption.

Ray always liked to start shit with anyone he found hanging around in the halls after school. Problem was he was a man amongst boys. Having failed the fourth grade twice, he was nineteen years old and the star lineman for the Raeford High Wildcats. Ray was a sum total six-foot-four and two hundred and eighty-nine pounds of pot-bellied redneck. And for some reason, he had decided to make Billy his whipping boy that year.

It was only the third week of school, and Billy had no intention of spending his entire senior year getting his ass kicked by Ray. Problem was a head-to-head confrontation with him was tantamount to suicide. Normal-sized humans had to rely on wit and guile to survive run-ins with Ray. That's how Billy came up with the plan he hoped would, as the guidance counselor might put it, 're-align Ray's priorities' or to put it in simpler terms, 'get him off his ass.'

School let out that day as the final bell rang and the student body burst through the doors like a covey of quail, leaving the ancient hallways all but empty. Billy was on his way to the locker room, his footsteps echoing in the silence, when he spotted Ray going into the boy's restroom. It was risky, but it was time to face his nemesis. It was time to try his new theory. And if it blew up in his face there'd be no witnesses. He would die and be buried on the schoolyard battlefield like thousands of nerd-warriors before him, but at least his annihilation wouldn't include public humiliation.

The way Billy had it figured, Ray was going to pound his head every day until he got creative and found a way to distract him. That's why he decided to ask him if he'd ever had any pussy—an exceptionally stupid question to ask Ray of all people, if he really meant it. One look at Ray and you knew he hadn't been near one since the day he was born—at least not one belonging to a human. Knowing his "agricultural" background, though, there may have been an unlucky farm animal somewhere along the way.

Billy slipped into the restroom behind Ray. Ray glanced over his shoulder and shuffled closer against the urinal. He was probably one of those delivered by a midwife in the country and never circumcised. You could always tell, because they often hid themselves, even in the locker room. Billy walked over beside him to take a quick pee.

"What the hell are you doin' in here, Coker?"

"Oh, hey, Ray. I saw you and was going to tell you something."

Ray finished and zipped up before backing away from the urinal.

"What?"

"Well…" Billy hesitated. He should have rehearsed. "Have you ever had any? You know?"

"Any what?"

Ray always seemed angry for no reason, and Billy found

himself unable to muster a pee, so he zipped up and turned to face him.

"You know, pussy."

Priming Ray first hadn't occurred to him, but it was too late. The fuse was lit. Ray began stuttering, then turned and charged like a rodeo bull. Grabbing Billy's throat, he lifted him off the floor and pinned him against the wall between the urinals. This wasn't the way it was supposed to happen. Bad timing, he figured, but he had to come up with plan 'B' quick or die.

"Wait a minute, Ray!" Billy said breathlessly. "Hold on a second. I need to tell you something, something important."

Ray hesitated with his fist drawn back as he held Billy there against the cold tile wall.

"What?"

His moronic little eyes came together like a pair of B-B's in the middle of his country ham face.

"What if I told you I know a girl who likes to mess around— you know? And she kind of likes you, too."

Ray's eyes narrowed even more until his brows nearly touched as he fought to focus on some shadow of a thought deep within. With this mask of total concentration covering his face, it seemed certain the cognitive overload was about to melt one of his two brain cells. Deep down in his heart Ray must have thought making love to a real girl was beyond the realm of possibility in his lifetime.

"Who?" he said.

Billy froze again. It wasn't that he didn't have in mind several of the finest specimens of female anatomy at Raeford High, but for some reason, he had a forevermore-unbreakable radar-lock on Sissy Conroy's most magnificent buns. This would never work. The mere idea was a desecration. Letting Ray have the misguided thought that he could dip into that little honey pot was totally repulsive. Death would be a better option, and for the moment, that possibility seemed imminent.

Skydiving couldn't have given Billy the adrenaline rush he had dangling there, his back against the wall and Ray's sledgehammer fist staring him in the face. He had to think. The toes of his tennis shoes barely touched the puddles of water on the floor, and Billy tried with all his might to come up with a name other than Sissy's. That was the one part of the plan he'd neglected. He needed a name—a believable one.

"Bonnie Jo Parker," he blurted.

The words no sooner left his mouth than Billy felt sickened by what he'd done. He was a loathsome jerk. He had just betrayed the girl who was going to help him graduate high school. Ray would trail her everywhere she went.

"I wouldn't touch that little pig," he snarled.

Guilt-ridden or not, it was too late to start over.

"Ray, I can't believe you would say that about Bonnie Jo. She's a little on the chubby side, but she's really a sweet person, and I think she likes you."

Billy's heart raced as he fought to catch his breath. Again, Ray's face became masked with concentration. Beyond the odor of Ray's bologna and mustard breath, Billy could almost smell his two brain cells smoking from the overload. Then slowly—so very slowly—Ray loosened his grip from around Billy's throat. His tennis shoes settle back onto the tile floor, and the smell of the urinal was like that of life itself, almost invigorating.

"What makes you think she likes me?"

It was think-fast-or-die-time again.

"I heard her say your name the other day while she was talking with some girls in the cafeteria."

Ray didn't say anything. That a female mentioned his name in conversation seemed an incomprehensible concept to him.

"I saw her looking at you in the hall, too."

Billy laid it on thick, and after a few moments the hormonal influence must have been too much for Ray's teenincy brain to overcome. He walked over to the mirror and gazed into the biggest section that wasn't cracked. With the heel of his hand, he pushed his larded locks into place. Billy was frozen in place, pinned by his own fear, unable to move. Ray was butt-ugly, and this lummox could go either way at any moment. Sucking down a deep breath, Billy took the first tentative step toward the door. Ray didn't seem to notice as he turned his head and studied his profile in the mirror. Billy bolted and didn't look back.

Sissy Conroy, the most glorious hunk of teenage womanhood in the school, owed him a big one. He had saved her from Ray, but since she was the heartthrob of most of the football team, crossing paths with her would probably never happen, at least in any significant way, such as undressing her and engaging in mad and passionate love making. She would never know how he had made Bonnie Jo her stand-in human sacrifice.

Taking another hard drag on the cigarette, Billy watched as the cherry stumbled down into the bunker. He was just another Ray Hokes. All he needed was the right motivation.

CHAPTER TWO

The Last Patrol

A fter a while it dawned on Billy that Lieutenant Busby might be calling him to the CP to send him back to Camp Eagle for out-processing—a little early, but it *was* less than thirty days until his DEROS. They called it the date of estimated return from overseas service, but he was almost too burned-out to care. Flipping the cigarette butt into a puddle, he headed up the hill toward the command post. As he made his way up the muddy path, he spotted the young lieutenant coming down past the latrines. He was such an antsy fucker everyone called him 'Bugsy.' The lanky platoon leader must have grown impatient and come looking for him.

With his helmet on crooked and a couple days growth of beard, Bugsy looked a little ragged as he wove his way through the shell holes pock-marking the ground. The NVA had just about decimated the officer ranks, and Bugsy was both covering as a platoon leader and acting as company executive officer. The two men met and crouched together in a mortar pit. Billy glanced up to make sure they were below the edge of the sandbags.

Canvas tarps were draped over the mortar tubes to protect them from the rain, and wooden crates of ninety-millimeter rounds were stacked all around. The two men were sitting on enough explosives to blast them into a fine mist and eternity, something Billy would hardly have noticed until now. Now, with less than thirty days left on his tour, he was seeing danger everywhere, but the only way to escape it was to already be dead.

Incoming mortars and rockets were almost as common as the rain, but the thing he hated most was the sniper fire. The NVA would crawl through the high grass to within five hundred meters of the perimeter. There, they lay in wait, sometimes for days, waiting for someone to get careless and stand in the wrong place for too long. A whispering crack of a round would break the silence, punctuated by the screams of the poor fucker who'd been hit—unless, of course, he got it through the head. When that happened, there were only the screams of his buddies calling for a medic, a futile gesture since medics weren't much needed when someone got the third eye.

There was a hill directly behind the firebase—Hill 819. It rose up out of the ground over a klick away, a huge monolith. The firebase sat on a plateau overlooking the highway, but behind it was this mountain of jumbled ravines and broken timber towering above all else. Billy and his men watched day after day as everything from artillery to helicopter gunships, Puff the Magic Dragon and F-4 Phantoms pounded 819. They dropped napalm, HE, and every kind of human exterminator available, and what wasn't destroyed was pretty much vegematic'd, but the NVA still came out of the ground every night and showered the firebase with rockets and mortars.

Straddling a wooden crate of mortar rounds, Billy sat with his M-16 across his lap while Bugsy squatted against some sandbags and lit a Chesterfield. He shook another one from the little C-ration pack and gave it to Billy.

"So, wassup?" Billy asked.

"CO says we have to send a patrol up 819 to poke around," he said.

Billy laughed. "No shit?"

"No shit," Bugsy said.

Bugsy was always pulling practical jokes or saying some off-the-wall-bullshit until no one believed anything he said. Still, he was better than most of the officers. He never took himself too seriously. Unlike some of the gung-ho, John Wayne types, he wasn't here to get his ticket punched. Like Billy, Bugsy took care of his men, but his jokes got old after a while.

Billy shook his head. "Try again, LT, 'cause if it was April, I'd tell you that's the dumbest April Fools' joke I ever heard."

Bugsy pooched out his lips and looked back toward the CP, as if he thought the CO might come down and participate in the joke.

"It'd take a reinforced battalion to recon that hill," Billy said.

The lieutenant still didn't smile, so Billy tried to humor him. "Lighten up, man. You should try that shit on one of the cherries. They'd take it hook, line and sinker."

"I'm not kidding, Billy."

Billy felt his face stuck on smile as he stopped laughing.

"What do you mean?"

"I'm not kidding. The old man says we have to send a reinforced squad over there to take a look around."

"No way."

Billy still didn't believe him. Bugsy always carried his jokes past funny.

"Look, Billy. Just get your men together for a briefing. I'm putting Curtis Teague and his gun crew with you, along with a couple extra riflemen. That'll give you two sixties and a total of fourteen men counting yourself."

Buy *Raeford's MVP* now on Amazon at:
www.amazon.com/dp/B01ANXHX80

.

About the Author

Rick DeStefanis lives in northern Mississippi with his wife, Janet, four cats and a male yellow lab named Blondie. Although many of his novels cross genre lines that include military fiction, southern fiction and historical western fiction, he utilizes his military expertise to produce the Vietnam War Series. *Melody Hill* (*Book #1*) is the prequel to his award-winning novel *The Gomorrah Principle*, both of which draw from his experiences as a paratrooper with the 82nd Airborne Division from 1970 to 1972.

Learn more about DeStefanis and his books online at www.rickdestefanis.com/, or you can visit him on Facebook at www.facebook.com/RickDeStefanisAuthor/.

Made in the USA
Columbia, SC
28 October 2021